Married to the Alien Admiral

Renascence Alliance Series Book 1

Alma Nilsson

Married to the Alien Admiral, Renascence Alliance Series Book 1 © 2019 by Alma Nilsson. All Rights Reserved.

All rights reserved. No part of this book may be reproduced in any form or by any electronic or mechanical means including information storage and retrieval systems, without permission in writing from the author. The only exception is by a reviewer, who may quote short excerpts in a review.

Cover designed by Yvonne Less, Art4artists

This book is a work of fiction. Names, characters, places, and incidents either are products of the author's imagination or are used fictitiously. Any resemblance to actual persons, living or dead, events, or locales is entirely coincidental.

Printed in the United States of America

First Printing: January 2019

ISBN-10: 1700188550
ISBN-13: 978-1700188557

Marriage is the only war where one sleeps with the enemy.

Mexican proverb

Note to Readers

In this book, I use anatomically correct vocabulary, which may alarm some readers. I believe the words vagina, vulva, and clitoris should be just as neutral and intoxicating by context as fingertips, lips, and tongue. In addition, the female main character is intimate with both men and women.

Also, if you have come to the Renascence Alliance Series from the Alliance Holiday series you might be surprised that these books are written in 3rd person omniscient and from a patriarchal perspective. This is because I did not consider writing in the 1st person or from a matriarchal point of view for the Alliance characters until December 2022.

Reader discretion is advised.

Abbreviations and New Words:

- **Alliance Empire**: A group of five planets occupied by a species almost genetically identical to humans but with grey skin tones.
- **Contracts:** A continuing list of legislative compromises between men and women in the Alliance Empire. The first of which gave men the right to learn to read, and the second gave men the right to their own language.
- **GC:** Galactic Court: A galactic governing body that tries to implement common galactic laws for the benefit of all its members.
- **IC:** Instant Communicator
- **Known Jewelry:** Jewelry bought and displayed by maximum class Alliance men to show what kind of men they are and what kind of husbands they could be.
- **Jahay:** Earth's alien ally and the Alliance Empire's enemy.
- **Watching:** A time in the middle of the night when all Alliance people are awake, either working, talking, praying, or having sex.

WAR

Admiral Tir of the Alliance Empire alpha warship *Refa* looked across the projection of the battle they were fighting with the Jahay. He took a moment to collect his thoughts and then said to his first officer, "Save the humans. It would be such a waste to let the women die given the Empire's current circumstances."

Captain Zan nodded and began giving orders to bring the small human starship, *Dakota*, into one of their docking bays. He instructed some guards and medics to attend to them.

Admiral Tir stopped him, "Don't waste our resources on the men, heal only the women, let the men die if they're going to die. Then put them into the brig. We'll send the women back to the Capital Planet on the next supply ship." The Alliance was the largest and most advanced civilization in the galaxy, but they were suffering from a demographic imbalance and desperately needed genetically compatible women. Unfortunately for the starship *Dakota*, the only other compatible women in the galaxy were humans.

After the battle was over and won and Admiral Tir had finished all his necessary reports, he decided to check on his human prisoners. He didn't need to but he was curious. As he walked through his ship's corridors, he tried to remember what he knew about humans. They were a beautiful species but foolish. They were known to spend most of their time on frivolous activities; they seemed to want to make everything around them attractive and had a strange obsession with their planet's wildlife. Due to humanity's peculiar obsession with beauty and fun, the Capital City Gossip Columns voted Earth 'the best party planet' in the galaxy every year. This award, by Alliance standards, was nothing to be proud of.

Tir had never been to Earth or met a human woman before. He *had* had the pleasure of meeting some unimpressive human men. But he expected human women to be like Alliance women, strong and independent. Instead of having grey skin and black hair, they would be all kinds of different human colors.

Tir was thinking about the *Dakota's* captain. He suspected she would be angry with him for not destroying them in battle. He was not wholly unfamiliar with the *Dakota* - its captain had lured many Alliance supply ships into danger and even managed to destroy a couple during this war with the Jahay. It was an impressive feat given that the *Dakota* was a completely inferior ship, but one thing everyone in the galaxy could agree on was that humans excelled at stealth. And they cleverly used their reputation as a technologically inferior species as an advantage. So, when Tir entered the brig, he expected their captain to be clever, fierce, and furious at him for taking them in such a way.

And to make matters worse, he was now going to take away her career as well, but it could not be helped. Tir needed to do this for the Empire. He had already decided that the best women to integrate into the Alliance Empire were those who already lived by strict routines in the human fleet. Tir judged them to be stronger than average human women and would probably stand a better chance at integrating properly into Alliance life, which was not for the faint-hearted. Rarely were off-worlders granted permission to live on any of the Alliance homeworlds. The reason was two-fold: first, everyone, believers and non-believers alike, had to observe the strict religious codes that maintained and governed Alliance culture and society. Second, many off-worlders did not feel comfortable living in a society where people were responsible for their own justice. As there was no official system for dealing with personal disputes, duels were fought between individuals to the death. Men's duels could be arranged and carried out in minutes. Women, being more civilized, had a two day waiting period. And the frequency of these duels was too high to entice other species in the galaxy to live there, despite the other lucrative opportunities that life in the Alliance Empire might bring.

Tir walked into the *Refa's* small brig. They rarely took prisoners, and Tir had only been in this room a few times before. When he entered, the three guards bowed to him as was the Alliance custom. He acknowledged them with his hand and then silently looked over the humans. He was looking for their captain, but they all seemed so disheveled he had difficulty telling them apart and making out who were the officers. He hated that humans did not identify their ranks with clearly marked jewelry as Alliance people did; it just made life so much easier to always know who you were talking to. Tir loathed having to ask for someone's rank. "Which one of you," he addressed the women held in a separate cell from the men, "is Captain Kara Rainer?"

All the women looked up, and then a beautiful, dark-skinned woman rose, moved forward to the edge of the forcefield, and answered him, "She isn't with us. Maybe you had her killed already?"

Tir ignored the anger in the woman's voice. He deserved her disdain. The crew of the *Dakota* had deserved to die in battle and he took that glory away from them and what he was going to replace it with might be worse than being a prisoner of war. He really didn't know how these human women were going to react when they found out his plans. "Human woman, you've been spared by the gods who have a better fate in store for you. Rest." Then Tir turned and went directly to his ship's sickbay without another word to the humans who had all started asking him questions about their future when they realized who he was.

As Tir entered sickbay, a wave of human odor overtook him. In the brig, their smell had been contained by the forcefields in the holding cells, but he could smell them here. It was the smell of unwashed bodies, and Tir wondered if humans had washing facilities on their ships or if they were just smelly creatures. Then he thought about the state of their vessel and assumed they had probably been running low on water. He walked through the different colored humans in varying states of health being treated on multiple medical beds. He was annoyed to see some human men there, given that he had given explicit orders to let them die, but he knew his doctor had a soft heart, and if he had the time, he would heal them all. Tir singled out his chief medical officer, Doctor Siu.

"Is their captain here?"

Doctor Siu pointed to a medical bed in the back of the sick bay, "She's there. Red uniform. She hit her head. Don't be alarmed, it looks worse than it is."

Tir wondered why Doctor Siu had not sent her to the brig then, but he did not want to question his doctor now. He reflected as he walked towards the back of sickbay that humans could get away with so much because people always underestimated them. And Captain Rainer had been no exception. She had been a menace to Alliance's supply ships throughout this war, and even in direct battle, the first time he had faced the human woman, she should have been hiding with her little ship, instead she showed superior strategical skills and bravery. Tir was impressed but also, at the same time, concerned. *Who knew what this human captain was capable of unguarded on his ship?*

Tir announced himself and the medics working immediately made space for him. He stood over this human female with short brown hair matted with blood and took in her status. The computer readout above her medical bed showed that she was not asleep but just had closed her eyes. Tir motioned for the medics to leave and then he addressed this human female, "Captain Rainer, I'm Admiral Tir of the Alliance Empire. You and your crew are my prisoners." Tir had to admit, she didn't look dangerous at all, instead she looked wildly attractive, but he quickly reminded himself, *This is how humans fool everyone, with their adorable colors.*

Kara opened her eyes and was stunned to see a good-looking, grey-skinned Alliance man with long black hair, the kind of hair people only wished they had, straight and impressively thick. He also had striking green eyes that were looking down at her inquisitively. She never thought about Alliance people being anything but a mute grey color. Racist humans often referred to them as 'zombies.' But this man was far from being a zombie or muted in appearance; he was extraordinary, he smelled of petrichor and something else pleasant, and his voice was so deep, she could not help but feel an instant attraction to him. She had imagined all the insults she was going to give to the Alliance commander who took them prisoner but now, at this moment, all she could say was, "I'd say thank you for saving us, for the moment anyway, I didn't think the Alliance took prisoners, Admiral." Kara reckoned it must be her head injury that was making her civil.

Little did she know that the Alliance gods were now at play and were manipulating her and Tir's conversation and thoughts. The Alliance gods had big plans for Kara and Tir.

"We're making an exception for the captain who was brave enough to disrupt our supply lines not once or twice but over twenty times with an inferior ship," Tir lied. He didn't know why, but he didn't have the heart to tell her her true fate. Not yet. Not like this.

Kara smiled devilishly. She was going to enjoy what she could of the situation. "I'm glad I made an impression." Human ships were nothing in the galaxy. When the Jahay had forced humanity to join this war against the Alliance, she knew they would probably die, but she would not go down without a fight. So, she had regularly used guerrilla warfare against her ally's orders because she refused to be used as fodder on the front lines. However, in all her scenarios of how this war would end for the *Dakota* and its crew, she had never imagined being taken prisoner. So Kara was intrigued, wondering what Admiral Tir wanted from them. She was trying to read his face as he stood over her. Their eyes were locked, but his green eyes revealed nothing, and before she could ask him a question, he was gone, without a word, only a small electrifying touch from his steady grey hand on her shoulder. *How long has it been since I've been with a man now? Too long if I'm finding the grey guys attractive.* Kara thought and closed her eyes again. She was trying to rest and figure out why the Alliance would go through the trouble of taking them prisoner.

Tir gently touched her shoulder before he walked away without another word. This little human had entranced him with her overwhelmingly sweet scent, not like the initial smell of all the other humans. And beautiful brown eyes, the color of eyes only humans possessed and her eyes saw directly into his soul. He could not deny his immediate attraction to her. So, Tir did the only thing he could do, leave and shake off her spell, but as he walked away, he found it challenging to get the image of her face out of his mind. He immediately tasked some guards to keep an eye on her, this woman had a certain kind of power, and he didn't want to take any chances.

Tir could not stop thinking about Captain Rainer, so after the evening meal, he had his guards bring her to him in his conference room so he could talk to her privately. When she entered, he was intoxicated by her scent again, and although she looked tired and dirty, he still found her very attractive. Tir was fascinated by how she moved very differently from Alliance women. He couldn't help but stare at her golden skin and pink lips. Her red uniform was tight and showed off all her curves. It had a zipper down the front, and all he wanted to do in that first minute of looking at her was to unzip that red uniform slowly to reveal her naked curves and check where else she may be pink on her body. *Where has your mind gone?* He questioned himself, momentarily wondering if she was wearing a pheromone enhancer. *Focus on the task at hand.* But he knew it would be a struggle; he had never had an immediate attraction to a woman like this before. In the past, he had always been in control of how he felt about the women he was intimate with. It had always been a choice. This was not a choice.

Kara was struck again by how handsome, strong, and tall Admiral Tir was. Now seeing him while she was standing upright, it was obvious he was well over two meters. And noticing his long loose black hair again, she suddenly, and irrationally, longed to run her fingers through it. She wondered why he wore it down, differently than most of the other Alliance men who seemed to wear theirs in different braided styles. She speculated it was because he was the admiral. Kara was also fascinated by all his ranking jewelry; she knew Alliance people wore this as proof of their status in the military and society. Then her eyes rested on his exquisite short sword, and she was reminded of two things, first the cruelty of Alliance culture that they still killed one another at the drop of a hat with these swords and second, of her position here as his prisoner, and she frowned.

Her brown eyes met his green ones. "Is this the first time you have ever seen a human in the flesh, Admiral?" She could not keep the amusement from her tone because he was drinking in her appearance like a dehydrated man in the desert who had just found an oasis.

Admiral Tir dismissed the guards and then said to Captain Rainer, "Yes, it's the first time I've ever seen a human woman, and, I must admit Captain, you certainly don't disappoint. Humans are rumored to be the most beautiful species in the galaxy, and I can't say that I agreed with that when I met human men for the first time, but your appearance lives up to the galactic rumor. Excuse my inappropriate behavior. Please take a seat." *I'm making a fool of myself,* he thought. After a minute of them just looking at each other, he decided to tell her his plans without any more preamble, "Captain, I'm going to send half of your crew back to Earth only if they agree that they will not participate in this war anymore."

"Only half?"

"The other half will be sent to the Alliance Empire," he was watching her reaction intently. Tir wondered if the tales about the Alliance's demographic problems had reached human ears yet.

Kara was trying to figure out why he would not send them all home. "What could you possibly want with only half of us? What value do any human prisoners have for the mighty Alliance Empire? Are you going to keep us in a zoo like pets?" It wasn't uncommon for human women to be abducted and kept as pets around the galaxy. The Galaxy Court forbid such practices, but it was only recently that they began implementing punishments for the abduction of humans.

"You misunderstand me, Captain. Human women are now considered Alliance citizens, as the order of the High Council Alliance date 4th day of the 28th week of the year 18903. So, you see, it is *our* responsibility, and in this instance, *my* responsibility to keep you and the rest of your female crew safe. You'll be sent to the Capital Planet in the Empire as soon as the first supply ship is ready to return." A second after he said the last sentence, he felt in his gut that this was wrong. *What if he kept her for himself? What if* he *was the first to marry a human woman?* The High Council would lose their minds. It's a ridiculous thought, but one that as daring as he was, he would entertain at least for a while. If it didn't work out, he could always say she died in battle. It happens all the time.

Kara looked at him in disbelief. "Admiral, I believe there's been a mistake. We're human and nothing more. We certainly aren't Alliance citizens. I'm not sure if this is some kind of Alliance joke?" She was rarely caught off guard, but this was completely unexpected. Alliance people were some of the most xenophobic aliens in the galaxy, and the idea that they would now allow human women to be considered Alliance citizens was unprecedented.

"No, Captain, you're Alliance now, and that comes before your humanity. Let me be the first to congratulate you on your new status in the galaxy," he purposely said it condescendingly. He was annoyed she was not pleased to be told she was an Alliance citizen. Tir, like most Alliance people, regarded his civilization as the best in everything and naturally assumed every person in the galaxy would jump at the chance to be a part of something as successful as the Alliance Empire.

After hearing this, Kara didn't know what to do with herself, so she went with her instincts and stood up quickly; she was furious and couldn't just sit there and listen to him tell her this as if it was 'a good thing.' Kara reached for where her gun would normally be on her hip and then realized of course she did not have it. Then she tried to make a move and run to the door.

Tir had been ready for this and got up quickly and had his sword at her small throat in seconds. He had no intention of hurting her but just wanted to prove a point. "Captain, your death won't change the facts. Neither you nor I made this law, but it is the law, and human women are Alliance citizens. You and your female crew will be returning to the Empire." Tir was lying. He helped push this law through the High Council. He had not liked the idea proposed by many of the Alliance women of many men sharing one wife.

Through gritted teeth Kara said, "We cannot return to a place we've never been and don't belong." She tried to struggle out of his grip but couldn't. "It sounds like you need me more than I need you, so I doubt you'll kill me," she said bitterly and tried to elbow him to get away, but it was futile. He just held her more tightly against his big strong body. Kara wanted to be repulsed by the action, but she was not. This upset her and she chastised herself, but quickly put her own shame to the side and thought, *Maybe I should have tried unzipping my uniform as a bargaining tool?*

Tir forced her back down into the chair. Still holding her with his sword to her throat, he activated the chair's restraints from the floor, bringing up laser cuffs on her wrists and ankles. He then resumed his seat across from her. He watched her struggle and heard a tiny sizzle every time she tried to break free from the restraints. Tir waited patiently for her to calm down while thinking about how she might be in bed. As terrible as it was, he could not help himself. Holding her so close and breathing in her delicious scent had almost put him over the edge. His mind raced through different scenarios of foreplay. He figured she would be feisty, and he had to admit that he found that arousing. He wanted a woman to tame in the bedroom. As he looked at her, his mind went through these scenarios, and he found it difficult to remember what they were supposed to be talking about.

"We will certainly not be returning with you," Kara said defiantly.

"If you are going to be difficult, I can be difficult too. I can execute your male crew and donate your ship to a museum. I'm doing you a favor, from one Alliance citizen to another, from one officer to another, by allowing your ship and male crew to go free. But, the choice is yours."

"Human women would rather die than be sex slaves or sex pets, as it were, in the Empire, Admiral. If you take us by force, we will not go easily, and we'll certainly not last long in captivity. Why not just let us all go free and return to Earth? None of us wanted to be involved in this war. It's no secret to anyone we were pushed by the Jahay. Why this farce of human women being Alliance citizens?"

"Captain, we aren't savages. We don't keep human women as pets, *anymore*. You and your female crew will be Alliance wives. This is an opportunity for you all to have better lives than you'd have ever had on Earth. This is a galactic gift. You should be thanking me."

"Why would the galaxy's most racist and powerful civilization suddenly want human women for wives?"

Tir did not answer but enjoyed watching her beautiful face while she figured it out. It was an easy answer to an easy question.

After a few seconds, she said regretfully, "I've heard whispers of what's going on, but didn't believe it. You think you can replenish your ailing genetic stock with humans? How arrogant of you, Admiral. I'm sure the GC will have something to say about this. You cannot just pillage human women. And who's to say whatever affects Alliance women's birth rates won't affect human women's too?"

"You misunderstand," Tir said evenly, knowing full well why the Empire has a demographic issue. "We're not abducting anyone. You've been given citizenship to the most powerful and prestigious Empire in the galaxy. You're *volunteering* to be the first human women to become wives to some of the best men in the Empire. Do you think the GC is going to waste their time on this? No one is going to think this is a crime. Humans are nothing. I think the GC would probably applaud us for bringing some humans out of the dark ages, even if we are taking a risk that whatever is affecting our women will negatively affect human women too, but trust me, I don't think it will. So, I will say it again, you should thank me, Captain. You'll be one of the lucky ones as we will only invite a select few to begin immediate integration into Alliance society."

Kara was frustrated. "Take that little sword you're wearing and kill me then. I'll not marry an alien, and neither will any of my female crew. Humans don't mix with other species. We find you and the rest of the aliens of the galaxy repulsive." This was a lie. Kara herself had been known to, on occasion, have the odd love affair with a passing alien trader, and even now, she found this Alliance Admiral incredibly attractive despite wanting to hate him for what he was telling her. "Nor do we participate in such archaic practices as *marriage*," she spat the word 'marriage' as she would talk about any other barbaric act. Humans might have been behind the entire galaxy technologically speaking, but they considered themselves quite sophisticated culturally and had given up religion and concepts of marriage centuries ago.

Tir was surprised by her ferocity. "I admire your spirit, Captain, so I've decided to make an example of you. Obviously, if I force you to do this, your female crew will fall in line. So, congratulations, you'll be the first to marry an Alliance officer of my choosing here onboard my ship tonight. If you resist, I'll execute a crewman from the *Dakota* every seven minutes until you agree." Tir was willing to execute all the human men anyway, except their doctor, who might be useful.

"My crew would rather die than see any human women barbarically forced to marry Alliance men."

"Really?" Tir asked in mocking disbelief. "Why don't we put this to the test then?" He ordered his guards to bring in two human male officers through his IC. Tir didn't need to specify that one of them should be her first officer. His guards were not ignorant of why he would ask some of her men to be brought in.

Kara's first officer and communication officer were brought into the conference room. They were bound together with a kind of laser. Her young communication officer had tears in his eyes and looked scared. Conversely, her first officer was ready to die for whatever the cause. But she could not let them die over something ridiculous like marrying an alien. Kara could run away from a husband, but she was no necromancer. In an instant, her mind accepted her current fate. And as was her nature, she had already begun scheming in those few seconds of how she could win the trust of an Alliance officer, steal superior Alliance weaponry, possibly even a ship, rescue her crew, and return to Earth. Before the admiral even gave the order to execute her men, she said promptly, "You win, Admiral. I'll marry an Alliance officer today. Let my men return to Earth."

Her first officer began to protest but was punched in the gut by one of the Alliance guards. Then he and her communications officer were subsequently led away by the same guards who brought them in.

Admiral Tir was pleased. He looked at this mesmerizing human captain. It would be very risky for him to take her even if she ended up 'accidently dying.' Any of his men would gladly take her as a wife, but in these few minutes with her alone, he had developed a favoritism for her, so he decided to pray on the matter. Taking a human would seriously jeopardize his status and future goals in the Empire.

Without breaking eye contact, Tir called in his guards, "Your men will be released after you fulfill your end of the bargain tonight. Guards, please escort Captain Rainer to my quarters where she may prepare for her wedding."

The guards were only momentarily surprised by his words but swiftly obeyed and escorted Kara out roughly by the arms.

Kara did not break eye contact with the attractive Admiral as she was led out. She thought *I guess we have a deal then, no handshake, no telling me who I am going to marry?*

Tir watched Captain Rainer be led out, left the conference room and went to the large shrine onboard the ship as soon as she was gone. Only a couple of other men were praying in front of the various gods' and goddesses' statues as he entered. The shrine was a dark room, lit only by artificial candlelight around the multiple figures. Tir stood before the goddess of home and said a prayer. He closed his eyes and prayed for the goddess to guide him.

Make no mistake, the Alliance gods were not only real but took a genuine interest in their people's lives, and at that moment, the goddess of home wanted to make an example of Tir, just as Tir wished to make an example of Captain Rainer. The goddess of home lifted her hand from her magnificent palace in the Alliance Heavens. She silently commanded Tir by infusing his mortal body with a blind lust for the human, Kara Rainer. *Marry her yourself, Tir. I have brought her to you to fulfill your destiny to the Empire. All your desires will be recognized through this human.*

Tir suddenly felt a deep longing and even protectiveness over the human captain. Not to mention, lust. Lust like he had never felt before. The combination of these emotions made him realize that he could not give her away to any of his men, no matter how honorable or sensible that might be.

Tir summoned his squire, Mux, and ordered him to procure Alliance dresses for Captain Rainer from the replicator and get her to wash. After his revelation in the shrine, he was confident of his destiny with Kara Rainer. He would marry her tonight, and as much as he wanted to unzip that filthy uniform and ravish her as an inferior human, he also wanted her in a respectable Alliance dress and clean. As this was going to be their wedding night, he did not want her to hold this little thing over him for the rest of their lives. He assured himself that he would have time to role play later with her human uniform, as he had no intention of returning her to the Capital Planet anytime soon.

Kara was taken to the admiral's quarters and guarded by the two guards in a dull sitting room with no patterns. The room only had grey, yellow and black colors. She sat on the sofa while the guards stood silently over her for about twenty minutes until a young man came in. Kara guessed him to be still a teenager.

"Captain Rainer, you must undress and wash." He knew she had a translator, but still, pointed to the bathroom. Mux had never spoken to a human before and found her coloring unnerving. She physically looked Alliance but in all the wrong colors.

"Ha," she laughed, "I'm not bathing. I said I would marry nothing more."

Mux did not know how to handle this. She was going to be his master's wife. As such, he had to obey her. However, he reasoned, she was not his wife yet, and the admiral would be furious with him if she were not presented as he wanted. Mux made a decision then and drew out his sword. He was prepared to force her to get clean. "Take off your clothes and get yourself clean, human. You are Alliance now, and we wash our bodies daily."

Kara took the opportunity to knock the young man hard enough that she could make a grab for his sword and nearly succeeded in getting the upper hand.

Mux was surprised only for an instant. Even though he was young, he had been training in the military since he was eight. He only struggled to get his sword back for an instant, and then he could easily pin the human back. She undoubtedly had some nicks from the scrap. "Stop this now, human. You cannot escape. Go bathe yourself."

Kara had to admit defeat and walked into the bathroom at sword point.

Mux said as he began to close the door, "I'll only let you out when you are clean."

Kara looked at the boy unemotionally and thought, *What a ridiculous situation this is?* After the door had closed and locked, she looked at her reflection in the mirror, and she had to admit, she looked like a woman who had been captured in war. Her uniform was dirty and had blood stains on it, and her short brown hair was very messy. She took off her clothes and entered what she supposed was the shower area. As she did, the shower spoke to her, and she jumped, almost losing her balance. Kara hated cleansing technology as it always caught her off guard.

"Please state your name, human," the shower ordered.

"Kara."

"Scanning. Be warned. The maximum water temperature is 25C."

The shower began raining water down on her, and she screamed as it was so cold.

Hearing the human shriek from outside, Mux rushed inside the bathroom quickly to ensure she had not hurt herself. He was momentarily stunned by the sight of her naked body and just stared.

Kara told him sternly, "Get out, boy!" When he had retreated, she stood deadly still and let the cold water run over her, trying not to shiver. She had some cuts from her scuffle with the young man, which stung when the shower provided her with soap and shampoo, but she had to admit it was good to get clean. The Alliance soap smelled rather nice, something flowery but alien, a reminder of how far she was from home.

When the water stopped, the shower dried her off with waves of chilly air blown from top to bottom. She didn't even think about her messy hair, which had dried very badly. Then she looked in the mirror, and the mirror lit up and switched on. The same automated voice offered a hand-held laser to brush her teeth. She used it. She suspected it was the admiral's, so she felt some small retribution in using his laser toothbrush. As she brushed her teeth, she tried to remember what his teeth looked like. She wondered if they were pointy, she could not remember. Kara had heard so many rumors about Alliance people in her life. She honestly did not know what she should believe. She did know one thing that was a fact; Alliance and humans were the only two genetically compatible species in the known galaxy. Thinking about that gave her a chill. She put the laser toothbrush back and took in her appearance. *I'm clean for this marriage thing, at least.* Then she could not help but smile at the ridiculousness of it all. *A human marrying, hilarious,* she thought. She looked for her uniform, which she had left on the floor, but it was gone. *The boy must have taken it,* she thought disdainfully.

Kara walked into the bedroom naked but clean and dry. She had expected to see the young man there, but she was alone. Not one to waste an opportunity; she took the time to look around the admiral's quarters. He had three rooms, a bedroom, a sitting area, and a dining room. Kara thought to herself, *Being an admiral in the Alliance certainly has its perks.* She opened his tall black lacquer wardrobe; inside hung three black uniforms, one stood out from the others, and she guessed this must be a formal uniform. Kara saw numerous black wooden boxes of various shapes and sizes stacked underneath the uniforms and was about to go through them when the young man returned. She closed the wardrobe and thought, *If I get a chance later, I'm absolutely going through those boxes.* If Kara was anything, she was curious.

Mux was surprised to see the human naked going through the admiral's wardrobe. However, as she would soon be his wife anyway, he felt he could not reprimand her for going through his master's personal belongings. So, he pretended he hadn't seen that and set three plain Alliance dresses on the bed.

Kara watched the young man and recognized the clothing as typical Alliance women dresses, not that Alliance women ever left their planets. Still, she had seen numerous videos and pictures of them. She knew from seeing them before that they would drape unattractively, like soft boxes, over her body. Kara reflected that Alliance women had very little curves on their bodies, so maybe that was why they liked the boxy look. But she did not want to wear one of these ugly dresses herself. She didn't even like human style dresses, she definitely didn't want to wear an alien one.

"Where's my uniform?"

"I threw it in the recycling," he lied. Admiral Tir told him to keep it and try to clean it, but he needed her to wear one of these dresses for the marriage ceremony. "Choose a dress. I made these based on your uniform measurements, and I even made them thicker for you, as you are human and a woman, so they will keep you warm onboard."

"Do Alliance women require more warmth as well?"

Mux gave her a look of disbelief. "Yes, women prefer a temperature of 19C."

"What's the temperature on this ship then?"

"Men prefer a temperature of 15C." Mux paused and added, "You may raise the temperature to 19C in your husband's quarters."

"How thoughtful," Kara replied and took the black dress. She was freezing without any clothes on. "Where are my undergarments?"

"We don't have such things in the Empire. Alliance women wear nothing but stockings under their dresses." He handed her some almost transparent stockings and then turned, putting the other two dresses in the admiral's wardrobe.

Kara watched the young man and thought, *Well good, at least Admiral Good-Looking is marrying me himself.* She had to admit it was honorable that he would not ask anyone of his crew to do what he was not prepared to do himself.

Kara looked over the other items the boy had brought. "Where are my shoes?"

"I didn't have time to have any made. You'll have some by tomorrow," he lied. Mux purposely did not make shoes for her as there would be less chance of her escaping without shoes. He knew who she was and that she was not a stupid woman. Her beauty may blind the admiral, but Mux was going to take all the precautions he could think of to keep her where she was supposed to be.

"I need shoes now," Kara demanded.

Mux shook his head. "Tonight, you'll marry, and I suspect, you'll not be leaving these quarters for many days. Shoes are not a priority for you."

Kara narrowed her eyes at the young man. She would make her new husband get her some shoes. Then she turned her attention to fastening the ugly dress.

Mux watched her struggle with the clasps. After a few minutes, he sighed and said, "Let me."

Kara moved her hands away from the clasps and watched the young man expertly close the dress. Unfortunately, he did it too quickly for her to see how he managed. However, once done, she had to admit that although the dress was unattractive, it was both warm and surprisingly comfortable.

In silence, Kara sat on the sofa with the young man across from her for at least an hour. She had tried asking him as many questions as possible to get any information that would help her escape, but he had been trained well and did not respond to her. So, in the silence, she finally nodded off to sleep after she had looked around the room for the millionth time. Soon her dreams drifted to a long-haired alien with a muscular body putting his hands and tongue all over her. She was awoken suddenly by the sound of the door opening and wondered if she had made any erotic sounds during her sleep. Her cheeks were flushed and she was soaking wet between her legs, but the young man's facial expression was still very much neutral when she looked over at him in the chair across from her.

When Tir came in, Mux rose, bowed, and left quickly. Tir took in the human, now washed and dressed in Alliance clothing, and was satisfied that this was what the gods wanted for him. However, he frowned at her messy short hair.

Kara stood up, waiting for the admiral to speak, surprised when he said nothing but just walked right past her into his bedroom.

Tir retrieved his comb and then handed it to her silently.

Kara was so surprised that she did not thank him but sat back down and began combing through her short hair, which had some knots and probably looked very wild.

Tir painfully watched her struggle with her hair for a couple of minutes before he could not take it anymore. He silently took the comb from her hand, sat next to her on the sofa, and said, "Just relax." Then he activated the smart comb and quickly combed her hair slowly and gently until there were no more knots and her hair lay as he supposed it was supposed to. If he was going to marry this human, he didn't want her looking like an ungroomed garden animal. And if he was honest with himself, he had wanted to run his hands through her brown hair since he had met her, and he was not disappointed. Her hair was soft and light. Tir could not help himself and purposely touched the back of her neck gently with his hand with every stroke of the comb. He was pleased she did not tell him to stop or move away. It was an electrifying touch for them both, which was good because soon, he would be touching her everywhere.

Kara was surprised by his gentleness. She found that she was becoming aroused by his actions, his closeness, the smell of him, like petrichor, and the power he had over her. His forcing her to marry him was a situation Kara had never imagined to be in, but against all of her instincts, she found there was something sexy about this whole thing. She turned to look around when he had finished combing her hair, and their eyes met. Are *you not going to kiss me? Do aliens kiss?* she wondered.

Her rapidly changing expressions amused Tir. First, it was evident that she wanted more physical attention, but then her expression changed, and it became apparent that something entirely different had crossed her mind. He caressed her cheek with the back of his hand and got up to return the comb to its place. When he returned to the sitting room, he found her in front of the locked door. He came up behind her and unlocked the door with his code. It opened in front of her.

Kara did not move but looked into the corridor. The admiral's heavily armed guards were there. They looked at her and then at the admiral towering behind her. She could feel him motion to them with his hand, and then they nodded. He then closed the door again and locked it. She still didn't move. He was standing right behind her. His hard body pressed up against hers and curse the galaxy if this wasn't sexy.

Tir put his hands on her shoulders and whispered in her ear, "You can't leave this room. You're still my prisoner until you prove yourself loyal to the Empire and me."

His breath on her ear sent shivers through her body. It took her some seconds to compose herself.

Before she could say anything, he guided her back to the sofa. "Have a seat."

Kara sat. She watched him enter his dining room and pour himself wine in a black ceramic cup. She admired his muscular figure in his black uniform and his jewelry, no doubt marking his bravery and battles won. Kara wondered how old he was. Older than her, but it was so difficult to know with aliens. Then a thought occurred to her. "Have you been married before?"

Tir thought this was a strange question. "No, why would you ask?"

"What do I know about marriage? How old are you?"

"How old do I look to you?" He was amused.

Kara rose and walked over to stand in front of him. She reached up and touched his perfectly symmetrical grey face. He had a few wrinkles, but his grey skin was still quite taut. She knew Alliance citizens lived to be about 300 years, so she said thoughtfully, "I'd guess you to be about 50 years old."

"Not too far off. I am forty-five."

"Young to be an admiral," she commented, wondering how he rose to such a high position so quickly.

"As you are young to be a captain, Kara."

Her body instinctually resonated when he used her given name. "How do you know how old I am?"

"Your ship is docked here. I've looked through all your files and many of your logs. Do you think I'd marry a woman without knowing as much as I could beforehand? Marriage is eternally binding."

"Until you kill me, that is," she said calmly.

"Touché, Captain," he was pleased to see that she was intelligent, but he hadn't doubted that. It was too far-fetched that all her many successes had been luck alone. "But I do hope that you and I," he motioned between them, "can make a good try of a marriage between us. Something for the Empire to see, a new chapter dawning for our people. Both Alliance and humanity." He touched her hair, "And you're nothing short of impressive."

"You're not worried I'll kill you in your sleep?" she asked in a sultry voice that surprised even herself.

"It's a chance I'm willing to take," he took a sip of wine, and then she took the cup out of his hand and finished it all.

Tir poured himself another cup of wine and watched her walk back to the sofa without saying anything more. He thought she still looked beautiful, even out of her uniform, although he could no longer see the human swell of her breasts or hips.

Kara realized they were probably waiting for something or someone to get this marriage ceremony over with. Or maybe they were waiting for him to have some wine; she had no idea but did not want to ask. So, Kara closed her eyes and tried to concentrate on making a plan. All she wanted now was sex, food, sleep, and escape, in that order. But the longer they waited, the more that sleep moved to the top position, and Kara felt herself drift off into a light sleep as she tried to remember what she knew about Alliance men. She knew they were rumored to be attentive lovers and brave soldiers but not much else. And what Kara knew about the Empire was even less, all she could remember was that they were a matriarchal society, but that seemed contrary now to how she was being treated onboard the *Refa*. She wondered if that had just been a rumor. Then despite the frosty air and her hunger for both a man and food, she drifted off to sleep.

Tir drank a couple of cups of wine while he watched Kara sleep. He did not know if he should move her to the bedroom or not. Although he was unwaveringly sure of his decision to marry her, he was unsure how to lead her into this union without a struggle. Alliance women usually led Alliance men in almost everything. He knew human men and women were equal, and he could already see this in Kara's behavior towards him, and he found himself at a loss at how to reciprocate that would be pleasing to her. He did not have time to train her to take the lead adequately, nor did he want to, as that would defeat his purpose of taking a human wife, but at the same time, he felt clueless about how to charm her into this partnership.

The door chimed, and Tir's chief medical officer came in without a word. Tir spoke to him quietly, careful not to wake Kara. "She's sleeping," he explained as he held out a cup of wine to his friend.

Siu took the wine, and they both looked at Kara silently.

Siu needed this cup of wine as much as Tir did. He and Tir, of course, had shared women before; they had been friends a long time, but this was different, it was marriage, and there would be no sharing with his wife. Siu was jealous of Tir and would have to refrain from joining in as he was supposed to be the witness to the consummation of their marriage, not an active participant.

"How long will you let her sleep?" Siu asked.

"She's been asleep for an hour, perhaps an hour more. She's tired." Tir did not care what Siu's other plans might be, this took priority over everything.

"Does she know who you really are?"

"What do you mean?" Tir answered ironically, "I'm an Alliance Admiral." Then he said more seriously, "It's all she needs to know right now. I want her to settle. I don't want her to have to worry about things that won't concern her for a while yet."

"You won't send her back with the others?"

"To be murdered? Can you imagine what they would do to her as my wife?"

Siu drank some wine and nodded. "You don't think your family would protect her?"

"It's questionable," Tir answered honestly, looking at Kara sleeping. "And right now, I'm not willing to take the chance. Besides, I want her here. Even though we are in the middle of a war, I still want my honeymoon."

Sui laughed. "How romantic you are? If this marriage lasts, I'm very skeptical it will, and she finds out she missed the real honeymoon at a real spa. She might hate you forever for it."

Tir smiled. "If this marriage lasts, hating me for missing the honeymoon will be quite far down the list of things she hates me for when she finds out everything."

Sui could not help but laugh again, and with his laughter, Kara woke up.

"Kara, are you ready to begin?"

Kara took a minute to take in her surroundings. She had forgotten where she was. She rubbed her eyes and saw the two tall grey men looking at her. She did not respond to the admiral's question. She was not ready. *Who was ever prepared to get married?* she wondered, suddenly panicked. This was not a joke. She was going to have to do this atrocious thing and she didn't even know how it was done. Her inner voice questioned how she could have been so calm about it hours before.

Tir walked over, stood before her, and repeated himself, forcing her to look up. Then, he bent down and put both hands gently on either side of her face, forcing her to stand.

His hands were cool, and his rings cold against her cheeks. Quickly her mind raced to where those hands and rings would be on her body soon. Kara's body wanted him without question. She felt betrayed by her desires, and then in a voice, she didn't recognize as her own, she replied, "Ready, Admiral." She thought of her lack of underwear and wondered if they waited any longer if her wetness would start to run down the top of her thighs and soak the stockings. She wondered why her body was nonresponsive to her mind. *I hate him, vagina, stop preparing for him to enter me.*

Tir did not remove his hands but softly said, "You'll be one of the few who calls me by my given name now, 'Tir.'"

"Tir," when she said his name, something resonated through them both electrically as if it felt right to call him this and as if she had said it a million times before. She stood deadly still as the feeling of déjà vu swept through her.

Tir felt the same déjà vu feeling, but he knew what this meant. The gods had destined them for each other, and perhaps they were already together in another timeline.

"Is there some Alliance magic at work here?" she asked quietly, looking into his large green eyes.

"No, human. This is what destiny feels like."

"Listen Alliance man, I don't believe in destiny nor do I believe in the galactic gods or any alien religion."

Their eyes were still holding, and he suddenly kissed her passionately. Tir was surprised that she was so warm. His tongue tasted hers. She was so human, so sweet. Then he began exploring her body with his hands. He was intrigued by her alienness, and after each new touch, he only wanted more. After a few minutes, he pulled away, realizing they were still not married. He had to give her his necklace and exchange vows to make this legal. He wouldn't touch her until then. But after the sacred words were spoken, he would have every centimeter of her and give every centimeter of himself to her in return.

Siu watched them and thought, *It's been a long time since I've seen such attraction, especially in an interspecies mating.* While Tir went to retrieve the marriage necklace, Siu poured himself another large cup of wine, settling in to be a spectator.

Kara was dumbfounded by waking up and suddenly being kissed by a man her body found irresistible. Her mind wanted to protest, but she could not find the words or the strength to do anything but wait and see what happened next.

Tir went to his bedroom wardrobe and returned with a heavy intricate necklace. He turned Kara around, so her back faced him and placed the chain around her neck. It was massive on her small frame. "Captain Kara Rainer of Earth, I pledge my life and honor to you in wedlock." He turned her back around. "Now you say it."

Kara turned around and put a hand up to touch the heavy necklace. "Is this it? Are we doing this now? Like this?"

Tir looked at her in disbelief. "Yes?" he was baffled as to why she was confused. "Say the words," he instructed her.

"If I say the words, then we will be married? Forever?" She could not keep the anxiety from her voice. *Or until you murder me,* she thought. Looking into his eyes she knew that he was the kind of man who did his own killing.

"What were you expecting? A blood sacrifice? We could do that if you wanted to, it's quite an ancient thing to do...."

Kara interrupted him, and Siu subdued a laugh. "No," she waved her hand. "I meant without any preamble. You are just doing this?"

Tir looked into Kara's brown eyes and thought, *How do I lead her to this amicably?* Then he explained, "We're a simple culture, Kara. Now, will you please say the words?" He wanted to avoid mentioning killing her crew during their marriage ceremony.

Suddenly, Kara looked up at this gorgeous man, and for some reason, she felt a calm wash over her and said, "Tir, I don't know if you have another name, from the Alliance Empire, I pledge my life and honor to you in wedlock." She could not help but put her hand on the large necklace again. "What's this? A lock?"

"It's a necklace to signify our marriage. Don't take it off." He was not going to mention that he had initially bought that and had it with him to give to another woman because now there was only his human, Kara. Tir took her hand away from the necklace and began leading her into the bedroom.

Siu followed with his wine in hand.

Kara looked over at Doctor Siu. "Is he going to watch?"

"We must have a witness," Tir replied casually, wanting nothing more than to consummate this marriage. Images of Kara with nothing on but the necklace already dominated his thoughts.

"Seriously?"

"Yes," Tir took both her hands and kissed them slowly, allowing her time to relax. After several minutes, he slowly let go of her hands and began exploring her body. He was touching her everywhere over the fabric of her dress. Tir loved lingering in the excitement of what was to be. Caressing her nipples through the fabric of her dress and bringing his hands up the full length of her stockings and then just brushing around the tops of her thighs where the stockings stopped. He could feel her wet arousal on the top of her thighs. Her scent was overwhelming him, and he could focus on nothing but pleasing her now.

Tir began undressing her little by little. He started with the top of the dress, pulling it down slowly, exposing the tops of her shoulders while he ran his lips along her collar bone.

Kara tried to close her eyes but kept looking at the doctor, who was watching them intently. She could not decide if this was utterly barbaric or sexy. Kara wondered if he was going to join in too or only watch. She lost her train of thought then and closed her eyes with pleasure when Tir reached her breasts and said sweetly, "Pink," then sucked and caressed her nipples equally with his tongue and fingers.

Tir had never seen such perfect breasts in his entire life. They fit neatly into his hands and were soft mounds with pink nipples, just like the color of her lips. He loved stroking and drawing on them with his mouth and, even more, the small, gratifying sounds she made when he touched them. Tir was grateful he had not given her to anyone else on the ship.

After about ten minutes, he pulled her dress further down, revealing the curve of her hips. He gently kissed all around her flat stomach and tenderly ran his hands along her hips, enjoying the Alliance floral taste of soap mixed with something else he could not identify, but found exotic and erotic. Tir drew her dress down further to reveal her vulva and was surprised to see a small amount of brown hair. He immediately reveled in the strong scent of her and guided her to lay back on the bed and began kissing around the patch of hair, gently stroking her, hoping that just as with Alliance women, there would be a clitoris there to make her orgasm. He scolded himself, *I spent hours looking through all the documents about her, how could I not check human women's anatomy?*

It had been a long time since Kara had been with a man who knew what he was doing. Most men had no idea about women's bodies and just went in for a good rut, and unfortunately, most human women allowed it, including herself at times. Now she thought, *It's ironic that here I am with an alien who cares more about my sexual pleasure than most human men.* She was so close to coming now, and it had only been minutes of him stroking her, and he had not even touched her clitoris yet.

Tir looked to his doctor across the room to ask with his eyes, 'Do human women have a clitoris?'

Siu nodded, and then Tir continued what he was doing. It was not long before he saw Kara's body opening up to him. She was so exquisite and pink. Gradually, he replaced his fingers, lightly caressing her vulva and thighs with his tongue. He licked her lightly everywhere before finally settling on her clitoris. Tir had not expected her to be on the verge of an orgasm so quickly. Siu would think he was rushing the sex if he made her come right away. So, he backed off and moved his mouth and hands back to her breasts.

Kara did not appreciate Tir moving. So she began wrapping her legs around him, trying to get herself off from the friction between her sex and his clothed body.

Tir smiled, put his hands on her hips, and pushed her down. He hovered over her and said, "Kara, open your eyes." She did. Her pupils were huge with desire, and it pleased him. "We're not nearly done here, I promise."

Kara was looking at this gorgeous alien through a cloudy, lustful haze thinking, *Yes, but I'm a woman. I can come more than once. Come on.* Her body was so on edge. All she wanted to do was orgasm, but he was far away from her now, and all she felt was cold air on her needy sex.

Tir was sucking her nipples, avoiding her clitoris, just trying to keep her on edge.

Kara desperately wanted release. She wanted him to lick her until she was writhing in his mouth. She tried to move one of her hands to take care of it herself, but he grabbed her hand and then put it with her other hand above her head. Tir held them there with one of his hands while he continued to pleasantly torture her with kisses and caresses in all the wrong places.

Tir was pleased that she was so close that she was willing to take matters into her own hands, literally. After he was sure she would not orgasm immediately, he slowly returned to her clitoris, kissing her all along the way from her breasts, stomach, top, and sides of her thighs. Then, he began to build her back up only with his tongue.

Kara had never experienced so much pleasure. She could not even move, she was frozen hoping his tongue would remain constant. She just lay as still as possible to take every ounce of pleasure she could from his attentions, and Kara knew that sometime very soon, he was going to make her orgasm harder than any other man before him, and that was all she could think about.

Then he stopped.

Kara was in such shock she did nothing for a full five seconds. Then she found her voice and said, "Don't stop," and put her hands on his head to urge him back.

"Don't stop, what?" he was looking up at her expectantly. He was confident he would be able to bring her back to come so hard in a few minutes; he wanted to play with her a bit.

All Kara could think about was her erotic desires being met. "Don't stop, Admiral?" she hazarded.

He didn't move, and his face revealed nothing.

She tried to shimmy her body closer to his face.

Tir held her thighs tightly to keep her still.

"Don't stop," she began and then was thinking and then almost cried with frustration when she realized what he wanted. She couldn't say the word.

Tir saw realization cross her face and her hesitation. He would not bend now.

Kara looked from Tir to Doctor Siu. She did not want to say this. It was one thing to say you pledged your life to someone, and he had technically saved her when he could have destroyed her ship, so she did not mind saying that, but to say what he asked now was humiliating and with an audience to boot.

Siu was clairvoyant. He could hear all of the human's thoughts and felt pity for her. He reached out to her with his mind to calm her and assure her that she was losing no respect by saying the word Tir wanted to hear.

Tir was becoming impatient. "Say it, Wife."

Kara almost moved away from him at being referred to as his 'wife.' It was an insult she had never heard but still stung as if it was the worst thing anyone could ever say to her.

Tir saw that she was frozen. Time was passing. He was losing his moment. He began stroking her sex with his finger, looking into her eyes to watch her reaction. He brought her back to the brink of orgasm again and then demanded, "Say it, Kara."

Kara's eyes were closed. She was so close coming. She was squirming closer to him. She wanted to find her release. He was holding her so tightly she was sure she would have bruises on her thighs. And despite all her squirming and struggling, all she felt was the cold air on her sex.

"Say, husband."

Kara opened her eyes, looked into Tir's expectant face, and could not bring herself to say it.

Tir waited and then began again with his tongue to bring her back. This time took longer, but he thought for sure she could not resist this now. She must be almost in agony.

Kara had never been so aroused in her life, and when he moved away from her this time, it only took a few seconds before she whispered, "Husband."

"Louder," he said sternly.

"Husband," she said impatiently.

Tir rewarded her by returning to her with his tongue and working her up again.

She wanted to come so badly.

He began putting a finger into her vagina and slowly moving it in and out while he licked her with his tongue.

Kara thought she was going to die from pleasure. She even repeated the forbidden word to him a couple of times more to make sure he would not stop again, "Husband...husband..." then it was just all sounds of her moans of the building orgasm. She cared nothing for the humiliation in the word she was uttering, although Kara knew she would regret it later when her mind regained control of her body that she was so shameless.

Tir was so aroused himself at the sound of her words and the smallness of her sex, he didn't know how long he could last without orgasming. "You are so tight, Kara." He had heard that human men had smaller penises, but he had not considered what this might mean for human women until now. His wife was warm, wet, and tight, making him crazy with lust. He had never wanted a woman so much.

Kara was in ecstasy and had no idea how long he licked her and teased her with his fingers entering her. But when he finally brought her to orgasm, it lasted for a few minutes, maybe longer, and then it took her several more minutes to recover. Then she began trying to take his clothes off but, unfamiliar with the Alliance clasps, her shaky fingers were clumsy and ultimately, she finally gave up and admitted, "I've no idea how to take off your clothes, but I want them off."

Tir watched her trying to figure out the clasps on his clothing and thought that humans might be the most adorable species in the galaxy. *I don't know who came up with the adjective 'adorable' to describe humans, probably the fools who write for Capital City Gossip Columns, but in this they weren't wrong,* he thought. When she finally gave up, he showed her how they quickly came undone by applying pressure on the inside of the clasp.

Kara undressed him now and touched his cold grey, muscular body with her hands. She noted that her hands looked surreal next to his grey skin. It was like touching a man who was an impossible color.

Tir was watching her pink hands, marveling at the diversity in color. He expected to be repulsed by an alien touching him so intimately, but unexpectedly, as everything else was with Kara, it felt natural.

Kara managed to take all his clothes off and marveled at his muscular body, utterly devoid of body hair. She immediately went down to her knees to take his large, ridged penis in her mouth.

"No," Tir said sternly. He wanted to explain that it went against the goddess for a woman to pleasure a man that way unless she was with child but could not explain it at the moment. He just took her hand and urged her up and back.

"I want to be on top," she said, wanting to be more of an active participant and take some control.

Tir was surprised but acquiesced to her request. He laid down, and she positioned herself, dripping wet over him.

Kara began slowly taking him into her, her hand around his large penis, "You're so big, and the ridges..." she trailed off. He felt so good inside of her vagina, stretching her so much she could not speak anymore, but she did remember the doctor was still there and made eye contact with him as she lowered herself onto Tir. It felt sexy that he was watching her, and Kara wondered if he would masturbate thinking about her later. That perverted little thought also gave her pleasure.

Tir watched Kara bring herself down enveloping him, *She looks like the embodiment of the goddess herself.* The handsome necklace was nestled divinely between her breasts so that it swung seductively with her movements. Her human vagina was so tight, wet, and warm. It took everything he had not to orgasm immediately. He tried to focus on something else and asked stupidly, "Human men don't have ridges?"

Kara was not going to answer him now. She was beyond talking. She would have married him without a fuss if she would have known about the ridges beforehand.

Tir instinctually grabbed her hips tightly to stop her from moving, "Kara, open your eyes and answer the question."

Kara was shocked. He stopped her. She opened her eyes, "Just smooth, no ridges, now let's get back to this. I don't want your doctor to think I'm a terrible lover." She looked up at the doctor again. She could see the desire in his eyes too. She looked back down at Tir and began moving, watching him watching her. Watching his large grey hands move over her hips and breasts. His rings felt like ice against her naked skin.

Tir let her ride him faster and faster, even though he knew he was flirting with his own end. He put his hands on her breasts. He loved watching them sway gracefully with her small movements.

"Put your hands on my hips," she said breathlessly. Tir did, and then she said, "Press me down harder against you."

Tir had his hands on her hips, pressing down in circular motions so that she could grind against him for a few minutes. He then urged her up with his hands off of him, "Let me lead you," then he balanced her slowly over him, lifting her up and down just so the tip of his penis would gently touch her, flirting with her sex.

"That feels so good," she said quietly. "I'm going to come again, but I want you inside me."

Tir guided her hips down on top of him so that his penis was entirely inside her again. He put his hands on her hips and moved one finger closer to her anus. He was toying with it there to see her reaction. He finally gently put his little finger in and saw her pleasure. He put his other hand between them to make sure that her clitoris was rubbing against his thumb while she moved on top of him. It was not long before she was coming again. He had to think of his engineering instructor at the military academy so that he would not orgasm himself.

As soon as she finished, he tenderly flipped her onto her back. "You are so beautiful, my human Wife. I'm going to enjoy having sex with you every day." Then he positioned his erect penis and quickly entered her again. The new position added new friction for both of them.

Kara was looking up at this gorgeous grey man who was now pounding into her and thinking that maybe being married to an alien would not be all that bad for the time being. She lifted her legs so high that she obviously wanted him to take them over his shoulders.

As if reading her mind, Tir held her ankles together over one of his shoulders as he thrust into her. It was not long before he lost himself in all the warm, wet exoticness of his human. And her hair roughly smashing up against his genitals with every thrust reminded him that she was not an Alliance woman. He groaned as he released his hot semen into her. Then he laid down next to her and pulled her close, but still caressing the hair between her legs, now drenched with both of their sexual pleasure. He thought this was disgusting as much as it was erotic and because of the latter, he couldn't take his fingers away.

After a minute, Siu rose and said, "May the gods be with you both and grant you many daughters." Then he let himself out.

Kara remarked lazily, "I forgot that he was here."

"No, you didn't. I saw you looking at Doctor Siu."

"It was shocking to have an audience."

"You are a terrible liar," Tir remarked. When Kara said nothing, he continued, "I'm sure Siu found it just as arousing to watch you as you did to be watched by him. You're gorgeous, Kara, and you certainly put on quite a show." Tir was still absently rubbing the exotic hair on her vulva as he talked.

"What do you mean?"

"Human women are much more vocal than Alliance women, all your wonderful sounds. I'm sure he has gone to relieve himself with another woman onboard, but he'll only be disappointed she isn't human."

"You've Alliance women onboard? I thought there were only men on Alliance ships?"

"Of course, there are women," he did not want to mention what kind of women they might be.

"Are we married now, or is there a blood ritual?"

"Yes, we are married, but we could add a blood ritual if you want? Like I said, it's an older tradition, but I do have a dagger and we could use a wine cup," he said seriously. He had no idea what humans did to mark special occasions, but he doubted it was anything that involved blood or pain.

"No, I'm fine without it," Kara replied, wondering how often Alliance people did include a blood ritual in marriage ceremonies. Her mind was running to how the blood might be used and if the witnesses were involved. Then she shook her head slightly to clear her thoughts and looked at Tir. "What do you expect me to do as a wife in your quarters like this?"

Tir had never heard such a ridiculous question. "We'll have children together in a monogamous relationship. The Alliance needs children, daughters."

"Is that it? How do you know we, Alliance and humans, can even have children together?"

"We know," he assured her.

"I'm not like a pet or anything. What am I bound by?"

"Your loyalty binds you to me and I to you. You're not a pet," Tir was beginning to realize Kara had no real concept of what a marriage was.

"Can I leave your quarters?"

"Not until you prove your loyalty to the Alliance and me, as I said before. But I'll allow you to see your crew off and tell your women what is happening under the supervision of myself and my guards. And don't doubt me; if you try to escape, you will be punished."

"How do Alliance husbands punish their wives?" she asked, baiting him.

Tir sat up and looked down at her. "Do you want me to punish you right now, just for the asking?"

Kara looked at him and was ready for him to take her again in all new ways. She wanted to see his dominant side. "I'm hungry and need food, but I also want to see you try and punish me for the asking… Husband."

DEPARTURES

"How much do you know about Alliance culture?"

"Not much," Kara admitted. "What does this have to do with food? Call your young man and have him bring me some food and vegetables if you please."

"Kara, we only eat at certain times of the day."

"It must be close to eating time, right?"

Tir shook his head. "We missed it."

Kara sat up in bed. She was still naked. "When is the next mealtime?"

"Seven in the morning."

"Tomorrow?"

"Yes."

"And we can't have any food now?"

"It goes against the gods."

"I don't believe in any gods. Get me some food," Kara demanded.

Tir sat up. "As an Alliance citizen and my wife, *you* do believe in the gods now. As such, you will pray to them every day and obey the prescribed eating times. You aren't a wild human animal."

"Did you just call me a 'wild human animal'? You insufferable grey-skinned arrogant Alliance man. At least I never had to abduct anyone I wanted to sleep with."

"I didn't hear any complaints from you an hour ago, Wife."

Kara jumped out of bed and tried to put on her dress, failing because she could not close the clasps. She stomped her feet in frustration and, without closing her dress, went out into the small dining room connected to his quarters, looking for food.

Tir did not bother putting on any clothing but simply got out of bed and followed Kara.

She was so angry at finding no food she took an empty ceramic wine cup and threw it at Tir's head, as he was standing in the doorway, amused.

He caught the cup quickly before it hit his face. Then he went over to Kara, picked her up, and carried her back to bed. All the while saying, "I'll make you forget you are hungry, and tomorrow morning I promise you'll have food."

Kara said nothing. She wanted to struggle but was too tired now and hungry. The last fight she had was in throwing that cup.

Tir removed her dress and lay her in bed gently. Then he lay down next to her. It wasn't long before his light caresses became more intense, and they were making love again within the hour.

Kara didn't know what time it was except that it was night. She was naked, lying next to Tir. They both were awake. She touched the heavy and ornate necklace he had given her. "Do your people always give necklaces away when they marry?"

Tir shifted in the bed so he could look at her. He ran a finger down the side of her cheek and neck and stopped at the necklace, admiring it against her golden skin. "No, we usually exchange bracelets, but I have none here. But we give our wives what is called 'known jewelry' as presents the day after we marry, so I thought this would do for now."

"Bracelets sound fitting, like shackles."

He frowned and looked into her brown eyes. "I know you think I've forced you into this, and in some ways, I have. But I also prayed on this, and I know," he touched his heart with one finger, "this is meant to be. We are fated Kara."

She assumed the finger over his heart meant he was speaking honestly. "You *forced* me to marry you," she said, while conversely running a hand down his muscular grey chest. "But I don't understand why we needed to be married. I find you attractive enough, but to be married as a human is a disgrace."

"As I have told you, we have...."

"I know, a demographics conundrum, you need women, but we don't need to be married to do this." She moved her hand lower to stroke his penis, and he closed his eyes momentarily. "Not that I didn't enjoy the little show we put on for the doctor, but I don't understand this need to say we belong to each other."

Tir removed her hand from his penis and pushed her on her back, holding her hands above her head. His finger found her vagina, and he followed with his erect penis while looking down at her. "Open your eyes."

Kara could hardly obey him as he was giving her so much pleasure. "This is your new life. You're an Alliance citizen, and that comes before everything you knew previously. Moreover, you are mine as I am yours. If you try and escape, you will be punished. If you manage to escape and I retrieve you, I'll kill you myself."

"I don't think you could ever kill me now that you have me. You enjoy me as much as I enjoy you, as strange as this all is," Kara said breathlessly. He was thrusting into her with his ridged penis in such a sensual way she could hardly think. Of course, she would try to escape, and she knew in the back of her mind he would probably kill her for it, but for now, there was this, and she was enjoying herself.

"Do you hear me?" he said a bit breathlessly.

Kara nodded, but she had missed what he had just said.

Had Kara been listening, she would have heard him mention a three-some with Doctor Siu after she became pregnant, but she had been enjoying herself too much to listen, so she had just agreed to it.

Tir let go of her hands and grabbed her hips to thrust into her more deeply.

She was lost in ecstasy.

An hour later, Kara lay across Tir's strong, grey, naked body. "Tell me again, what are the differences between humans and Alliance citizens?"

He answered quietly while running his hand through her short brown hair absently. "We all have grey skin and black hair with green or grey eyes. We aren't as colorful or as beautiful as humans. And as you noticed, ridges in certain intimate places."

She smiled and put her hand down to feel the ridges on his penis, but they were only noticeable to the touch and not protruding against his skin as they did when he was aroused. She wondered why human men had not developed such a fantastic enhancement, given the two species were almost identical. "Do Alliance women have ridges on the inside of their vaginas that match up?"

He laughed. "No."

"Are there more differences?"

"Well, there is the heat; Alliance men are comfortable at 15C, whereas I think you and other women like it at 19C?"

"Try 23C, but it is not like I'm going to die at 15C. I just need warmer clothes."

Kara got up, went into the bathroom, and then admitted, "I don't know how to work your toilet."

Tir joined her in the bathroom. He could not help but touch her arm gently as he passed her. He loved how she looked wearing the large, colorful necklace with nothing else on. It hung beautifully between her breasts as she stood waiting for him. He touched a section behind the toilet on the wall, and a virtual menu appeared.

"I can't read Alliance," she said. "Human translators are for the spoken word only. Maybe you could get me an Alliance translator? Then, I could speak and read with everyone in the galaxy."

"Not until you have proven yourself loyal to the Empire and me. Until then, I don't want you having access to everything in my quarters, so you will just have to memorize the basics." He then showed her which buttons to press. "The toilet will remember you after this." Then he left the bathroom and closed the door to give her some privacy.

Kara sat down on the toilet that had now adjusted for her height and thought about her situation. She decided she would turn her translator on and off when she could, to try and learn not only their written language but their spoken language as well. She figured it could not be too difficult as she spoke a few human languages and was surrounded by the Alliance language everywhere onboard his ship. Moreover, she guessed it would be a good trick to have up her sleeve when she needed to escape.

Humans still loved their little nuances, so unlike the rest of the galaxy, where every civilization had one language, humans still had many, so their translators could be mentally turned on and off. It was also true that humans took the time to learn other world's languages as well, something that aliens found useless and a waste of time. Kara smiled to herself. *Not such a waste of time now as she knew how to learn a foreign language, how to look for patterns and practice.*

Kara now focused on the task at hand. It took her some time to relax and pee. She took in her physical self as she sat on the toilet. Her vagina felt like it had been well-used by his large penis, her nipples raw from all the attention they had just received, and she was somewhat shaky from all the orgasms, but surprisingly, she was still aroused. After she finished, the toilet cleaned her, which was probably the most embarrassing part about smart toilets. Then she looked at herself in the mirror, her naked body and the necklace around her neck. She absently touched the Alliance jewelry, the foreignness of it, and thought, *This isn't forever.*

The mirror greeted her, which she disliked. "Good evening, Kara. You lack nutrition and are dehydrated. I recommend some food and water."

"I know," she answered the mirror, "Tell me something useful, mirror."

"You have Admiral Tir's semen inside of you," said the mirror in a matter-of-fact tone.

"How do you know that?" She could not believe she was talking to an alien smart mirror, but she was too curious to walk away now.

"It's in your urine," answered the mirror.

"Stop talking to me," Kara half-whispered as she turned on the tap and splashed her face with ice-cold water.

"Would you like the water temperature warmer, Kara? It is set for Admiral Tir now."

"No, stop. Turn off. I don't want to talk to you, mirror."

Tir heard Kara's conversation with the mirror and thought, *Ah, this is why they call humans the most adorable creatures in the galaxy.*

When Kara came out of the bathroom, she looked at Tir naked on the bed. He looked so good, healthy, and muscular. His ridged penis was resting, but she knew she could get it to come alive again. Her mind raced to all the things she could do now, but then a hunger pang struck. "I've hardly eaten all week. I would love some food."

"It's still an hour before breakfast." He didn't appreciate that she used the word 'love' but he wasn't going to chastise her for it now.

"I'm human and I'm hungry." Kara realized by his stoic facial expression that these lines were getting her nowhere. She tried again, "I cannot get pregnant if my body thinks I'm starving. My crew and I have been on low rations for weeks. And I guarantee you, my body thinks I'm starving."

He looked her over and thought that was probably not true as his doctor would have seen to that, but since it was only an hour and she had waited throughout the night, he would allow her some food now. "Just this once, Kara. What would you like to eat?"

"Vegetables and bread. Humans don't eat meat." She could not hold back a smile at the thought of food, and feeling a bit happy, she could push him into this. But she didn't congratulate herself too much as it was only an hour away from breakfast.

"You must have meat," he said as he contacted his squire on his IC beside the bed.

"It'll make me ill, so I'll not eat it."

Tir looked at her and remembered his doctor's words, 'Make her as comfortable as possible.' So, he consented to her request with a nod. "For now, I'll not force you."

When the young man arrived, Tir left the bedroom naked to speak to him in the sitting room. Kara smiled to herself at this behavior, *I guess you can be naked and do whatever you need to do onboard an Alliance starship and no one thinks twice about it.*

When Tir returned, he found Kara under the covers in his bed. "Are you that cold?"

"How about we turn up the heat to 23C, and I ask you if you're warm?"

He liked her sass. "Get up and put on your dress. It's been specially made to keep you warm. Your vegetarian food will be here shortly."

Kara jumped out of bed and tried to put on the plain, black Alliance dress, but again and again, she struggled to get the clasps to close. She knew how to open them from taking off his clothing, but his squire, as he had called him, had completed her clasps before when she had put on this dress the first time without explaining how it was done. She was frustrated. *I can install sophisticated machinery on a starship under pressure, but I can't figure out some clasps on a dress. Pathetic Rainer,* she thought to herself.

Tir watched her struggle for a minute and then moved beside her to show her how to close the clasps. Their fingers touched. Kara looked up at him as he finished, and she could not help herself as she ran her fingers through his hair to bring him closer for a kiss. Even though this was a forced marriage, she inexplicably still found him irresistible.

She whispered in his ear, "I'm so drawn to you. I can't explain it," and then sucked on his earlobe.

Tir made a pleasurable sound and began taking off the dress he had just finished putting on her. "It's because we are destined to be together. The gods will it." His hands were on her firm breasts, licking and pinching her pink nipples. "I've never seen such perfect breasts," he said as he could not resist gently kneading them and watching them go taut under his touch. Then he began making his way down her body, slowly kissing and licking her. "And your skin is so soft and warm." His hands were on her hips, now pulling the dress down to take it all the way off. "And I adore this hair," he said, looking up at her while he softly rubbed her vulva. "It's so primal." He breathed in her scent from between her legs. "The exotic human smell of you. Gods, I want to make you come from the touch of my tongue again."

"I'm all yours, Admiral," she said with her head back, not realizing her mistake until he stopped touching her.

Tir could not believe she had just called him by his title. It was a massive insult as they were married now. He looked up at her and soothed his anger by telling himself that she was enjoying herself so much and that is why she forgot. However, he still took his right hand and smacked her hard across the bottom for indiscretion.

"Oww," she said and looked down at him questioningly even though she had liked the tingling sensations on her skin where he had smacked her.

"Who am I to you?"

"Tir," she said.

He frowned and smacked her again.

"Husband," she corrected herself but could not help but add the word "Admiral" afterward.

Tir gave her a small smile and then smacked her rear again, harder. The sound of his hand against her made a loud slapping sound through the bedroom.

"Who am I to you?" he was on his knees, so close to her that his lips were only millimeters away from touching her nether hair.

Kara knelt to be on the same level and kissed him passionately. She was thrusting her hot tongue into his mouth, and her hands were in his hair, pulling him towards her and holding him as steady as she could. In between kisses, she murmured the forbidden word, "Husband." She kissed his neck. "Husband." Licked around his ear. "Husband." And sucked on his right nipple. "Husband." Her hand was on his ridged erect penis, stroking it back and forth. "Husband, I want this inside of me again. I want those ridges rubbing against me."

He pushed her on her back onto the cold floor and moved down her body with more kisses. Everywhere he left, a kiss was followed by her skin feeling the cold air, making her even more aroused. By the time he was stroking her vulva and the top of her thighs, she was begging for him to make her come, "Please."

Tir looked up at her, his green eyes filled with amusement and desire. "Please, what?"

"Please make me come, Husband. I love the way you lick me." Tir then began licking her clitoris in earnest. But then stopped and bit her labia lightly. She screamed.

"Don't use the word 'love.' It's forbidden."

Kara didn't know what to make of this transgression but after thinking about it for a second, she didn't care. "Okay."

Tir decided to leave the conversation for another time. He wanted to bring her to orgasm again. He wanted her to come all over his face so he moved his head between her legs with his hands on her buttocks and his tongue on her clitoris.

Kara was frozen. It felt so good. She did not want to move in case she broke the trance. After a couple of minutes, a massive wave of pleasure overtook her.

Tir was tightly holding her thighs so that she would not move away when the orgasm began to hit her. He had never been with a woman so responsive to his touch, and he thought again, *It is because we are destined to be together.* But because they were destined, he was under no illusion that it would always be so easy. The gods, of course, would make it this easy to begin with but then make things more complicated. It was blasphemy to think the gods did this for their own pleasure, but sometimes he believed they did.

After recovering, she tried to take his penis in her mouth, but again he would not allow her.

"Why not? Don't people in the Alliance do this to pleasure each other?"

"Of course, we do, but it is forbidden unless you are with child," he left off explaining the other part, 'or another man or slave artist.' He knew that no one in the galaxy liked to talk about Alliance slaves. Very few understood Alliance culture and the Empire preferred it that way.

"Not even if you don't come?"

"There's always some before, so, no," he said casually as he flipped her onto her stomach and pulled her up towards him. "But I've no doubt you'll become pregnant soon as we are so enamored with one another. So I'm sure I'll have the pleasure of your mouth on me soon enough." Tir positioned his hands on her hips tightly, and then he entered her so vigorously and quickly from behind he heard her moan with pleasure, *and a little surprise,* he thought.

Kara felt his large, erect penis with its ridges were hitting all the right spots inside of her, and she loved it and toyed with the idea of saying, 'love' again just to annoy him, but was enjoying herself so much she didn't want to interrupt his thrusts. She also kept it to herself that she was on birth control, so she would probably not get pregnant anytime soon. As he was pounding into her, she vaguely thought it was perhaps a good thing to keep that information to herself until she could gauge the whole situation. However, it did cross her mind that he would probably trust her more if she *were* pregnant.

Tir's hands were on the curve of her hips as he powerfully thrust in and out of her. He was intoxicated by the feel of her tight, wet vagina, taking the entire length of his penis like this. And she was making the sexiest little pleasurable sounds. The only thing he did not like about this position was that he could not see her breasts moving in a delayed rhythm with their movements, so he tried to urge her onto her back.

"No. This feels too good. I want you to take me like this, faster. Harder." She loved the feel of him, and she thought, *For the first time in my life, a man might make me orgasm while having sex.* Kara was urging him on, and then it happened. She came again without any more clitoral stimulation, and she thought, *We will have sex every day before I try to escape.*

He came then shortly after. Tir was unaware of how good she found sex with him. Of course, he was enjoying being with such a responsive and exotic human woman, it was something he had never done before, but making a woman orgasm often during sex was normal for him. Alliance women expected it, and the men performed accordingly.

Kara and Tir were motionless for half a minute, then he stood up and put his hands on her hips to help her up.

She looked up at him and said sarcastically, "Thank you for helping me with the clasps on my dress."

"The food is here. I heard my squire come in while your vagina was enveloping me." Tir picked up the discarded black dress and began to dress her again.

Copious amounts of semen and her natural lubricant were running down her thighs and into the stockings she was wearing, but Kara didn't care. She was starving. She figured everything she had on, including her body, would need to be washed anyway. She walked, wetness and all, into the dining room where one plate of food was waiting. Alliance food was famous for being bland and terrible, so she did not expect much. Kara sat down quickly before the food and ate with the three-pronged fork next to the plate. She thought to herself while she was shoveling food into her mouth, *I love eating with a trident.*

Tir came in and sat across from her at the silver table. "The gods be blessed. We are not breaking any laws. It is the breakfast hour now."

Kara was eating and only paused long enough to ask casually, "So Tir, how religious would you say you are?" She was thinking, *No fellatio, because it goes against the gods, no eating outside mealtimes because no doubt this angered the gods too...*

"As religious as most Alliance citizens. Are you spiritual at all my wild human wife?"

"No," she answered evenly. Then she concentrated on eating the blandest food she had ever had.

"Privately, your spiritual life is your own, but publicly as my wife, you must abide by Alliance religious traditions. Do you understand?"

"Or else you will punish me?" She looked into his green eyes with desire and a little humor.

"Yes," he said calmly. "I mean it, Kara. I hold a high rank in Alliance society, and religion is essential to Alliance culture. You must be seen as a believer."

"I'm a terrible liar as you've already discovered."

"Don't play with me," he replied harshly, but already his mind was rushing to all the ways he could punish her for a minor transgression. Finally, his mind rested on one particular punishment he would subject her to when she was done eating.

Oblivious to his devious thoughts, Kara took the wine jug and poured herself some wine to help combat the blandness of the food. She didn't care that it was breakfast. They'd been at war for months and on such small rations she was going to take everything she could get when she could get it. "What happens now?"

"What do you mean?"

"We're married, and then what? Will I live here with you forever?"

"For the time being, I'll keep you here with me, yes. As long as the war is going on, I can justify your presence by saying that you are providing useful information against the Jahay. Which, by the way, I fully expect you to do, not that I think they would share too much with a human, but you must know something useful."

She dismissed his prejudiced comment. "Great," she said sarcastically. "I've always dreamed about being a traitor to my people and allies. Thanks for the opportunity."

Tir frowned at her. "Being my wife is a gift, Kara. You're an Alliance citizen now. Your loyalty is to the Empire. The alternative is death. I hope I won't have to remind you of this every hour of every day that we are together. It makes you look ungrateful."

Kara wanted to tell him to stop reminding her that he saved them, but before she could do that, she reminded herself, *Keep him happy, so he trusts me, and then I can run away with technology, credits, weapons, and possibly even a ship.* "I'll admit you did save my crew's lives and my own, and I do owe you some gratitude for that. And, of course, it goes without saying that the sex between us is amazing, but otherwise, you're still the enemy, and I'm still human. I don't feel like an Alliance citizen. I'm your prisoner. When will you be prepared to treat me as an equal? Only then will I feel some loyalty to the Empire. As I see it, I'd rather donate my eggs to you and be off back to Earth. Why can't we do that? Why all the charade?"

"It goes against the gods to tamper with fertility," Tir said, evenly annoyed by her questions. "You're my wife. Once you have proven your loyalty to the Alliance and me, I'll give you a ship in my fleet," he said gravely. "Earth will become a vassal to the Empire, and we'll need to protect you with a human fleet. And it'd be a waste if you didn't get a command again, you're too good of a strategist to do anything else."

Kara tried not to be charmed by his compliments, but she could not help it. He was an Admiral in the Alliance Empire, they were the most powerful and feared species in the galaxy, and she doubted he got to this position by his good looks alone. "You mean you need a fleet to protect human women in our little corner of the galaxy before anyone notices that we are yours now and sees an opportunity to hit you where it hurts the most?"

"More or less. Don't look at me as if this is the worst thing that could ever have happened to you or to Earth. Alternatively, you could be dead, or humans could be our slaves or enslaved people to the Jahay. None of those things will happen now."

"Why didn't the Alliance just ask humans to consider helping you with this demographics issue before this war started with the Jahay?" Kara knew enough about the Empire to know that they *never* acted rashly. She suspected this invitation to human women had been brewing for quite some time before they acted on it.

"We didn't want to waste our time if you said 'no,' and to be honest, I don't think the pride of the High Council could have taken it if humans, the most technologically un-evolved civilization in the galaxy, had denied us."

"Charming," she said sarcastically.

"I'll not mince words with you, Kara. And you can't tell me that you are unaware of your species' status in the galaxy."

Kara wanted to change the subject back to her getting a ship, "When I've proven my loyalty to you, which won't take long, will I get my own ship again? Will you give me the *Dakota* or an Alliance ship? An alpha ship?"

He laughed then. "Kara, once you prove yourself and your loyalty, I'll give you a beta ship in my fleet to begin with, and if you're perfect, I might even let you bring some of your crew along. As for the *Dakota*, it belongs in a museum. By the way, tomorrow morning, you will see your crew off; if you want to retrieve anything from your ship, you should take it then. Of course, I'll send your male crew back in the *Dakota*. Don't get any ideas, though. You'll be guarded the entire time. You aren't going anywhere."

Kara was still going to try and escape whenever a good opportunity presented itself. She was under no illusion that he thought his words would change her mind about that. "I still need shoes, your young man or squire or whatever you call him, said he didn't have time when he gave me the dress, and I have no idea where my other shoes are. I refuse to walk around barefoot and be your wife."

"We are still in the middle of a war. My squire had other things to attend to. I promise you'll have some shoes by tomorrow." His squire's attention to detail amused Tir. Of course, it had been a gamble. No one knew if a human woman would walk around without shoes.

"I guess I don't need pajamas either?"

His translator translated this as 'clothing for sleeping,' followed by a beep to let him know this was not a direct translation as it did not exist in the Alliance language. "We don't wear such things as they are considered unhealthy and go against the gods' wishes, especially if you are sleeping with your husband. Skin-to-skin contact is best for peaceful sleep and good health. I wonder what other kinds of human habits I'll have to break you from? I'm not above punishing my wife." Tir looked at Kara, imagining all kinds of wild things he had heard about other species in the galaxy, and wondered if any of those things could be applied to his wife.

"I'm going to miss pajamas in my new life," she said, resentfully more to herself than to him. Then she decided she would defiantly bring hers from her quarters on the *Dakota*. He would have to deal with it. It was too cold in his quarters not to have pajamas.

Kara finished eating, drained all the wine in her cup, and then looked at him questioningly. "What should we do now? Are you very busy since, as you keep reminding me, we are in the middle of a war? Or do you want to do some more sleeping with the enemy? Or not sleeping, as it were?"

"Kara, you're no longer the enemy. You're my wife and an Alliance citizen. I'll repeat this until you believe it. Although, I'll admit that you are still my prisoner until you recognize and start acting accordingly. As for my professional responsibilities, my first officer will contact me if there is an emergency. Otherwise, I've another day to spend with you, and I believe your words before were something like, 'Feed me and then punish me for asking, Husband.' We can move on to the punishment now that I've fed you."

Kara could see the desire in his eyes. She wondered then how many times a 45-year-old Alliance man could have sex in a day. "I'm impressed by your stamina, old man."

Tir smiled at her. "It's only because I have such a wild and beautiful specimen from a far corner of the galaxy before me that requires some lessons in Alliance obedience." He stood up, "Come." He walked behind her with his hands lightly on her elbows, guiding her back into the bedroom. Tir then left her standing in the center of the room while he went into his wardrobe and brought out some black ribbons. He gently took off her dress again, touching and kissing her body as he went. After some minutes, she stood in the center of the bedroom naked, and she allowed him to tie her wrists together behind her back with one black ribbon, and then he put the other ribbon over her eyes, so she was blind folded. Then in quite a different tone of voice than before, he ordered her, "Don't move." Then she heard him walk out of the bedroom.

Kara was excited, just standing there in the cold, bound and naked, waiting for him. Her nipples were stiff with excitement, and she could feel her sex wet again in anticipation of what he would do to her. *How would he punish her?*

Tir made her wait five minutes, which he thought was long enough given that this was the first time they were doing this and that she couldn't see what he was doing. Little did he realize that humans could not see in the dark, and he would have scared her if he had just turned out the lights, but he had not thought of that because Alliance people could see well in complete darkness. When he walked back into the room, he kneeled in front of her and ran his fingers lightly up her legs. When he reached her inner thighs, he said, "So much wetness here. You must like your husband's touch a great deal." He gently ran his fingers over her inner thighs, then through the hair over her vulva and back near her anus. He was mixing her wetness and his semen. "Do you like the feel of my semen running down your legs?"

"Yes," she said. *Punishment with an alien was going to be different,* she thought, *I hope I don't laugh.*

He smacked her bottom hard.

She corrected herself, "Yes, Husband."

"Now, what was I punishing you for, my wild human wife?"

"For asking about punishments."

He smacked her again.

"Husband." She had purposely forgotten that time, and she thought, *Yes, spank me harder.* Kara was no stranger to these kinds of sex games, and she was pleased that neither was he. However, as he was an alien, she hoped it would not go too far or get too ridiculous.

"Asking about punishments. Usually, an Alliance man would never punish his wife, but you are human and must learn our ways, so I have no choice. I'll punish you as I would an enslaved person."

"A slave?"

He smacked her hard again.

"A slave, Husband?" She tried not to smile but could not help herself, so he smacked her again, and that time really stung, but she was enjoying every moment of this.

"Yes, slaves brought to the Capital City usually must be trained with rewards and punishments. I'll do the same with you." This was a lie. The Empire had not had slaves from other species for at least ten thousand years and the organic slave class in the Empire only held the title of 'slave.' In reality they were far from being at the beck and call of anyone. But this was role play and he suspected she didn't know any of this, which made it fun. He rubbed her rear. "Now, your punishment for even asking about punishments will be 20 lashes with this little whip I have here. Put your hands out, palms up so you can feel it."

Kara did as he said.

Tir rubbed the small whip along her palms. "Feel the length of it, Kara," he ordered her.

Her fingers ran along the little whip, and she noticed it had two short tails, and she could not help but become aroused thinking about him whipping her with this. She inadvertently squeezed her thighs together in anticipation.

"I'm going to whip you with this across your backside, thighs, and vulva for the asking. Twenty lashes."

"Yes, Husband." *Do it*, she thought, *Oh yes, do it.*

"Lean forward to receive your punishment," he stood behind her, still fully clothed but completely aroused by the whole situation. He wished she would be a bit feistier, but he suspected that she was tired or that maybe she had never done this before and was unsure how to behave.

"Can I put my weight on the bed?"

There she was his feisty captain. "No. Bend over and keep your balance." He took the whip and struck her across her behind with it. "Count."

Kara bent over, keeping her balance. The weight of her necklace felt like it kept her head parallel to the floor. She closed her eyes, waiting for the first strike. "One, two, three, four, five." He kept a slow and steady rhythm. On number five, he purposely struck her vagina, and she winced with pleasure and pain. A tightness between her legs began to tingle.

"Did that feel good?" He was rubbing the whip up and down against the length of her vulva down to her vagina's entrance. "You're so wet my little wild human. I think you might be enjoying this too much. We should make it a bit more painful, or I'm afraid you won't learn your lesson." He struck her then across the backside harder than before.

Kara winced but loved his strength, "Six, seven, eight, nine, ten."

Tir had taken a small break and was caressing her now, her breasts, her stomach, her neck, her hair. Then he grabbed her hair roughly and brought her close to him to whisper in her ear, which gave her shivers.

"Ten strokes left, Wife, tell me where you want them." Tir pinched her nipples, "Here?" Then his hand moved down to her vulva, and he stroked the long length of her, pulling a little at the hair there and she jumped at her sensitivity to his touch when he grazed her clitoris. "Or here?" He knelt then and began kissing her bottom, which was raw from the whipping.

Kara jumped again from the touch his mouth and the surprise of his actions.

Tir held her thighs still as he continued to kiss her behind. He heard her moan a little with pleasure as his tongue circled her anus. "Where do you want the last ten lashes, Wife?" he asked between licks.

She was overwhelmed with cold and hot sensations. She wanted Tir to continue. She wanted him to lick and kiss her everywhere. Kara could hardly think and could not speak.

Tir kept kissing her and licking at her from behind. "I'm waiting."

"Here, Husband," she said, pointing to her vulva. "Whip me here. Make me scream."

Tir looked up at her and smiled, although she couldn't see it because she was blindfolded. He sprang to his feet and stood behind her. Then he guided her to lean back against his chest, put one arm around her, his hand gripping one of her breasts, got a good angle, and began whipping her.

She had not been expecting the sensation that exploded in her body when he softly smacked her. She jumped and forgot to count.

"Count," he ordered quietly in her ear, his breath causing shivers to run down her body. He also pinched the nipple of the breast he held.

Kara was melting in his arms. She could not remember what number she was on, "Eleven, twelve, oh…" He rubbed the whip up and down, slowly, touching her clitoris as he went. Kara was so close to coming. "Thirteen, fourteen, fifteen…"

Then he took a break and was rubbing her again, and she moved her hips to create even more friction between her body and the whip.

Suddenly another smack.

"Sixteen, seventeen, eighteen, nineteen, twenty."

When he finished, he walked away from her and just left her alone wanting.

She heard him get on the bed. Kara suspected he was watching her. She wanted him to come and finish this. To touch her. To do something. She tried to take the blindfold off but couldn't because her hands were tied behind her. Now she began to struggle to get them out, to get the blindfold off and to bring herself to climax as she was so close it was almost painful.

"Don't struggle," he said from across the room. "Just wait."

"Wait, for what… Husband?" she added his new title at the last minute to gain some favor.

"For me to decide how long I should punish you for."

Kara stood there thinking, *I hope it won't be too long. I want him. I need him to touch me.*

Tir left her for ten minutes. He would have left her longer, but he realized how tired she was when she began to waver. But he was impressed that she did not ask to be released again. He guided her to the bed. "How do you want me to enter you?"

"Like a dog," she said breathlessly.

"What's a dog?" he asked.

"Never mind. From behind, like before." She got on her knees on the bed, and he held her wrists with one hand and her hair with the other.

"Primal," Tir said as he entered her, impaling her rhythmically.

Kara was tied, blindfolded, and he was holding her so tightly she was completely at his mercy. He was controlling everything now, and she screamed, "Yes, harder! Pull me against you harder."

Tir had never been with a vocal woman before, and it made their sexual connection even more powerful. He grasped her wrists with a strength he had never used with a woman before and increased his thrusts to be stronger and deeper. After a minute, he was rewarded by her coming again, which triggered his own orgasm.

When she thought she would collapse out of pure exhaustion, he held her as he took off her blindfold and untied her wrists, but Tir noticed that she almost fell when he released her, so he effortlessly picked her up into his arms and took her into the shower.

Tir looked down at Kara in his arms and said, "This is probably going to be very cold for you." The water began to fall in that instant.

She screamed at how cold it was. It was not the 25C she thought was cold before, this was freezing.

Tir set her down but held on to her, so she did not escape or fall. Soon the shower was providing soap, and he was spreading it all over her body gently. He whispered in her ear, "This won't take long. I know it's cold for you. But your covered with the remnants of our sex together. What kind of husband would I be if I didn't clean up my own mess?" After he washed her and himself quickly, the shower turned off. He grabbed his comb, the same one he had used last night and combed her hair. Then his own, and activated the dryer.

Even though she was clean and dry now, Kara was still shivering. She barely registered that the shower had scented her with some artificial smell she recognized from his scent, and she found it mildly revolting. Humans didn't mask their odors.

Tir carried her to the bed. He put her under the covers. "These blankets will adapt to the temperature you require so you will not be cold. I'll join you in a minute. Try to warm up."

Kara nodded and then disappeared entirely under the blankets. She was so cold she wanted her head and everything under them. It was not long before she began to warm up, and she was relieved that he was right about the blankets.

When he returned, he got in and held up the blanket to look down at her. "Are you okay down there? Or do I need to call the doctor?"

"I'm getting warm."

He moved down the bed, under the covers, so their heads were at the same level and their faces only centimeters apart under the dark covers. He stroked Kara's short brown hair. "Kara, we will try to come to some compromise about temperature."

She looked into his green eyes and nodded. Kara had never been so intimate with a man she hardly knew before. She wondered if she would get to know him for better or worse by such close intimacy so soon. *She thought to herself and then questioned again, How long will it take for him to trust me? A year? After some children?* She frowned and firmly ordered her mind to stop thinking and to work on warming her body, nothing more. *Take each moment as it comes,* she reminded herself. So, she closed her eyes then and allowed herself to drift off into a deep sleep.

Tir watched Kara fall asleep as he stroked her hair. Unexpectedly, under the blankets like this, just the two of them, he felt the connection between them was so natural. And every moment they had like this, he was even convinced she had been sent to him by the gods. But, he could not help but remind himself that even though they were destined for each other, she still had a lot to learn about the Empire and could not be trusted. Not until she at least bore him one child, he decided.

His doctor had investigated all their information about human women's fertility and briefed him earlier this evening before their wedding. Women from Earth ovulated more often than Alliance women and were fertile for fewer days per cycle, but Alliance men's sperm was stronger and would last longer once inside her body. Doctor Siu reckoned that he would be surprised if it took longer than two of Kara's cycles for her to become pregnant, given her age and health. However, he did warn Tir that stress and past lack of food during the war could contribute to her not becoming pregnant. Tir was still stroking her hair even though he knew she was fully asleep and thought to himself, *You are strong and willing. We will have a daughter. It is the will of the gods.* Then he stopped stroking her hair, pulled her close against him and brought both of their heads above the blanket, and tried to go to sleep himself.

Sometime during the night, Kara woke up, and she was confused. She did not know where she was. She sat up.

Tir put a gentle hand on her arm, and she instinctively swatted him away and tried to jump out of bed.

"Where am I?" she said into the darkness.

Tir could see that her eyes were open and realized that humans could not see in the darkness. "Lights on," he said and got out of bed to try and comfort Kara. She was looking at him, confused. He wondered if she was still sleeping. "Kara? Kara?" She didn't answer him, so he tried to take her arm, and she backed away. "Kara," he tried to grab her wrist again and succeeded. He held her close against him and stroked her hair. "You are safe," he said quietly to the top of her head. After about five or ten minutes, he could feel her begin to relax in his arms.

Kara had been so scared when she woke up and didn't know where she was and when the light was turned on, she was so confused. She had been dreaming, and her own people were interrogating her for being a spy because of him. She kept saying that they weren't married because, in her mind, she would never be married, she was human, but no one believed her. Kara breathed deeply, closed her eyes, and tried to clear her head and think, everything had been so bizarre since she had said his name for the first time, and it felt as if the galaxy had been turned upside down. She didn't believe in religion, fate, or destiny, but she didn't know what to make of all of this and needed to ask a question that had been at the center of her dream. "Are you the Emperor?"

He stopped caressing her hair. "Why would you ask me that of all things?"

"I had a nightmare. My people interrogated me for being married to you, and they said you were the Emperor. I know that the Alliance has one; I just don't know who that is or how that works. Surely the Emperor wouldn't be in the Alliance Fleet."

"I can assure you I am not the Emperor," he said softly. He could feel her relax, so he almost felt guilty about the lie, but he knew now that the gods had sent her that dream to her to warn him to be honest with her or face their consequences. "But I am the successor." He could feel her stiffen again.

"What does that mean?"

"Successor?" He wondered if her translator was malfunctioning.

"No, I know what 'successor' means, but does that mean you will become Emperor tomorrow? Next year? What are you going to do with me when that happens? I know your people don't like aliens. Will you discard me, kill me then?" She was asking all the same questions now that both her interrogators had asked her in her dream. She felt so weird, like different realities were colliding. She was herself, but not herself.

"It is five years before I am supposed to succeed to the throne. And you are right, the Alliance would never stand for a human Empress, but when I saw you, I had to have you as my wife. Now I will probably abdicate, but that comes with its own issues. I wasn't going to trouble you with this information now, but it seems as if the gods thought you should know."

"You don't have a brother or something to take it and grant you a pardon or something for marrying an alien?" Although men and women had been equal on Earth for centuries, because the Alliance still practiced religion and marriage, she assumed it was more like ancient Earth.

"It doesn't work like that; the position of emperor is based more on merit than birthright. Important people will be angry because they will feel I wasted their time. I won't lie to you. They will want to kill us for it. But if we take imperial power in five years, they will be upset because you are human and want to kill us for that too." Being Empress of the Alliance was one of the most important positions in the galaxy. They would both be killed if he even attempted it with Kara. *But who knows what the next five years will bring? But at the moment she is far from ready from holding any important imperial positions.*

"Wow. When were you going to mention this to me?"

"I don't know. Perhaps after we were so in rapture with each other that you would not kill me for it." He touched her face lightly with the back of his thumb. "Please, Kara, let's not think about this anymore. You are safe. I'm never going to let your people imprison you. It was just a nightmare."

"Stop lying. Everything here is strange. Why do I feel like I know you, but I don't. We just met. And now I have a nightmare only to find out that some of it is true. Did you put hallucinogenic drugs in my food?"

"No," he said, offended. "We don't use drugs. Our relationship, our marriage, our connection, this is all the will of the gods."

"I don't believe in religion."

"Well, come up with something yourself because I believe. I'm glad you had this nightmare. Now you know what you have married into."

"Tir, I don't want to be Empress and die for it or die because you forced me to marry you. I'm not an Alliance woman. All I ever wanted to do with my life was be a starship captain. I wanted to have an interesting and exciting life out in the galaxy. I never want to be a mother. I definitely don't want to be a wife."

Her words cut him deeply, but he answered her stoically, "The gods chose you for me for a reason; only time will tell where our true destiny lies. You should forget about your inconsequential human life before you met me."

Kara raised her hand to slap him.

But Tir grabbed her hand forcefully. "Don't you ever raise a hand to me, you barbaric human. I will tame you if it is the last thing I ever do in this galaxy." He saw the shock on her face and wanted to take back his racist comment but could not. He had already said it.

When Tir let go of her hand, she slapped him hard. "Don't you *ever* call me a barbarian. You're the one who forced me to marry you. Sex is one thing, but marriage is an archaic and cruel practice which is why most of the galaxy, as you well know, my dear illustrious Alliance Admiral, gave it up centuries if not millennia ago."

Tir looked at her and said icily, "Would you rather I had married you off to one of my junior officers? I could have. I thought you deserved better than that." He wanted to add, 'But I didn't because I have adored you since the moment I set eyes on you.' Instead, he said, "But I would not have trusted you to have married anyone less than your equal; otherwise, without a doubt, we would have had a mini-revolution of human women on our hands in less than a couple of years." Even though he was paying her a huge compliment, she still looked angry.

"Kara, listen to me. We're going to have fantastic sex — we're not going to be murdered by anyone anytime soon if we can help it. You're going to get your own ship again, and we'll save both the Alliance and human civilizations. But we need human women to balance our numbers. The sooner you and I have a child as an example to the rest of the Empire, the sooner our demographics problem will be stabilized and the better we can figure out what has happened with our own women. In return, the Alliance will protect Earth, and you must admit you need protection. The Alliance will allow humans to develop as they would choose, except for a few differences, women and protection. As my wife, you are not a pet, but you are still my prisoner for the moment. The sooner you accept your position, the sooner I can trust you, and then you can start freely enjoying your new status in the galaxy as an Alliance citizen." When she did not reply immediately, he asked, "Right?"

"I guess when you put it like that, it does not sound too terrible, given my other option was death by your command." She did not add that, 'And it still might be.'

He mistook her face expression. "I know you don't hate me. We don't know each other well, but there is something between us. To feel it, you do not have to believe in religion or destiny."

She nodded. "Fine, I just want to sleep now."

They got back under the covers, and he turned out the lights. He held her, and after a long silence, she said, "I think the gods sent me to you to keep you from being emperor. I always want to be on a ship free in the galaxy. I don't want to live in the Empire, not ever."

"I agree. I have a suspicion we wouldn't last long."

In the morning, Tir woke up before her and got out of bed to check his ships' statuses. Nothing out of the ordinary had happened during the night. He made sure his squire had her shoes made by the time he brought breakfast for them. He went into the bedroom to wake Kara when breakfast was laid out. She was sleeping so soundly he did not want to wake her, but he knew she would be upset if she missed another meal, so he said her name gently. She didn't stir. He touched her arm, and she shooed him away. Then he picked her up and stood her up on her feet, and instantly, she tried to get back into bed. He picked her up again and smacked her rear.

"Really?" she murmured, rubbing where he had smacked her.

He noticed she had some bruises from last night, and he wanted to kiss those away but reminded himself that he would have to do that later as they had things to do this morning.

"I didn't want to wake you, but I knew you wouldn't want to miss another meal." Tir left her standing naked next to the bed with her eyes closed. He went to his wardrobe and got a clean dress for her and some warm, black stockings. He placed them on the edge of the bed. "Or do you want me to dress you?"

Kara ignored him and slowly began putting on her clothes. First, the thigh-high stockings, which felt nice and warm, and then the navy dress. After some minutes, she struggled with the clasps and had only managed three out of ten clasps before he came to her rescue. "I'm making progress," she said sarcastically.

"Of course you are."

"Thanks," she said when he had finished helping her.

Tir then handed her the necklace he had given her to signify their marriage. "You should wear this."

"Every day?"

"Alliance women would wear it often at intervals with the jewelry they already had."

"I will skip today as my interval."

Disappointment crossed his face.

She couldn't believe it would mean so much to him. "It's heavy, and I'm not accustomed to wearing any jewelry. Get me something much smaller, and I'll wear it daily if that makes you happy," she lied.

"Don't lie to me. In the Empire, your jewelry reflects my status. If I got you something small, people might not think I'm much more than a beta captain."

"How many Alliance men are married to human women?"

"One."

"One other than you?"

Tir motioned his finger between them. "Only us. And you know it."

"Good. Then there will be no confusion. Everyone will know I am your wife dressed in these clothes as I guarantee there is a good reason no other women in the galaxy ever willingly wear Alliance dresses, and I need not wear any of your jewelry to signify my position or your rank." Kara said the last lines and pointed to all the jewelry he wore to further prove her point. "But I do need shoes."

"You think Alliance dresses are unsightly?" he asked surprised. He thought they were attractive.

She looked at him in disbelief.

Just then, the door chimed, and the young man who was becoming a familiar fixture came in with shoes for her. He laid them at Kara's feet. They were flat, black boots and looked warm and comfortable. Kara put them on immediately and felt much better, almost good enough to wear his jewelry as she reminded herself to try to make him as happy as possible.

When the young man left, Kara asked, "What is his name?"

"Squire Mux, you can refer to him as Mux. Now let's eat."

Kara sat down to another bland breakfast of some form of bread and bland vegetables, like potatoes but with less texture, if that was even possible. She was still starving, though, so she ate everything and then asked, "Do you have coffee or tea? A warm drink, perhaps?"

"No, only water or wine. In the Capital City, we have begun importing human drinks and food. When you move there...."

She interrupted him, "I'm not leaving you given that I could be assassinated now that I'm your wife. I want my ship. Don't forget."

"I can only keep you here as long as the war continues. After that, you will have to leave or join my fleet. It might be you need to spend some time on the Capital Planet alone."

"No, you will give me a ship after the war if not before," she said determinedly.

"We'll discuss it when the time comes. As I've said many times, you must prove yourself, and I mean really prove yourself." He had not considered that she would want to remain with him. It was forbidden, of course, but if he was honest with himself, he never wanted her to leave. "Now, you must go to your ship and get your things, then inform your crew of their futures. I would prefer it if you wore the necklace I gave you yesterday, not for your crew but for mine. We are married."

Kara said nothing but nodded acquiescence.

Then they both rose from the table.

Tir retrieved the necklace from the bedroom and put it on her. "Let's go," he said, and they walked out the door together trailed by four large, heavily armed Alliance guards.

"You're not taking any chances, are you?"

"You managed to take out more than one Alliance ship with your inferior vessel. One ship could have been luck, but any more than that was skill. I'd never make the mistake of underestimating you."

They arrived at the docking bay, and there was her *Dakota*. The admiral and his guards followed her onboard the old ship. She was not ashamed; it was a great ship and had served her well. She would be sad to see it go without her. Kara went to her small quarters, just a room with a bunk and a desk. Only the admiral followed her in. She got a duffel bag and started putting clothes and things in it. She had an extra uniform and asked, "Do you mind if I wear this to speak to my crew, it might be the last time they see me for quite some time."

Tir stopped investigating all the random human things he had become fascinated with on her small desk and considered her question. "Fine, but this is a favor I am doing for you. Do not forget it. I'll want something in return later."

Kara nodded, took off the dress and necklace, and laid them politely on the bed as she took out a pair of underwear and a matching bra; she never thought she would be so happy to see them and put them on. She specifically chose the one sexy pair she had onboard, thinking Tir may appreciate them.

"What are those ghastly things," he asked, looking at her bra and underwear with slight disgust.

"Undergarments. Human women like to wear them for comfort."

"Those undergarments look unattractive," he said and wondered if human clothing was so uncomfortable humans had to cover their more sensitive areas with extra clothing. "If you wear those undergarments under your Alliance dresses, I'll cut them off with my sword."

Kara turned around half naked and gave him a skeptical look.

"I'm giving you fair warning."

Kara was not one to be intimidated. "I'd love to see you use your sword to do that without hurting me. Don't think for a second I would just stand still and let you ruin some of my clothing." She smiled, thinking *Alliance men probably found the ugly dress I had on before attractive if they think black lace bras and underwear are unattractive.*

Kara put on her red uniform and zipped it up. She felt much better now. Then Kara slipped the dress and necklace into her bag with her other things. She was also sure to grab some old-fashioned pictures of her parents from her desk, a book, her computer, and all her other items that were the most important to her. When she finished, she turned to him. "We are going to take some coffee and tea too, come on," and she led him to the mess where she pillaged coffee and tea and some spices.

"Is that everything?" Tir asked.

She nodded.

Tir motioned for one of his guards to take her belongings. "Take Captain Kara's personal items to my quarters after thoroughly inspecting them for weapons." Tir did not want to take any chances.

Kara was annoyed by the incorrect use of her name and that his guards would inspect her things. She emphasized the improper use of her name first, "That's not my name," she admonished.

"Your family name is now the same as mine, and we do not use family names in general conversation, so yes, that is your name, 'Captain Kara,' and that will be the name for the rest of your life unless you leave the military or gain or lose rank. Now come, we must send off your crew."

Kara walked with him out of the docking bay and down the corridor. She wanted to correct him again, to defend her name, a name she would always have, but soon they entered the brig, and she became solemn seeing her crew behind the forcefield. They all stood up and saluted her. She had never felt so guilty in her entire life.

Kara addressed her male crew first. She had no doubt they had heard what had happened, that she had been forced into marriage with the admiral to save their lives.

"All male members of the crew *Dakota* will return to Earth with the promise to the Alliance not to engage in this war any further as terms of the agreement I have made with the Alliance Empire through Admiral Tir." After she finished her announcement, their forcefield went down, and her male crew was hastily escorted away by the extra Alliance guards who had accompanied them in before she could even say proper goodbyes. But Kara made eye contact with all her men as they walked by her in a single file line. Their faces all said one thing to her, 'This is not over, Captain,' and she wholeheartedly agreed. This story was far from over.

Then Kara moved to stand in front of the holding cell where her female crew was waiting to hear their fate. She looked at them all evenly. "All female crew of the *Dakota* will be sent to the Alliance Capital Planet to be married to Alliance men. The rumors are true. The Empire is suffering from a demographic problem. We must sacrifice ourselves to preserve both the Empire and humanity. I have been assured that fewer human women will be taken if we cooperate." Kara had been assured of no such thing, but she couldn't tell these women that they were just being taken as wives, a social practice only observed by the most backward civilizations in the galaxy. "Alliance men will treat you with respect, and there are laws to protect you. Ask for new translators once you reach the Empire so you can read and stay in contact with each other. Be strong and be proud to be human. Don't forget that they need us more than we need them right now. I will find you all." Kara felt guilty and silently vowed that she would escape and free them from this Alliance slavery, even if it took the rest of her life. These women were her responsibility, and no one owned human women.

Kara looked at her crew and let them protest. She hated that she was doing this to them.

Tir looked at Kara. "Calm your crew, Wife." He purposely used her new title to humble her in front of her crew because he knew humans thought it was a disgrace to be married.

Kara pretended she didn't hear him. She knew he would do nothing to hurt her or them. The Alliance desperately needed human women as they were too religious to employ their superior medical technology to manipulate natural fertility. When she saw the last woman go through the door, she said under her breath, "Don't give up on me. I'm coming for you all."

PRISONER

Kara watched the last of her female crew from the *Dakota* walk onto the transport that would take them to the supply ship and then on to the Alliance Capital Planet. "It's marginally better than being dead, I suppose."

"The sooner you assimilate to your new lives, the sooner you will be together again on a beta starship in the Alliance fleet," Tir said frankly. "Living superior lives that could have never been possible on Earth or in the human fleet."

"Why do you keep saying that?" She wasn't trying to be rude, as she wanted to win his favor and escape as soon as possible, but keeping an even temper when he kept repeating this ridiculous notion of her and her female crew having better lives in the Empire was grating on her nerves. "Not everything in life is about being the best. We are human. I'm human. My heart will always long for Earth." She looked up at him. He was a bit shocked by her little speech. "You better get used to hearing that, as it will not change as long as I live."

"We'll see about that, Kara. Alliance citizenship is a gift. You must begin to come to a compromise in your heart." He lightly touched her chest where her heart was located to mark his meaning. "The gods demand it."

Kara was just annoyed by his words and actions. She felt guilty for putting those 26 women from her crew in this situation.

When Kara didn't follow Tir immediately when he began walking, his personal guards pushed her forward a little then she started walking behind him to their next destination. She wished she was heading back to Earth with her entire crew, not here married to this alien, not sending her female crew off to be alien brides. And underlying everything, she was especially upset with herself for enjoying his touch.

Her little speech about being human amused Tir. He liked her pride and loyalty to her own people, despite them being so lowly in the galaxy. At least when he had earned her respect and trustworthiness, he knew it would be real.

They made their way to the conference room. He was going to have a strategy meeting with all his captains and he wanted Kara to be there to put her on the spot about Jahay locations and ships. He had purposely not told her about this so that she would have no time to prepare adequate lies. He only wished he could have kept more than her doctor behind as a hostage to hold over her head, but it would be better for the Alliance and his relationship with Kara if he showed compassion towards the humans in his care.

After a few minutes of walking, Kara realized they were not returning to his quarters. Her mind was racing with possibilities, all of them terrible. *Was he going to torture her for information about the war and the Jahay?* Tir was correct before in assuming that the Jahay did not share such information with her. Still, she and her crew had easily intercepted and decoded their communications, and she knew a lot more than she was supposed to. However, now that her crew was gone, he had very little leverage over her. She wondered then if he thought she would tell him what he wanted, she reckoned he would be arrogant enough to think so.

One thing was clear for her, though, she had no loyalty to the Jahay. True, they had never enslaved Earth or tried to colonize them, and they were supposedly humanity's ally. But, they had forced humanity into their war, over disputed space that had nothing to do with Earth, and it was because of them that she and her crew were now in this strange situation with the Alliance.

And the admiral had saved her entire crew, granted he had ulterior motives for the women, but he had still saved them from death and allowed the men to return to Earth free and unharmed. So, there was no clear moral path for what she should do now. But as was her custom she would make a decision in the moment based on her gut instinct.

When they arrived at the large conference room with a table and twenty-some chairs all occupied by Alliance officers, she then knew what was going on. There were two chairs empty, one at the head of the table and the other next to it on the side. Tir pointed to a chair next to his for Kara to sit down, and she sat without speaking. She was happy she wore her uniform to show that she was not just some human woman married to Admiral Tir. Every time she remembered she was married, it sent a wave of humiliation through her. Although she righted herself now and looked back defiantly at all the curious Alliance men, who were staring at her. They all had the same color grey skin and long black hair, but their facial features varied. She then looked up at Tir and thought, *Well, at least I don't find you attractive because you are exotic to me as an Alliance man. You are good-looking among your people too.*

Tir did not look at Kara but addressed his captains, "As you all know, the last battle with the Jahay was a success."

Kara doubted he used the word 'success' often by the reaction of the other men. And she could verify it from her end as well, and it had been a clean and well-won victory.

Tir brought up a virtual map above the conference room table of this section of the galaxy with Alliance and Jahay ships marked. He began discussing the battle, fast-forwarding through to different events, stopping at other times to talk about how things had happened to criticize or praise some of his captains.

Kara was surprised that he even mentioned her ship at one point in criticism against one of his captains for letting her get so close as to do a bit of damage. She was even more surprised that he turned to her then and said, "That was well done, Captain. You have a brave crew considering had my captain been faster to react to your maneuvers, neither one of you would be sitting here with us now."

Then, Tir talked about where they thought the Jahay might have regrouped and their strategy for the next battle and the rest of the war, which he hoped would be over soon. Then he looked at Kara and said, "Captain Kara, please show us where they have regrouped on the map."

Kara looked up at him without expression. "I'm sorry they never told human ships where the rendezvous points were until it was sure we had survived the battles or reconnaissance missions."

"I believe the Jahay would have kept this information from you. They realized for some time now that we would do everything we could not to harm humans. However, Captain, I know you aren't the kind of woman who would wait for an alien species like the Jahay to tell you where to go and what to do. Now tell us, where is the next rendezvous?"

Kara just looked at him. Of course, he was right. But she was not just going to give him the information so easily.

"Captain, your doctor is still in our brig. Does that refresh your memory?"

Kara sighed. She would not let John be tortured over what he did not know. And it was obvious Tir would have this information from her either now or later, after real torture, so she decided to save them all the trouble. She looked at the small virtual console in front of her on the large conference room table and tried to figure out how to bring up the coordinates, but without her handheld translator, she could not make out the Alliance written language. So, she stood, walked around the table to the amusement of the Alliance men, and pointed to the places on the large virtual map that were displayed.

Tir was pleased that she was clever enough to realize her situation and resign herself to it. He also had to admit that he enjoyed watching her walk around the table in her tight red uniform. He still had his fantasy about her wearing that as foreplay. However, it unnerved him that his men were also admiring her figure, and Tir was shocked by his own emotions. Jealousy was the most frowned upon emotion in Alliance culture. In the Alliance, everything and everyone shared according to their position.

Kara returned to her seat, and Tir began making more plans with his captains. Surprisingly, Kara found she was less cross with Tir the longer the meeting went on. She watched and listened to him discuss the war's progress with his captains. His men seemed to respect him in a way that she found a bit cold, but she reasoned that it could just be their culture; Alliance people were not known for their warm personalities. Sitting in the meeting, not being expected to participate again, she could observe him and learn more about him and his culture. He was tall, even for an Alliance man. Unlike many of the other men, who wore their hair in a braid or multiple braids, he always wore his loose or had in the last 48 hours, and she wondered if this was a status hairstyle, as everything in one's appearance in the Alliance Empire was connected to rank.

Kara wondered what kind of culture the Alliance really was. There were so many rumors around the galaxy, it was difficult to know what was true and what was false. It was often said that the Alliance culture was brutal and archaic, especially regarding honor and women. Kara knew for certain that Alliance women rarely left the Empire and were forbidden from serving in the military. So, she looked at him now and wondered if he really would give her an Alliance ship once she gained his trust. She had no reason to doubt him. He had not lied to her yet, and if the Alliance needed human women and not as sex slaves, it was better to entice humans with what they wanted and needed in the galaxy, which was more technology. It occurred to her then that maybe that was the Alliance's plan all along, to begin with the women serving in the starships and have a kind of trickle-down effect to women on Earth who might even come freely to be wives in the Empire. She had some friends back home that read a lot of historical romance novels and would probably love to be married, even if it were to a grey-skinned man that lived on a cold and dark planet with strange religious beliefs.

Tir asked Kara a question and she almost missed it as she had been daydreaming about her friends at home. "Captain Kara, how many Class One Warships does the Jahay have in sector two?"

She looked at the virtual map between them and found sector two by identifying the stars as she could not read the Alliance hieroglyphs. Kara closed her eyes, trying to remember the maps she had seen from their intercepted communication. "I believe only one, Admiral." She assumed that she should not call him 'husband' here, but didn't mind if he whipped her again privately for the misdemeanor later.

"You are sure?"

"As sure as I can be for only seeing the information once three days ago."

"Good enough."

Tir was finishing his well-organized meeting now.

Kara was surprised that all his captains rose and bowed to him after he formally ended the meeting with a religious prayer. She stood but was not going to bow to him, although she could not deny that she was completely aroused that he commanded so much respect from his men. Despite whatever rank he had been born into in his society, he had definitely earned this position of admiral, of which she was glad. She could never have been with someone who was a fool. But then she reminded herself she probably could have escaped already if she had been forced to marry a fool.

Tir ended the meeting and then waited for everyone to leave. He sent his guards outside the door and then locked it with his DNA. He walked directly over to Kara and began fervently kissing her.

Kara had not expected him to just come to her with so much desire, here in the conference room, only 30 seconds after he had just finished a meeting. But after a couple of minutes of kissing each other, she did not care that they were in the conference room and his guards were right outside. Tir's hands were on her hips, pushing her body against his, she could feel that he was aroused already, and his tongue was exploring every area of her mouth. She knew this would be different than the sex they had had in his quarters, that this was fantasy sex. But she didn't mind. She had thought he was sexy while he talked about the battle that had brought them together and future strategies about crushing the Jahay. It was partly the Jahay's fault for her position now anyway.

Kara's suspicions of Tir wanting to play out a fantasy were confirmed when he said, "Ever since I saw you in here yesterday, I wanted to do this. And watching you walk around the map with your fitted uniform and all my captains' eyes on you was," he struggled for the word, "invigorating." He would never admit to being jealous.

"If we do this," she said between kisses, trying to sound like she could stop kissing him at any moment. "This is your favor for letting me wear my uniform."

"I know," he said between kisses. "Why do you think I agreed so easily when you asked to take off the dress and put on your uniform?"

"This is what you thought when I asked to change my clothing? This moment?"

"It was the first thing I thought of, yes. Then I considered how it would look to my men, and I decided the prize outweighed the embarrassment of my wife not wearing her jewelry the day after we married. Now come back here my wild human wife, I want you."

Kara had scooted away a little in disbelief.

"Kara, I'm not a complete brute. Although I have never had a prisoner before, I'm trying to make this as civilized as possible. And there's nothing wrong with a little alien role play."

Kara looked into his green eyes. "I don't think you can use the words 'civilized', 'prisoner' and 'wife' in the same sentence. But I will admit one thing; I *love* it when your hands are on me." She could not help herself; she used the forbidden word to annoy him.

"I'll allow you that word since we are human role playing."

She looked at him, his large penis already erect tenting his uniform and her body wanted him so badly, although her mind warned her against her physical desires, Kara easily dismissed those warnings. Instead, she tried to wiggle off the table to remove her uniform quickly. "Wait, it's better if I stand up." Then a thought occurred to Kara. Something she knew Tir would die for. She jumped down and commanded him, "Sit."

Tir sat down in a chair as Kara stood in front of him, only about half a meter away. She was going to give him a little show. One of her hands on her uniform zipper, innocently playing with it, looked at him and said, "I heard the Alliance never took prisoners. What are you going to do with me then? I don't want to die."

Tir tried not to smile at her words, mocking what he had said to her just moments before. Of course, he was more than pleased she wanted to live out this fantasy as well, "What do you have to offer, human?"

"Well," she said in a sultry voice, slowly beginning to unzip her uniform. When she reached her belly button, she smiled at him seductively. "I've never been with an alien before. Should I be scared? You know there are all these rumors about Alliance men in the galaxy, and

I'm just a little human woman. We don't mate outside our species. I'm so afraid of you, but I don't want to die either. Please be gentle with me." She was running her index finger up and down the sliver of exposed skin from where she had unzipped her uniform.

Tir was surprised she said that and wanted to say something clever and sexy back, but his mind was blank. "Let's take it slowly. I wouldn't want you to pass out from your fear. Unzip the rest of your uniform."

Kara looked at him and then slowly ran her hands seductively over her body, cupping her breasts and biting her lip, before she began slowly unzipping her uniform further. When she had it open all the way, she turned around and looked over her shoulder at him while she slowly worked it off her shoulders. "I'm very shy. I've never done this kind of thing before. I feel so naughty. I hope you're not going to spank me for doing it wrong."

"You are the worst liar. If I weren't enjoying this so much, I would laugh," he said quietly and heavily. He felt that this was a show she had done many times before, *And why not? She was so sexy in that uniform.* "I permit you to be as naughty as you want, Captain. Maybe it will help your situation here as my prisoner. I've heard humans are very naughty," he said, playing along with the fantasy.

Kara put her finger in her mouth, looked at him, then took it out with a seductive pop and said, "As naughty as I want? You dirty alien man. You've no idea how wicked my mind can be."

"Oh my wild human, I give you permission to be as wicked as you want to be then. I want to see *everything* you have to offer."

Kara still had her back to Tir; she slowly pulled the rest of her uniform down and stepped out of it. She was crouched down seductively and then ran her hands slowly up the back of her legs over her bottom, skimming her hips through her short, brown hair until her arms were high above her head. After a couple of seconds, she lowered her hands to rest on the back of her neck and looked back at him again. Then she ran her hands back down to her black lace underwear and began rubbing her rear. There were some bruises there. "As you can see, I have already been so naughty and adequately punished for it. But you know I loved being punished and then well, I can't say, I'm too embarrassed." Then she began pulling her underwear up to cause friction against her clitoris and anus. "But you know what I mean? You know what I want don't you? Do aliens you know, in the same way?" Then she ran two fingers over her pulled underwear. "But I can't help it. I'm so bad and need punishment from a big bad alien like you. I need you to put your hands all over me and teach me how to be in the galaxy."

"You'll have to show me more bad behavior if that is what you want. So far, you've done nothing wrong here," Tir said barely able to remain seated.

Kara gave him a feigned look of confusion. "I'll do my best." Then she turned, put her hand down the front of her underwear, and stroked herself while she bit her lip and looked at him with innocent eyes. "I'm so wet already thinking about having an alien penis inside me. That is the extent of my naughtiness now. All the while you were talking to your men, I thought about your strength and power. I wanted you to strip me down and take me in front of all of them, to show them who I belonged to," she guessed from his reaction to his doctor watching yesterday that this would also be an Alliance man's fantasy.

Tir was impressed. "Keep touching yourself like that, and I promise I'll thrust into your vagina so hard you'll never want to have sex with a human ever again. You'll only desire Alliance men and only me."

"Are you sure? I mean, how do you know? Have you ever been with a human? Maybe you won't like the way human women feel on the inside? We are so much warmer than Alliance women. Maybe you won't like the feel of that warmth? Or maybe our vaginas become too wet and slippery for your penises?" she asked, coming closer to him. "Maybe you won't like how tight I feel once you're inside of me? You know, humans have all these curves," she ran her hands down over her hips to her bottom. "And we have breasts," she touched her breasts over her bra until she could see that they were hard with arousal. "And we have hair, do you want to see?"

"Show me the hair between your legs."

Kara gave him a coy look. "I'm too embarrassed. What if you don't like it? I'll be so desperate for sex then; what will I do? I'll have to use my fingers to bring myself to orgasm and that will be so shameful, and even then I know it won't be enough to satisfy me now after I've imagined your alien penis impaling me."

"I'll like your hair. I promise."

"You promise to still have sex with me? I need you inside of me. I've been so naughty. Throughout the meeting, I was looking at you, thinking about you, hoping that you might find me attractive enough to have sex with."

"Show me the hair on your body, human. I want to see it and run my fingers through it."

Kara slowly bent down in front of him again, and she was so close to where he was sitting that her rear almost touched his knees. She slowly pulled her underwear down, giving him a nice view of her bottom. Then she stood up slowly and turned around, her hands over her vulva. Her head was down in feigned embarrassment.

Tir could not take much more of this. She was driving him crazy. He could smell her desire. "Show me that little patch of hair covering your most private parts."

Kara slowly moved her hands away, and once she did that, he pulled her to him and began kissing her passionately. Tir ripped off the bra and was sucking her nipples as if he had never seen them before. In no time, he had her up on the conference table and was kissing her all over while his finger was moving rhythmically over her clitoris in a way that he was finding worked for her here and now. Tir knew that she was close to coming. He whispered in her ear, "You are so wicked and so wet."

"Barbarian," she whispered breathlessly, and then she orgasmed hard against his fingers.

"I adore your face when I make you come. You look like the goddess herself," Tir said before he tore down his trousers. He entered her quickly and forcefully and completely enveloped by her slick vagina.

Kara's legs were on either side of him, and he was enjoying the sight of her as he thrust into her again and again. The way her breasts bounced with every thrust.

After some minutes, Tir flipped her over and held her hands behind her back, her breasts pressed hard against the conference room table. "You're so wicked; I bet this is going to make you come again." He spanked her rear a few times before entering her again. Fast and hard.

Kara could not believe he was pounding into her on the conference room table right after a meeting. She knew it was his arrogance, but then she thought, *He is right; he will make me come again.* She wondered if she would ever be able to leave if they were going to have sex like this every day. Kara hated herself for enjoying this ecstasy so much and for being unable to turn him down. But then she thought, *This is aiding in my escape.*

Tir climaxed shortly after she did a second time and pulled out of her. Semen and her wetness dripped from her empty vagina now. She sat up. He pulled up his trousers and then grabbed her uniform from the floor.

"No, I need to put on my underwear first," she instructed him, and he handed her the black lace underwear. Kara put on her underwear to somewhat stop the flow of semen running down her legs and then looked around for her bra, which he had thrown in the heat of the moment. She jumped down and went across the room.

"Where are you going?"

She picked up her bra off the floor and held it up to him as an answer but did not put it on as he had ruined it, so she kept it in her hand.

Tir brought her uniform over. He looked her up and down before giving it to her. Then he ran his fingers over her labia through the fabric of her underwear. "I want you to wear those for the rest of the day." Then he gave her her uniform.

They had made a mess of sweat and sex on the table. "Should we make an effort to clean that up?" Kara didn't know anything about Alliance housekeeping habits, but compared to her ship, everything was spotless. And had she done this in her own conference room, she would have put in a little effort to make it not look like what they had just done.

"No, a slave will do it."

"Tir, it's not like we spilled some water."

"I don't understand you. You're my wife. Everyone onboard knows we were just married. For a culture that does not get married anymore, you can be very prudish. I'll send the slaves in to clean the table."

"You keep slaves onboard?"

Tir looked at her and realized there was still so much she did not know about Alliance culture. "Of course, we always have slaves with us.

I'll explain it over the midday meal. Right now, I need to return you to our quarters because I've some *actual* work to do." He could not help but run his fingers through her hair as he looked into her big brown eyes. "Thank you for helping with the Jahay strategies."

"How do you know I wasn't lying?"

"Because I already knew where the rendezvous point was located from the intelligence I received this morning. You just confirmed it." Then he smiled a little and added, "And we both know you're a terrible liar. And you're not stupid, so I'm sure you only lie as a last resort. Today wouldn't have warranted that risk."

They walked back to his quarters in silence, followed by his guards. The crew they passed in the corridors bowed to him and looked at her curiously.

When they reached his quarters and Tir escorted her in, "All your possessions are here. I'll do my best to keep you onboard the *Refa* with me as long as possible. Take your things and put them where you want. This is our space now." He paused, considering, and then finally said after a couple of seconds of hesitation, "I'm guessing you're going to go through my things as soon as you're alone, but to save you some time, I'll just tell you, there are swords in the bottom of my wardrobe. But don't bother trying to use one to escape if you've never used a sword before. Other than that, there's nothing else of interest to you in these quarters. I'll be back soon."

Kara did not like his smug attitude. She was going to go through his things, and she was sure she would find something to help her escape. As much as she loved the sex she couldn't stay with him. As soon as he left, the first thing she did was go check out the swords at the bottom of his wardrobe. Sure enough, there were short swords like the one he wore in the black and yellow boxes. Kara quickly went through her things from the *Dakota* and found her handheld translator. Then she held it over the engravings on the swords. She got bored after a while, and they were all awarded for his different ranks throughout the military. Nothing was surprising about them at all. She put all the swords back in their boxes and back at the bottom of the wardrobe.

When she returned her handheld translator to her bag, she got the small painting her father had painted for her of the beach near their house at sunset. She put it next to what she would assume would be her side of the bed as she slept on that side last night. And lay down looking at the small painting, "What would you think of this now, Dad?" she said quietly to herself. She could not help but wonder, *Will I ever be there again to see a sunset on that beach?* Suddenly Kara became very sad and was happy she was alone because she needed a good cry for all that had happened in the last weeks, especially in the previous 24 hours, and the shower was way too cold to have a good proper cry in.

Kara let her emotions go completely. Better here alone than in front of anyone else. She cried for being married, losing her ship and half of her crew, and for not dying when maybe she should have instead of accepting this marriage deal. And then she cried for humanity, for wasting so much time on frivolous things instead of military, technology, and defense. After she had cried for all those things, she wiped her eyes and felt much better. Kara always felt that hitting rock bottom with a good cry was the best way to propel herself back up more quickly.

She went into the bathroom to splash water on her face, and the mirror began talking to her again. "Good afternoon, Kara. Would you like the water warmer? It is currently set for Admiral Tir."

"Leave me alone mirror."

"Do you need some help shaping your eyebrows?"

"No, what's wrong with my eyebrows?" Kara asked, touching one of them looking in the mirror. She had never done anything to her eyebrows. She had always considered them one of her natural beauties.

"I can recommend different shapes..." the mirror suggested, and Kara interrupted.

"Absolutely not. Can you tell me when my next period will begin and what Alliance women do for that?" Human women still used a menstrual cup because humanity was all about being close to nature. Still, she suspected that Alliance women would have something much better with all this technology and Kara was ready to embrace that technology.

"Processing," the mirror said, then continued after about a minute, "Kara, I have insufficient data to confirm your next period as you have only been aboard a short amount of time. Please seek advice from Doctor Siu in sickbay on deck five, section two."

"What can you tell me then, mirror?"

"I can tell you many things. Ask me a question."

"How many women has Tir brought to his quarters in the last year?"

"Admiral Tir has brought three slave artists to his quarters in the last year."

"What?"

"Admiral Tir has brought three slave artists to his quarters in the last year."

"I heard you. Turn off mirror," Kara said as she went to sit on the toilet and take all this information in. *Slave artists*, she thought to herself and felt a bit sick.

When Kara finished in the bathroom, she went into the sitting room, armed with her handheld translator again, and turned on his computer. She tried to bring up any basic files on the *Refa's* crew complement but was locked out of almost everything but internal communication, and she knew that was on purpose. Then she got out her inferior computer and began looking through the little cultural information humans had about the Alliance. She scanned through all the statistics until she found the part about slaves, but it just said that the Alliance had a class of slaves. She slammed the button to close her virtual computer and thought, *Useless.*

Kara sat in silence in the sitting room and thought, *Why am I so upset? Was it because he was with other women before me or because they were slaves, or was it both?* She thought about it for many minutes and concluded that it was both. Kara had to admit that she was fascinated with him, and she was jealous, even though these feelings were ridiculous because she had just met him and was planning on escaping the first chance she got. But when she thought about what the mirror had told her, she was not only upset that he had been with other women and slave women, but she couldn't help but imagine that he had taken advantage of his position to be intimate with them. And in her mind, this meant rape. But it was difficult for her to imagine him raping someone given that he was a very considerate lover, he did not seem like the type, but then she reminded herself you never really know about people until they have committed the crime.

Mux chimed the door and came in without Kara saying anything to allow him entry which annoyed her. He greeted her by bowing and explained he had brought the midday meal and would lay it out in the dining room. After he finished, he told Kara that Admiral Tir was on his way soon to join her.

"I just have one question, Mux."

He stopped and looked at Kara.

"How many slaves are onboard, and how many of the slaves are women?"

"I don't know exactly. At least 100 slaves and probably 35 of them are women."

"And why are the women onboard?"

"They are artists," he said as if that explained everything.

"I didn't think the Alliance produced any kind of art," she said suspiciously.

"No, artists in that they recite some of the ancient myths, dance, and provide basic entertainment."

"Entertainment? For money?"

He nodded. "Of course, Captain. Is there anything else?" Mux did not want to discuss slave artists with his master's wife.

"No, thank you."

It was not long before Tir returned, and he was pleased that she had waited for him to begin eating. "Shall we eat now?"

"Wait. I want to ask you about something."

He could tell she was annoyed about something, but he was perplexed about what could be bothering her as she had just been sitting in his quarters for the last 40 minutes, putting her things in order and no doubt going through his things.

"I was talking to the mirror," she began and realized she sounded like a crazy person but tried to hurry past that fact and be serious. "And it said that you had three slave women in here this past year. Explain to me why you would need to rape a slave woman?"

It took all his self-control not to laugh at her for getting jealous from what the bathroom mirror had reported to her, or be furious about the assumption he would ever take advantage of a woman. "Kara, I'd never rape a woman. I'm offended that you would even think that. Second, slave artists are here of their own free will, and they don't do anything they don't want to - ask any man on this ship. Not only that, they're making a lot of UCs off of all of us for their time. I can ask one to come and join us now if you don't believe me. They recite ancient myths, religious texts, history, and battle stories. They keep us all sane when we are so far from home and our families. We have been a spacefaring civilization for a long time. Sex is a physical need; slave artists, both on the ship and on the planet, provide release. It's only sex."

"Why are they called 'slaves' if they are here of their own free will?"

"It's an old class marker, and maybe millions of years ago, they were enslaved people because of their closeness to the gods, but no longer. Slaves own land, have their own UCs, and control their destinies as far as the gods allow for any of us in the Empire."

"But what about the Alliance's slave planets?"

"That is a completely different thing. Those people are not slaves but merely live in territories we took. They are not citizens of the Empire. But still, no one is raping anyone there that I know of. I've never raped anyone, and I don't know of anyone who has committed rape or been raped. We marry, and I understand that you find this barbaric, but we don't rape. Understand? Can we eat now?"

She stood up. "I'm still uncomfortable, three women, Tir?"

He put his hand on her shoulder. "Gods, we've been married for one day, and you are jealous about three women I had to pay to come here over the last year? Shouldn't you be feeling sorry for me? Three women is not a lot, and I can assure you, despite my good looks, they charged me a fortune."

She frowned. "I'm not jealous about the women as much as I am that you had to pay them." But if she was being honest, she was jealous thinking about him with someone else.

He looked at her and didn't know what to say for a minute, this was a normal part of his culture, and no one had ever questioned him about it. "Of course, I had to pay them. I didn't emotionally connect with any of the women; it was just sex." He almost smiled then remembering the threesome he had with the slave artist Sera and Doctor Siu.

Kara looked at him and did not know what to say. Prostitution was legal on Earth, of course, but she herself had never bought sex, but then again, she had never needed to either. "Why did you do it?"

"Pay for sex?"

"Yes."

"Because the woman I was courting was on the Alliance Capital Planet, and I wanted to have sex. These slave artists choose their positions. They are famous throughout the Alliance; they cost a small fortune and prey on the men who are off-planet for long periods."

"You make it sound like you are the victim here."

"No one is a victim," he looked at her and thought he was explaining this all wrong. "This is a matter of consumerism. I don't understand why you are upset."

"Do you plan to still sleep with those slave artists now that you are married?"

"Only if you want to."

"Like a threesome?"

He nodded.

"I can't suck your penis until I'm pregnant, but threesomes are okay? What kind of gods are the Alliance worshiping?"

"Threesomes only with other women until you are pregnant," he clarified as if that would make more sense to her.

"You must be joking?" Kara let out a laugh then. Then her mind was racing. "What about orgies?" she asked as a joke.

"All the same rules apply," he said, not understanding how strange this sexual practice was for her. In the Empire there was sex for good health that could include many people and there was romantic sex between a husband and a wife.

Kara looked at him in disbelief.

"I don't understand why you find this shocking. Sex is a natural desire. Should I call a slave artist here now? I wouldn't mind seeing one again," he suggested provocatively.

"No. I can't believe you get married but then still sleep with these slave artists. How is that logical?

"How do you track your ancestry on Earth if not through marriage? Humans do not have a large population. Aren't you worried about incest? We never procreate with slave artists, only those who we are married to."

"Tir, we are not wild beasts and don't have a problem with incest. We always run genetic tests at special centers before we decide to have children together. But we usually don't sleep with other people if we decide to be exclusive with someone."

He saw his opportunity to change the subject and took it, "What do you mean, 'decide to have children together?' Certainly, procreation must *just happen* with a lot of the population without government or religious involvement?"

Kara was so fired up; that she forgot who she was talking to, "We're all on birth control until we decide not to be."

"Women take birth control? Are you on birth control now and didn't say anything?"

Kara looked at him blankly. She hesitated.

"Are you on birth control, Wife?"

She answered him, "It's technically still in my system, yes. Unless your doctor did something to make it inactive?" Kara noticed his expression and tried to appease him, "I was going to mention it when you mentioned getting pregnant, but then you took my breath away the first time we were having sex. Afterward, I forgot I hadn't been able to tell you. Don't be so cross; not much time has been wasted. We've only been married for a day."

Tir rose from the table, came to her side, took her arm gently, and escorted her down to sickbay. Their food remained untouched on the table.

Kara was surprised to see her doctor John working with Doctor Siu.

Siu looked up when they walked in, excusing himself from John, and escorted Tir and Kara into a private room. "Is something the matter?"

"Human women are on birth control," Tir said, annoyed.

Kara was surprised Doctor Siu looked so horrified by this information. He then politely asked Kara to lay down on the medical bed and began running a handheld device over her, looking at the results on the little screen.

Kara was watching Siu's face as he worked and remembered how he watched her have sex with Tir at their marriage ceremony, if you could call it a 'marriage ceremony' she thinks of it as 'that night I slept with an alien and his alien friend watched.' Then, she could not help but wonder, *Did you find one of these slave artists and have sex with her imagining it was me, Doctor?* She had to admit to herself she was aroused again, thinking about him watching her, and then she wondered, *Do his scans tell him I am aroused too?*

Siu was good at blocking thoughts that did not concern him. He had to be. Most doctors in the Alliance were bred to be empaths and telepathic, and Siu was no exception. But he decided he could listen to Kara's thoughts because they did concern him, and he had to use all his self-control not to smile and say, 'No, my machines don't tell me you are aroused, but your eyes and thoughts do, and I would happily watch you have sex again. And I'm looking forward to you becoming pregnant because then I might be able to share you with Tir.'

Siu finished running scans and professionally said, "The human birth control is at such a low dosage, it wouldn't inhibit Alliance men from impregnating human women, but I'll flush it from her system and let our doctors know of the situation on the Capital Planet. I don't doubt Doctor Anu can easily take care of this at Space Port One." He looked at Kara then and said sympathetically, "I'm sorry that you were ever put on birth control. I cannot imagine what a backward place Earth is."

Kara was very confused now. She sat up. "What are you talking about? We aren't backward. Do Alliance women breed a thousand babies not being on birth control?"

"No, Captain, you misunderstand. You have it the wrong way round. Women's bodies are sacred. You are the bringers of life. To interfere with women's health is to interfere with the gods," explained Siu. "Also, from a biological point of view, it is much less invasive to have men use metabolized birth control."

"Alliance women never take birth control?"

"Only slave artists are allowed, as they have a special agreement with the gods. But even then, it's not necessary as most men are on birth control."

Of course, slave artists have a special agreement with the gods, thought Kara. She could not believe she was going to have this conversation with a doctor but then decided that he had watched her have sex with a man she was forced to marry, so there was nothing professional about their relationship. "Do people only have sex with slave artists before marriage then?" Kara wanted to double-check what Tir had told her. She did not see any reason Siu would lie to her about this.

"No."

She looked from Tir to Siu and waited for more information, and when she did not get it after a short pause, she asked, "Are you going to explain this then?" Then she looked at Tir. "I'm assuming you are not on birth control?"

He looked at her, annoyed. "No, let's go. I'll explain all of this later." He wanted to go and eat. If they hurried, they could return to their quarters in just enough time to eat the midday meal.

"Wait," she said to Tir and then, looking at Siu, asked, "What do Alliance women do about their periods? As you might have guessed, we are very old-fashioned on Earth. I'm sure there is something better here."

Siu looked at her and could see in her mind the shape of a small cup filled with blood. He suppressed a shiver from the savagery of it and the waste of blood down the toilet. "We have a little device Alliance women call, 'the tab.' We have some here in sickbay, but I'll have to look for them. When I find one, I'll call for you and show you how to use it. I think it will be much more convenient than your cup."

"How did you know?" she trailed off.

Siu smiled at her.

"Alliance doctors can read your thoughts," Tir told her.

Kara blushed, thinking about all the sexy things that had been going through her mind over the last few minutes.

Tir and Siu smiled at each other, and Tir did not have to wonder too much what she had been thinking about that made her blush.

"Wife, do you have any more questions for Siu?" Tir asked with a bit of humor in his voice.

"No, I think I've asked enough for today. Thank you, and do not forget to look for that tab, Doctor."

When they walked out of the private room in sickbay, Kara looked for Doctor John as she wanted to speak to him, but he was nowhere to be seen. Then she asked Siu, who was walking behind them, "Where has Doctor John gone?"

"He has gone to eat the midday meal. Should I call him back?"

"No, I'll speak to him later." She was so hungry herself she wanted to eat too. Kara and Tir left sickbay and began walking back to his quarters. "I'm starving."

"I hate to tell you this, but we have missed the meal."

"No," she said in disbelief. If John was eating, there was still time. "What are you talking about? The food will still be there, right?"

"No, the midday meal ends in just a few minutes. Mux would have taken it away by the time we returned. We must wait until evening now."

"You've got to be kidding."

"Kara, next time you want to talk about something, wait until after we have eaten."

"So, we have missed the meal; what about Siu? Did he also miss the meal?"

"Yes. If I come in there, Siu has to attend to me whether it's mealtime or not."

"Why didn't you say something? I'd much rather eat lunch than question you about women from your past."

"Good. You'll remember this then. I thought I made it clear yesterday, but maybe I shouldn't have allowed you to eat when it was not a time for eating sanctioned by the gods."

When they entered his quarters, she went immediately to check the dining room; sure enough, there was not a bit of food to be found there. She did pour herself a cup of wine. "I'm so hungry. How long until the next meal?"

"Six hours."

She took her cup into the sitting room, and he gave her a disapproving look. "What now?"

"No food or drink outside the dining room," he said and thought, *Gods, humans are primitive.*

"But yesterday?"

"We had wine outside the sitting room. It's true. I do break the rules sometimes, but you need to be trained first, then you can break the rules. Stay in the dining room, human."

Kara went back into the dining room, sat down with her cup, and scowled at him angrily through the doorway.

Tir sat on the sofa and began reading something on his IC as if everything was fine.

Kara could not help but wonder how often he had missed a meal, which is why he was so fit. No doubt there would be countless times that he was busy with work and would miss the meal. Suddenly she felt sorry for him and all these Alliance men; they must be hungry all the time.

Kara drank her wine and then poured herself another cup and wondered again how difficult it would be to escape, how she would even begin to plan such a thing. His guards were always outside; even if she could get past them and get to a transport, she wouldn't get far. His ships were too powerful. She resigned herself to learning the language and gaining his trust unless another opportunity wildly presented itself out of the blue, but she doubted that would happen. Kara finished her second cup of wine and reckoned it would probably take her having a baby for him to trust her. And if that was what she would have to do, that is exactly what she would do. She had to get home and back to Earth. She would not allow her emotions to get in the way.

But she looked at him and asked, *Are you strong enough to have a baby and leave it with him? What kind of man is he? Would he kill it? Could I escape with a baby too?* She thought about all this while she watched him quietly reading something on the sofa.

After she finished her third cup of wine, she joined him in the sitting room.

Tir looked up as she sat down. "Better now?"

"I'm not a child," she said, a little drunk from the wine.

"Don't act like one then," he admonished her.

"Humans eat whenever we want," Kara said, and he gave her a

disapproving look. "Don't look at me like I am a wild animal. We've mealtimes, of course, but they are more just guidelines."

Tir looked seriously into her brown eyes. "And now you are an Alliance citizen, and you'll act in a civilized manner and obey Alliance mealtimes sanctioned by the gods themselves."

Kara held his gaze for a long time. She could not believe he had again suggested humans were uncivilized. She thought, "You *carry a sword, practice marriage rituals, and still believe in religion, and you are calling me uncivilized?* But she said nothing to him while she calmed herself; then, she asked, "On the path to civilizing me, could you please teach me some Alliance written words so that I can at least make out the symbols in the bathroom and the internal communications?" he frowned so she added sweetly, "Or you could reconsider and just give me a proper translator? I'm your wife, after all."

"You're my wife, but you are also my prisoner. I'll introduce you to the program we give to children learning to read." Tir opened a virtual program on the small table between them. He flipped through the menu.

Kara could not help but smile when she noticed that the last thing he had used this table for looked like a strategy game.

"Do you like games?" she asked.

"Yes, do you know how to play Uki?" It was an Alliance strategy game; many people in the galaxy knew how to play it. He had no illusions that he would be able to win against her once she learned to play.

"No, I've only heard about it, but I'd like to learn."

"I'll teach you, but now it's better if you learn to read a little first. I've no intention of giving you an Alliance translator soon, especially after you failed to mention the birth control."

"We've been married for one day, Tir."

"And how often did I make it clear that we need to have a child? I know you are far from being a fool, so do not take me for one either."

"Show me how to work the children's reading program," she said politely, wanting to change the subject.

The learning program began and spoke to her like a very young child, but it explained their written language perfectly. Unfortunately, Alliance was not entirely phonetic, but she was not completely put off by that. Many of Earth's ancient cultures had not used phonetic writing systems, and humans still managed to use them. Once she listened to the explanation in English, which went through all the hieroglyphs in the first chapter, she mentally turned off her embedded translator and listened to it again in Alliance. When she heard Alliance spoken, she was disheartened, it was tonal, and there were so many tones, at least more than five. Then, she realized that learning Alliance would not be as easy as she thought. But she thought she might as well know it to aid her escape. There were locks on high-security weapons and information that were only accessible to native speakers; even humans had them, even though no one had ever tried to take anything except some art from humans.

Tir said something to her then, but she didn't understand him because her translator was off. "Sorry, what did you say? I was concentrating." She mentally turned her translator back on.

"It shouldn't take long to learn the core hieroglyphics and our complementary phonetics, and Alliance children learn to read at a basic level in 30 weeks."

"And your great civilization never thought about a completely phonetic alphabet? Our children learn to read in days."

He shrugged. "What is 30 weeks of study in a child's schooling? And just because human children can pronounce all the words after a few days does not mean they know them. It's just a different way." Tir had never had to defend his written language to an alien before and felt defensive.

"True," she smiled at him, "Now let me get back to the first hieroglyphs."

Tir didn't reply or smile back but thought, *Gods, let me not be so taken in with how enchanting my wife is every second of the day, even when she is uncivilized or questioning Alliance culture.* He decided then that after she had finished chapter two, he would take her to the bedroom and then in the shower. Then they would have the evening meal, and he would have a slave artist visit them afterward.

———

Kara finished the second chapter and was ready to begin the third when Tir interrupted her by showing her a hieroglyph on his IC.

She didn't recognize it. "Should I've learned that one?"

"No, they do not teach it to young children."

"Sex?"

"Close. Try again."

"Orgy."

"No."

"Anal sex."

"No, and we can't do that until...."

She interrupted him, "I don't want your ridges going in there, ever."

"Some women enjoy...."

"Not me. A finger occasionally, maybe, but that is all. No ridges ever do you hear me?"

He smiled at her. "I understand; it's not something I prefer. But maybe in the future, you might want it. Have you figured out the word on my IC yet?"

"Just tell me what that word is. You are getting me out of the mood talking about anal sex, and I can see from the size of your pupils you are aroused."

"Masturbation."

She laughed a little. "Why are you showing me that?"

"I want to watch you masturbate."

She began to get excited by the idea, "While I was trying to learn how to read Alliance, that is what you were thinking about?"

Tir nodded. He did not understand why she thought this was an odd request. She was his wife, and he wanted to know her inside and out. If he could not bring her to climax as fast as he could for himself after a year, he would feel that he was failing her as a lover and a husband. Part of his understanding would come from him watching her pleasure herself.

Kara got up and went into the bedroom. She looked at him, waiting for him to follow her. "Do you want me to wear my uniform as you had that fantasy earlier?"

"No, just naked. I'll turn up the heat to 19C in the bedroom." Tir was so pleased she would do this. Most Alliance women would have made him wait a year, if not more, as they would feel they were giving their secrets away that men should have to work for.

Kara took off her uniform, and the cold air immediately grabbed every nerve in her skin and gave her goosebumps. She got on the bed and lay back on the smart blankets that were thankfully already heating up to make her back feel warmer. When she knew he was watching, she closed her eyes and began touching herself lightly with a finger.

A few minutes passed before he said, gently and softly, "No, Kara, touch yourself like I'm not here. I want to know you, not what you think I want to see."

Kara opened her eyes and looked at him; green eyes met brown, "All right, but then I want to flip onto my stomach."

Tir smiled and thought to himself. *Yes, I thought so.* Then he got up and lay down next to her. Although it was difficult to see her hands, he could still sense her movements.

Tir was far enough away that she could not kiss him, but if she reached her hand out, she could easily touch him. She lay flat on her stomach and gently touched her clitoris with her right hand. Then as the minutes passed, she increased the speed and pressure. About 15 minutes had passed, and she was quickly caressing her clitoris with big, strong circles while her breasts were pressed against the warm bed.

Tir turned her a bit to the side then as he knew that she would only welcome his mouth on her breasts, and she came within minutes.

"Happy?" she asked while he was still casually sucking on her left nipple.

"Yes," he touched her cheek. "Your face gets so pink after you come. It's the only time I see you with such a tranquil expression."

Kara moved her naked body closer to his clothed one and he wrapped his strong arms around her. She lay her head against his shoulder. He caressed her soft, brown hair as he liked to do, and they said nothing for a while. Then Tir began caressing other areas of her body, and she wanted him again. She looked up, and they kissed. He used his teeth to grab gently at her bottom lip, and she began quickly undressing him but could not manage to get his jewelry off. In the end, she left it. She did not care, she needed him again. Her lust for him was insatiable.

Tir hovered over her, his ranking necklaces falling down against her breasts and torso. He spread her bent legs wide as he slowly entered her vagina. She tried to grab him to make him change positions so he would enter her with more force, but he shook his head.

"Touch yourself now. I want to watch you again."

"I can't," she said, thinking there was no way she could orgasm again so quickly. That's not what she wanted right now.

"It doesn't matter if you don't come again; it makes me so aroused to watch you," he said and entered her faster.

Kara began touching herself and closed her eyes.

"No, look at me, Kara," he commanded. "Look at your alien husband." Tir wanted to see her beautiful brown eyes filled with desire as he orgasmed inside of her.

Kara felt as if the galaxy were standing still again. Tir was making love to her, and she could see him, but she also felt like she was watching him on a video com link that had some issues and that he would change. He was still him, and she was still her, but they were different. The longer she looked at him, the more the other Tir was in focus. "Do you see that," she murmured confused by what she was seeing. He was him, but a different him, and she had the urge to call him by a different name. It was on the tip of her tongue, but she didn't know it. This was all déjà vu again.

"I only feel *you* in the whole galaxy right now. This is the way the gods wanted it," he managed to say as he could barely focus. Tir flipped her over letting his carnal desires take over. He knew she wanted him to take her like this and began thrusting hard into her. The sounds she was making only urged him on faster and harder.

At that point, Kara lost all thoughts about an alternative timeline as he would make her orgasm again. Those ridges and this position, it was ecstasy. She did not care anymore what kind of Alliance magic was at play. She wanted him like this more than anything she had ever wanted — more than a primal, spiritual desire. But Kara would never have acknowledged it as she closed herself off from ever believing in gods, religion or the supernatural.

Tir was also in ecstasy, but primally and spiritually. He knew already that this was the will of the gods. And when he felt the déjà vu again, he was reassured that they were already together in alternative timeline.

When they both found their release again, they lay on the bed together for a short time before Tir picked Kara up and carried her to the shower.

"Absolutely not. No Tir, I am not taking an ice-cold shower with you again." She tried to squirm out of his arms, but he just tightened his grip on her.

"You need to take a shower, and I want to shower with you."

"How about we turn the water temperature all the way up for me, and you can watch, and then you can have your shower?"

"How about I override the system, so you can turn the water up to 40C or whatever it is you want by tomorrow, but that right now you have one last cold shower with me?" Tir knew that an engineer would have to override the bathroom's safety settings to allow the water to become so warm for her.

Kara nodded because she didn't want to be covered with his semen for another day, and they went into the shower together. She screamed again when the freezing water hit her.

"Your surprised sound is adorable. You knew the water would be cold yet you screamed anyway."

Kara ignored him because it was so cold. Soon he was washing her body everywhere because she could not move. Thankfully they were out of the shower after ten minutes and then dried with the cool air from the shower dryer. She raced out of the bathroom and then to his wardrobe to grab herself the last dress hanging there. Her hands shook as she put on the red dress and looked for the stockings. "I've no idea where the stockings are. Can you help me? And do these clasps."

Tir came up behind her, showed her where the everyday stockings were, and handed her a pair. "You look good in red, Captain."

"Honestly, are you trying to make me angry?"

"It's just a little joke."

"It's not a joke to me. You took away everything," she said accusatorially.

"And I'm giving you an opportunity at something so much grander, you obviously cannot even comprehend it at the moment, and I'm beginning to suspect that's the problem."

Kara pulled on the stockings and stood still as he helped her fasten the dress. "Is it time to eat dinner yet?"

"Soon. We can have some wine beforehand if you want?"

"I'm never going to start a conversation before mealtime again."

"Good, you'll be civilized in no time."

After a couple of cups of wine, he wanted to tell her about the slave artist coming after dinner. "I've organized a surprise."

"What kind of a surprise?"

"A slave artist. I want you to understand this part of Alliance culture now that you are an Alliance citizen."

"Was this supposed to be a good surprise or a bad surprise?" Kara asked, thinking this was a pretty bad surprise, then reminding herself that he thought she looked good in this ugly dress with no form whatsoever, so obviously, a lot of Alliance culture was contrary to hers.

"A good surprise. She can recite a myth or an exciting segment from Alliance history."

Kara could tell that Tir was excited by this. She remembered that the Alliance had very little entertainment and culture, so she looked at him and half-smiled, "I'm sure it's going to be entertaining." She poured herself another cup of wine. "And just so we are clear, I'm not having a threesome with this slave artist."

"We'll see, they can be very convincing, and I know the slave artists are desperate to have sex with a human; we may even be able to get a discount. You know humans are rumored to be the most beautiful species in the known galaxy."

"Even if it was free, I'm not having a threesome."

He looked at her in disbelief. "Kara, if it's free, I would offer you a ship right now to have a threesome."

Kara couldn't help but smile. "Well then, maybe I will try to turn on my human charm." She stood up and turned around, "What do you think? Are the rumors true about humans being the most good-looking species?"

Tir took in Kara's lovely form, brown hair, golden skin, and pink lips. "I've never seen anyone more beautiful than you. Especially in that Alliance dress, you're just missing the necklace I gave you."

Kara frowned and sat down, hoping to avoid having to wear the ornate necklace he gave her to signify their marriage. It was a public sign of her imprisonment.

"Kara, go and get it. People will think you are ungrateful for your new position."

"Or merely human."

Tir rose from the table and went into the bedroom. He returned the necklace she had left in her bag with the dress she had been wearing earlier. He placed the chain around her warm neck, caressing her as he did so. "Now you are perfection," he said and kissed the top of her head.

"I thought you said I was perfection and the goddess herself when I was naked? I'd rather be naked than wear this heavy necklace."

"You must become more refined. Only then will you be able to enjoy everything the Empire and I offer you, and then, I guarantee you will not be disappointed. Please leave your human prejudices about what it means to be civilized in the galaxy behind. You are an Alliance citizen now. I'll not stop reminding you until you begin to believe it."

Slave

Mux came at exactly seven o'clock and laid out the evening meal for Kara and Tir, who had already had more than a couple of cups of wine while they waited for the food. Kara had learned her lesson now about mealtimes in the Alliance and that they were not something to be trifled with.

Mux set down the lukewarm vegetables in front of Kara, "I never thought I'd be so delighted to see these texture-less and tasteless vegetables again, but here we are."

"Be grateful for what the gods provide Kara."

"You know most people in the galaxy eat anytime they want?" she said casually.

"And who controls most of the galaxy?" he asked condescendingly. "Not any society that cannot control themselves to eat at appropriate times, certainly not humans. Because the Alliance follows the gods' edicts so closely, we are rewarded in our mortal lives. Do not be so obstinate about becoming civilized, my human wife; it'll only annoy us both, and it is a battle you will most certainly lose."

Kara wanted to throw a vegetable at him but resisted because she was so hungry. "Listen up, my darling husband." She noticed him bristle when she called him that and decided it was better than throwing a vegetable. "I'm not a pet that needs to be trained. You forced me to marry you, knowing full well that I'm human. I'm not going to give thanks to any gods for something I know was procured only by mortal hands. Show me the gods doing something for me, and then I'll give them thanks."

Tir just looked at his wild human and wondered how he was going to get her to behave in a more dignified manner. Humans were the most beautiful species in the known galaxy but were unorganized, undisciplined, impulsive, and heathens. And it did come as a surprise to him that she did not want to embrace Alliance culture and thank him for marrying her. When they were intimate, things were easy between them, they had a strong and natural attraction to one another, but when he was trying to instruct her, to civilize her, gain her loyalty, she stubbornly refused to obey. Tir had saved her ship and crew, none of them had been harmed, yet she seemed ungrateful. True, he denied her some things, but it was only because he could not trust her. Tir knew, though, that once she was loyal to him and the Empire, she would be a strong force to be reckoned with, not just an annoying, mostly harmless human hanging around the galaxy attacking supply ships.

"Kara," he said more gently, hoping that a softer hand might work better. "Do you remember the first time we said each other's names?"

"Yes," she said softly. They had both felt something larger than themselves resonate between them. "It was only a few days ago."

"How could you think those feelings could come from anything but something greater than ourselves? Those feelings were sent to us from the gods to guide us."

"I don't know. Maybe you are drugging me?"

"Drugs are forbidden for the maximum class," he said in a matter-of-fact way that made her curious.

She looked at him confused then and decided to take this further, she needed as much information as she could get about the Empire, and until she could read properly, she had access to nothing but the people around her. "I know so little about Alliance culture. What do you mean, maximum class?"

"Alliance people are separated into three distinct classes, maximum, middling, and slave."

"Are you born into them?"

"Yes," he said, watching her. "We're born into our class and our House."

"What do you mean?"

"Almost every Alliance citizen is born into a House, regardless of class. This is the first point of identification." Tir pointed to one of his necklaces with the illegible inscription. "This is my House. We don't say it because you can see it. Everyone wears a necklace like this, from slaves to the emperor."

"That must take the fun out of many initial conversations."

"It saves time. We don't waste time talking to the wrong people."

Kara could not even comment on that; it sounded so terrible to her ears. "What about those people not born into a House? Are they just unlucky?"

"Yes, the only reason not to be born into a House is that your parents married outside their class or the child was conceived before marriage."

"You're really selling the Alliance to me as such a great place, please continue," Kara said sarcastically.

"I didn't make the laws. And again, shall we compare the high standard of living in the Empire with that of humanity's?"

She was humbled then. "No. So what happens to these people who are born without a House?"

"They are not abandoned, but they can never hold an official post in adulthood. Most of them become traders or pirates in the galaxy."

"Are there many of these Alliance people without Houses?"

"A couple of million, not many for a population as large as ours. But people fall in love with the wrong people all the time," Tir commented.

"Why not change the laws then? What's the point of keeping people who love each other apart?"

"It's not up to us. It's up to the gods, and they still forbid it."

Kara wanted to ask, 'You cannot believe that?' but she held her tongue.

"Everything will make more sense to you when you know more about our culture."

"I ..." she began but was interrupted by a chime at the door.

Tir grabbed Kara's hand from across the table and said, "It's someone to teach you more about Alliance culture." Then Tir led Kara to the sofa and then went to open the door.

Kara watched Tir let in the female slave artist. She did not know what to expect as she had never seen an Alliance woman more than at a distance or on media, let alone an Alliance prostitute. And Kara had certainly not expected to see the woman who walked in with Tir now.

"Captain Kara, this is slave artist Sera, the most charming woman in the Empire."

Kara did not know if she was charming or not as Sera had not spoken yet, but she could not deny Sera might be the most beautiful creature she had ever seen, despite being grey-skinned and wearing an ugly green Alliance dress that looked like a box. Sera wore a lot of ornate jewelry that added more shape to her dress, and now Kara could understand why Alliance women wore the jewelry to add definition to the boring dresses. Kara was taking in her appearance with fascination. She reckoned Sera must be wearing at least five to eight necklaces, all of different lengths and made of other metals with stones, as well as many bracelets and long earrings that almost touched her shoulders. She also had her black hair pulled up in the most intricate braids with many jeweled hair accessories. Finally, Kara looked at her face, which was a perfect heart shape with sharp grey eyes almost matching her skin and high cheekbones *This is what physical perfection looks like*, she decided. Her skin looked so perfect that even Kara wanted to reach out and stroke her.

Tir offered Sera a seat and some wine; she took both but only had eyes for Kara. She had never seen a human woman before and was startled by her short brown hair, big brown eyes, and golden skin. She wished that Kara had not been dressed in an Alliance dress as it revealed nothing of her figure, which had already been rumored around the fleet to be so seductively curvy that people were saying she looked like the goddess of home herself. Sera smiled at Kara. "What would you like me to entertain you with this evening?"

Kara took a sip of wine, assuming Tir was going to answer this question, but when he did not answer, she swallowed the wine and asked, "What would you suggest for someone who has been forced into marriage and knows almost next to nothing about Alliance culture? Is there a story about that?"

Sera smiled at Kara and looked to Tir for approval to grant this request. He nodded. "There is the ancient myth about the Lost People I think you would find interesting."

"Is it a long?"

Sera smiled. "No, it is not long. Would you like me to recite it for you?"

"Yes," said Kara realizing that she had to ask Sera to do something since Tir was no doubt paying her to be there and entertain them. *This is so bizarre*, Kara thought.

Sera stood up then and dramatically began telling the story of the Lost People:

Long ago, when the Alliance was still an infant and ships got lost, an unknown force pulled a fleet of explorers and scientists to the other side of the galaxy. Unable to return, they found an almost inhospitable planet, too bright, too hot, but uninhabited except for some small animals. They sent a message back to the Empire explaining their situation, begging to be rescued. The message took over one hundred years to arrive. When it was received, the Alliance had already counted those in that fleet for dead. The Empress and Emperor then were greedy and did not want to waste time and resources to look for some citizens who may or may not still be alive or waiting to be rescued. The imperial family decided to conceal the information about the Lost People. They had the message destroyed. From that point forward, everything only improved for the Empire; technology, military, colonies, and Alliance civilization in the known galaxy soared. No one thought about the rumored Lost People again until we discovered a species almost like our own. They called themselves 'humans'. We sent ships to investigate them before they had the technology to understand what we were doing. We believed that these humans were most likely the Lost People. However, since the Empress and Emperor of the past had all the original documents destroyed, no one remembered the exact location of the Lost People. So, it was decided, conveniently, that humans were not the Lost People, and the Alliance continued to expand and almost completely ignore humanity. But now, the gods are punishing the Alliance for not retrieving the Lost People when we were twice allowed to do so. They are making us suffer with low-female birth rates and catastrophic disruptions to our perfectly ordered society. We have been given a third chance to accept humans back into the fold or die from our pride.

"Who believes this?" asked Kara, a bit spellbound.

Sera looked at Tir and then back to Kara. "All of us who consider ourselves to walk in the light of the gods."

"All of you?" Kara confirmed.

Sera nodded. "Humans are the Lost People; you must feel that in your blood. Our skin colors are the only difference between us."

"No. I liked your story and you performed it well. But we aren't the Lost People. Do you have any proof? Where did all the Alliance technology go from Earth then? We've been the last civilization to modernize almost everything in the known galaxy. If we were the so-called Lost People, we wouldn't be far behind the Alliance."

"It's possible that the first Lost People destroyed their Alliance technology to start over. We don't know why or how, as there's no official record on Earth or in the Empire, although there are many conspiracy theories about it. One thing we all know for certain, humans are the only other species in the galaxy genetically like us, and now, ironically or fittingly, humans will have to save us. The myth and the reality are aligned now. You've no proof that you are not the Lost People. Nothing you can hold up and say, 'See, humans are organic to this planet,' because you are not. There are too many similarities, not only in genetics but in your ancient cultures. You are us. Thanks be to the gods who light our paths."

Kara just drank some more of the bland wine considering this. She knew so little about Alliance culture and religion, so there was no way that she could compare it to ancient Earth cultures and religions.

Sera watched Kara thinking she was so lovely, and hoped that she would be able to stay longer, but she had to be invited to do so. So Sera was determined to be as charming as possible. "Did you enjoy the myth even if you do not believe in it?"

"It was very interesting as far as myths go. I think it makes for good propaganda now when trying to get human women to have children for you and conform to your archaic beliefs of marriage."

"Even if it is only propaganda, do you think it will work?"

"I think the Empire would have a better chance if they would have asked us for help instead of insisting on making us marry. You're just forcing us to do things that we find barbaric and it won't result in compliance. Think of all the children that will be born out of anger because of this. That can't be good for the Empire, Earth, or the galaxy, can it?"

"Will our children be born out of anger, Kara?" Tir asked evenly, clearly annoyed.

"If you continue to keep me on the tight leash you have me on now, then most definitely yes. I'm quite used to being as free as you are, Tir. And I doubt you would like to be as confined as I am for the foreseeable future."

"This is true, but you are on the losing end of getting what you want. You came to this war expecting to die in your little ship and I changed that future. It does neither of us good to have you dead."

She bristled at him, calling her ship little, although it was little compared to his.

"And you didn't die, I saved you, but instead of gratitude for saving you and your crew and even marrying you, you continually deny your destiny, a destiny set out for you from the gods. And instead of gratitude, you are only trying to escape."

Kara looked at him in disbelief. "And you wouldn't do the same in my position?"

"No, I'd accept my new fate. And in some ways, I've given up more than you have. I have jeopardized everything by marrying a human."

Kara was getting angry now. "Then why did you do it? Why am I not dead or with the rest of my female crew?"

"You know why. It was the will of the gods. You've experienced the same as I have in these last few days. They've thrown us together forever. Our paths are linked, and the sooner you stop acting like you are alone in this galaxy and that you have any control over your fate, the better. I'm tired of dragging you along and reminding you of your place."

"Tir, we are in control of our fates," Kara said calmly.

Tir rose, but then Sera interrupted them before this argument escalated, "Captain Kara, I've never met a human before. I know little of human culture; could you tell me why you find Admiral Tir so disagreeable? In our culture, you owe them yours if someone saves your life. This is why the admiral struggles with your stubbornness not to give yourself to him in every way."

"He definitely has my gratitude," Kara said, answering Sera but looking at Tir seriously. "But I cannot just give myself to anyone. Humans don't marry anymore, and we are in control of our destinies. I just cannot walk away from my beliefs because I got lucky. It's just not something I'm comfortable with. I'm not willing to give up my freedom to Tir or mythological gods."

Sera and Tir were shaking their heads at her. "The gods control all of our destinies here. You were meant to be with Admiral Tir. You know it, Captain. Everyone on this ship can see it between you two, but you resist every time you remember something about your life before. Open your eyes and accept your fate. Think of your human life as having died on your ship. Now is the time for your Alliance life to begin."

"I've been forced into marriage and seen my female crew off for the same fate, and just because I don't mind having sex with Tir does not mean we were meant for anything. I've enjoyed sex with a lot of men in my life. It's a primal animal instinct. There's nothing spiritual about it."

Sera smiled. "I agree with you, sex is an instinct all species have, but it doesn't always stop there. I know you're clever enough to understand that, even if you don't believe in the gods or fate. Humans must fall in love, excuse my use of the word here, may the gods forgive me, and even if you do not marry, you do decide to spend a considerable amount of time with people you consider special in your life, don't you? I don't know much about humanity, but I can't imagine it being so different than Alliance culture. Regarding you and Admiral Tir's relationship, I am just telling you what I know and see. I can also see that the truth makes you very uncomfortable right now, so let's talk about something else. As a slave artist, I represent the living and breathing culture of the

Alliance Empire onboard this ship. I can tell you anything you would like to know. Please ask me something."

Kara looked into her grey eyes. "Tell me how you think my female human crew is faring now on your capital planet being married off like animals?"

"Oh, they would not be just married off. I heard that Admiral Tir pushed you a bit...."

"Coerced," Kara corrected her.

"But I also heard that you had an instant connection, so even if he might have pushed you for marriage, you don't look completely unhappy, nor are you chained up here."

Kara had to admit that this was true. Had she met Tir under different circumstances, she did not doubt that they would have fallen in love. She was unsure about the marriage part, but they would have definitely fallen in love. "I'm not physically chained, no, but I'm locked in as a prisoner, nonetheless. Who told you we had an instant connection?"

"Someone who witnessed you both together came to see me afterward," Sera said with a knowing smile.

Kara knew that it must have been Doctor Siu. In her memory, she replayed the image of his eyes on her as she rode Tir. "What did the good doctor say about us?"

Sera smiled seductively. "You have nothing to worry about, Captain. He said that your beauty was unparalled and that your body was the most perfect female form he had ever seen. Doctor Siu was jealous that he couldn't touch you as Tir did and that he could only be a spectator."

Thinking about that aroused her and she tried to get control of herself, before this turned into a threesome. "Sera, how do you think my female crew will find their alien husbands? Will they be physically forced?" Kara did not add, 'as I was' because she was not forced to have sex with Tir. Not once. She had wanted him every time, and despite the irritating way he spoke about their destiny, she still desired him, and his body against hers. He was like a drug to her and she had never felt this way about anyone before.

Sera looked into Kara's eyes and realized she did not know. "Admiral, you need to take care of your wife and not give the impression we sell women like slaves," she admonished him. "Captain, your female crew will be given lodgings, clothes, food, and whatever else they require, including an Alliance education and suitable work. Then they will attend what we call 'The Assemblies.' At these Assemblies, they will have the opportunity to meet eligible men for marriage. As human women are the most striking in the galaxy, and there are so few Alliance women to compete for the men, I think your crew will find themselves with reasonably successful husbands in a very short amount of time. I'm sure anyone who doesn't will probably be given a reprieve, but I'd be surprised if any of them would not want to marry. I've even heard it gossiped that your young doctor with the fiery hair already has a ban on her from an eligible suitor from an imperial House. You see, your crew is in good hands."

"What do you mean a ban? More archaic barbaric behavior?"

"A ban is a special condition a man can pay to put on a woman. It means that no man of lesser rank can speak to her, and no man of equal or higher rank can court her without challenging the man who banned her to a duel."

Kara looked at Sera in disbelief. "I'm sure my junior doctor will be thrilled to learn someone put a ban on her," Kara could not keep the sarcasm from her voice, but it seemed lost on Sera. "What else would you like to know about the Empire?"

"How *bad* is the demographics issue?"

Sera looked to Tir then, and he nodded, letting her know she could tell Kara the truth. "It's not good. This year we had a seven percent decrease in female babies born, and we still do not know why. Our doctors have been working on this problem for over a decade now. The decision to begin taking human wives was not something the Empire took on lightly."

"But why would you not just ask? Humans desperately need technology. We would have volunteered ourselves in exchange for UCs and equipment."

"What if you were to say 'no.' The Empire is too proud to risk lowly humans rejecting us publicly."

"As you all keep reminding me," said Kara looking at Tir. Then Kara had another moment where she felt she had heard this all before but that it was all different. "Do you feel that?" she asked Tir about the strange feeling of déjà vu.

"What do you mean?"

"I've heard this all before but not just from when you said it earlier."

"I think you are just adjusting to being in a new environment in a new situation. It's culture shock. It's natural. You're the only human here."

"That's not it; this is more like, I'm on the verge of realizing something, but then I lose it again before I can figure it out. This is the third time this has happened while I've been looking at you, Tir. The first time was when I said your name, and then you felt it too. Remember?"

"I did feel it, but that was just the gods' way of confirming our union and our destiny, as I told you then."

"Then, tell me, what are the gods trying to do now, make me feel like I am losing my mind?" she took a deep breath. "Because if that's their plan, they're well on their way if they keep this up. Every time this happens, it's like a tremor in reality."

"These episodes you mention can you see other people? Other Alliance people?" asked Sera.

"No other people. Not really, just different versions of the same. It feels like I've done this before, but things were different like this is a bad dream, or the other is the nightmare, I can't figure out which one, but only one is real, I know that for sure. And I'm stuck in-between both reality and the nightmare without a good connection to either. Thankfully it always passes quickly as I've never felt this way before in my life. It only started happening since I came onboard the *Refa*, so you can imagine how suspicious I'm about possibly being drugged."

"It may be a glimpse into a parallel universe," said Sera seriously. "Be careful you don't fall through."

"Impossible," Kara dismissed her suggestion but looked over at Tir. She could not read his facial expression.

"It's not drugs. Members of the maximum class are not allowed drugs." Sera noticed Kara's confused face and said, "Each class in Alliance culture has made compromises with the others to ensure everyone feels equal. Our maximum class is the highest but also makes the most sacrifices in terms of pleasurable activities. As such, they are allowed no drugs except for wine. But you see, I'm part of the slave class. I can do what I want when I want."

"You mean you do not have to eat when the gods decree it?"

"I don't have to, but as a slave, as we are closest to the gods I always do." Sera wanted to change the conversation; if it stayed this depressing, she would never be asked back or asked to stay longer. "Has Tir given you any jewelry besides that impressive necklace?"

Kara instinctively touched the heavy and ornate necklace. "No, should he have? I'd have appreciated a bracelet or a belt that was also a weapon."

"I didn't expect to get married during the war on my ship. This was all I had with me. I've ordered jewelry and clothing befitting my wife that will be on the next supply ship," Tir said defensively. Then he looked directly at Kara and said, "And some of the human food you like from the Earth Store in the Immigrant Ring on the Alliance Capital Planet will also be delivered."

Kara had not expected that. "You bought me some human food?" *As if I am a well-looked after pet,* she thought.

"Just more of what you brought back from the *Dakota* and a few recommendations from the store's owner," He wanted her to be as comfortable as possible even though she was still his prisoner because she was also his wife.

"You know, in the Alliance, women have lots of jewelry to show their status and complement their beauty," Sera explained. She did not want to discuss something as boring as food from Earth.

"It must be something you have to grow up with. I'm not accustomed to wearing jewelry," she touched the necklace. "And I don't like the weight of it. I hope, Tir, you don't expect me to wear too much all the time? I'm happier in a uniform than a dress."

"You'll have another uniform soon enough if you conform, but the jewelry is a part of our culture, and you will have to become accustomed to wearing it," Tir commented lightly. "Not necessarily *that* necklace all the time though."

"I'm surprised to hear that. You're such an exquisite woman, but without jewelry, you only show half of your beauty and half of your status," Sera commented gently.

"Only to Alliance eyes," Kara said.

"Are there any other eyes here?"

Kara said nothing.

Sera stood up and moved to sit next to Kara on the sofa. She looked at Kara's ears and ran her fingers over Kara's pure earlobes, and said to Tir, without taking her eyes from Kara's. "She does not even have her ears pierced, Tir," then she reached out and took one of Kara's hands and brought it to her breast and said, "And I doubt a nipple pierced either." She began moving Kara's hand over her dress enough that she could feel the outline of the elaborate nipple ring she had. "See Captain Kara, in the Alliance, we like to decorate ourselves as much as possible. Maybe it's because we all have grey skin? Maybe it's because we are not nearly as curvy and diverse in shape as human women? But regardless, we wear a lot of jewelry, and enjoy how it defines us and breathes beauty onto our forms."

Kara was surprised Sera had brought her hand to her breast, but she didn't pull her hand away. She was too curious. "Doesn't that hurt?"

Sera was still holding her hand, rubbing it lightly over the fabric of her pierced nipple. "No, it feels good. I've never been so close to a human. I'm curious about you. Your hand is so soft and warm," Sera slowly moved closer to Kara and stroked her hair and face. "And your hair and eyes are so attractively brown."

Kara had never received advances made by a woman. She did not know how she felt about this. Sera was the most gorgeous creature, but did she want to do this? She didn't know, but Kara was interested in this alien experience, so she decided to let this go just a bit further and see how it felt. She had to admit. She loved how Sera's cool, soft hand felt on her skin. And she was now curious to see what kind of jewelry she had attached to her nipple that her fingers had fully explored.

Sera saw a flash of desire in Kara's eyes and decided to move a bit closer now, and she stroked Kara's hair and face again, but instead of stopping at her chin, she proceeded down to her neck and the top of her chest. Her fingers lightly made circles there as she still held Kara's hand against her nipple. After a couple of minutes, Sera leaned in slowly, never breaking eye contact with Kara and kissing her. She pulled gently away with Kara's lower lip seductively in her mouth and then whispered in her ear, "I greatly desire to see what a human woman looks like without her clothing on and tastes like between her legs. Would you let me lick you while your husband watches?"

Kara now knew what it was like to pay for sex, but in this moment she didn't care, this was so different it was taking her mind off everything else in her life, and all she could think was, *Tir, now I understand. It's still wrong, but I don't want to say 'no.' I feel so alive right now doing this thing that's just like marriage, it's so wicked.*

Sera began kissing Kara in earnest; then, her hands explored Kara's clothed body. She was so curious about this human. She could feel such curves as she had never felt before through her dress and was tantalizing them both by slowly caressing Kara's human body over the fabric. "So many curves, Kara. I'm in awe of you already." Then she began putting her hand slowly up Kara's dress, along the side of her stockings which she made sure Tir had a good line of vision for as Alliance men were aroused by seeing stockings touched by others, even the black everyday ones that Kara was wearing now.

When Sera got to the end of the stocking, she circled the top of Kara's thigh with her finger leisurely. "Such soft and warm skin. I'm going to begin licking you from there, but I want to take your dress off first. Human beauty, let's stand up so I can see you fully."

Sera slowly stood up, guided Kara to do the same, and then undressed her with her skillful and seductive hands and lips. Pinching here and kissing there as she slowly took the dress off, pleasuring Kara while at the same time giving Tir the show she knew he wanted. When the dress fell completely to the floor, she took in Kara's body with more kisses and caresses. "Doctor Siu was right, you are just as magnificent as the goddess of home. It's no wonder that Tir had to marry you and that Siu was so obsessed he had to have sex with me, imagining you, telling me all about you as he thrust into me." She sucked on one of Kara's nipples while her other thumb and finger brought the other to a point and switched after a couple of minutes. Then she worked her way down with her hands and her mouth following. "I had heard that humans had hair here, but I had no idea how intoxicating it would look or smell." Sera leaned in and smelled Kara's sex. "May I lick you in front of your husband, Kara? Would you like that?"

Kara didn't answer her.

Sera asked again while she ran one cool finger over her vulva lightly. "I think he'd like me to lick your legs, thighs, and sex while he watched. I think he'd like to compare his performance to mine. Should we give him a chance?"

Kara opened her eyes and made eye contact with Tir. She had never seen him so aroused as he sat in the chair, watching them. His irises were hardly visible. She then looked down at Sera, who was on her knees before Kara. "Sera, use your professional mouth and show Tir how it's done."

Sera took Kara's hands then and positioned her on the sofa to get a good angle to pleasure her, but also for Tir to watch everything. Sera looked back at Tir before she began and licked her lips. "How delicious does your human wife taste? Will her scent linger on my lips and tongue for the rest of the night?" Sera did not wait for an answer before turning back to Kara and, as promised, began licking her inner thighs where her stockings ended.

Kara initially jumped with the wonderful sensations when Sera kissed her thighs again. She put her hands above her head as she did not want to put her hands in Sera's hair and mess up her elaborate hairstyle. Kara had no idea how many minutes passed while Sera just teased her with her tongue until finally, she settled on her clitoris and then a finger, then two fingers in her vagina. "You're so wonderfully warm and soft. If I were Tir, I'd not even be able to show up for duty. I'd want my penis in you every second. The taste of your desire on my tongue every day. You're so lovely, soft, tight, and warm," she said as she moved her fingers expertly in and out of Kara's wet folds. "Tir's penis must stretch you so much. I hope I can watch him mount you and take you later. But at the moment, Kara, how am I doing so far? How do I compare to your husband?" Sera was consciously saying 'husband' as this kind of thing was a turn-on for Alliance couples. What she did not realize was that it was a bit of the opposite for Kara.

"About equal, Tir is good, but I'm sure you can do better if you stop talking, Sera," Kara said breathlessly.

Sera took the hint and stopped talking. It was not long before Kara reached her climax and Sera then slowly and casually caressed her body marveling at the differences and running her fingers through Kara's pubic hair, almost petting it.

Tir was watching everything, completely aroused as both women could see by his tented trousers. He had so many fantasies now about what they were going to do. He hesitated only for a minute, deciding. He adored watching Kara being pleasured by another woman. Especially now that it felt so terrific as she was his wife, and they were aboard his ship. This was something that should not even be allowed to take place under existing Alliance laws, but then it was war, and she was a useful prisoner.

Sera was licking outside of Kara's vagina entrance again. She could not help herself. She was intrigued by this human woman Tira had married. "You're so aroused, Kara. I'm glad. All this wetness. I want to taste all of you." With that, she surprised Kara by suddenly sticking her whole tongue into her vagina and then continuing to go in and out with her tongue.

Kara gasped and put her hands on Sera's head "Don't stop doing that."

Sera continued to use her tongue for many minutes to thrust in and out of Kara. She appreciated the small sounds of pleasure Kara was making. She pulled back after a suitable amount of time and then began licking her vulva up and down, with big strokes from top to bottom, before she played around her clitoris, finally coming to that special place and so lightly licking it.

Kara felt like she was going to lose her mind. It was not long before Sera had her fingers inside of her again and brought her to orgasm again.

"It's so sexy that you are coming in front of your husband again. I'm sure he can smell you across the room. You are so wet and fragrant. Look at him; he's so aroused waiting for us to finish so he can have his turn. But I think you both must admit, I'm better at making your human wife come."

Kara looked at Tir through her lustful eyes and said quietly, "Who says we want him to have a turn?"

Sera laughed. "Would you like to punish him, Kara?"

Just then, Sera was bringing Kara to a whole new level of ecstasy by playing with her breasts, and she forgot to respond. After a while, Kara opened her eyes, and she had never seen such a great desire reflected in Tir's eyes. Then she closed her eyes again because she felt so good and wanted to concentrate on the pleasure Sera was still building up again in her. Suddenly, Tir came and picked them both up and carried them to the bed. One woman in each arm.

Once on the bed, Kara began undressing Sera. "I want to see an Alliance woman's body, and I want to see how you've adorned your body with jewelry. I want to feel that cold jewelry against my skin. I want to rub my nipples against yours." Kara removed Sera's clothing and was surprised to see a very athletic grey body with pierced nipples, long hanging nipple rings with jewels, and a belly-button jewel. Kara was beginning to understand the jewelry now. If you had no curves, jewelry enhanced everything. Kara put her hands on Sera's pierced nipples. "These are stunning." Then Kara kissed each nipple.

Afterward Sera was completely naked, she kissed Kara, and their naked bodies rubbed against each other with desire. Kara's breasts were meeting Sera's pierced nipples. Kara loved the cold sharpness of Sera's jewelry against her naked skin. She thought to herself, *This is so different being with a woman, and I have never been so aroused in my life with Tir watching everything and the expectation of him inside me afterward.*

Tir watched from the side of the bed some time again, wondering when he would join them. There was no question that he would. After half an hour of watching them, he decided it was his time. He began taking off his clothing, but Sera immediately noticed and took off his trousers for him, kissing him everywhere, and then took off his shirt and jewelry. She didn't want to neglect him.

Kara watched Sera undress Tir. She was fascinated that Sera did not do it the awkward way she had done. For starters, Sera had not struggled with the Alliance clasps that were invisible once closed. But even more interesting was that she took off his shirt and then the jewelry and kissed everywhere the jewelry hit before removing it, like she was showing each piece of jewelry reverence. It was also so odd to Kara that Sera only kissed his penis and did not take it into her mouth as would have been the natural thing to do if they were all human. Kara had the strong urge to take Tir into her mouth and pleasure him in a way that she knew was forbidden, but Tir moved too quickly to achieve what he wanted with her and Sera once he was naked.

Now that Tir was going to participate, he positioned Sera on her back without speaking, and had Kara hover above her mouth. He was sure Kara would have mixed emotions about him having sex with another woman, even though that other woman would be expertly licking her. Still, he wanted to watch Sera lick Kara again in this position. He thought it was so sexy.

"You're going to enter her first?" Kara asked.

"Yes and she's going to lick you while I do it. Hover your sex over her face. I want you to orgasm again, wife."

Sera looked up at Kara. "Please," putting her hands on her thighs. "I want to run my tongue over your delicious human body. Don't deny me now."

Kara couldn't resist Sera, her touch was like magic. She positioned herself over Sera's mouth and closed her eyes.

"Open your eyes Kara. I want you to watch," Tir commanded her as he entered Sera and he kept eye contact with him while thrusting into Sera.

Tir wondered how long he could do this before Kara's jealousy took over. And as quickly as they started, Kara got up and moved Sera to a seated position, and Kara began to get on her hands and knees to lick Sera's sex and enter her with her fingers as she had done to Kara. Sera smelled like exotic flowers to Kara, and she was surprised at how cool her skin, even the inside of her vagina, felt, so alien and strange. Kara loved licking Sera while her rear was up in front of Tir. He was playfully caressing her anus and vagina. Kara finally took a break, turned her head around, and said, "Tir, please."

He loved watching her lick Sera. He did not want to hurry things. Tir thought Kara was so intoxicating as she turned around and begged him to enter her that he could not deny her. He positioned himself and penetrated her vagina slowly, and she moaned a bit from his pleasure inside her. His hands were on her hips as he moved back and forth, grinding into her. He was holding eye contact with Sera. He wanted to tell her how jealous Kara was, but he assumed she already had figured it out. He loved being inside of his warm tight human. He was thrusting faster and faster, and even though he did not want to orgasm yet, he could not help himself.

Afterward, they all lay together on the bed, and then after a few minutes, Sera quietly excused herself. When she was gone, Kara said, "You are never allowed to put your penis inside her ever again."

Tir smiled, but Kara could not see it. He put his arm around her and pulled her close. "But I am so glad you are still calling this a 'forced marriage,' Kara."

Kara did not know if she could ever get the image of him having sex with Sera out of her mind, which almost made her physically ill. She didn't know why. She had never considered herself a jealous person. And she knew she was not in love with him, but some serious lust, she guessed. "If we have to be married, which we do because I can't do anything about it, then I don't want your penis in anyone else. I think that's how humans used to behave within a marriage in the past, and I can see why now. You're supposed to be mine, forced marriage or not."

"I enjoyed watching you and Sera together, I thought you might feel the same," he hazarded.

"No, I didn't. I only felt jealous," she admitted quietly.

He ran a hand through her short hair and felt touched by this strange emotion she was having over a slave artist. "I'll not have sex with Sera as long as you say you do not want me to." That was the best compromise he was going to give her right now.

After a couple of minutes of lying in each other's arms on the bed, Kara got up and got one of her bags from her ship that she was supposed to have unpacked but hadn't and pulled out some of her favorite pajamas and put them on.

"What are those?"

"Pajamas."

"Stop," he sat up then and noticed a small bloody scratch across her breast; he gently touched it.

She looked down and said, "It must have been one of Sera's piercings that cut me." Kara went to put her pajama top on.

He stopped her and looked at it again, and then kissed the small wound. "We must make sure it does not scar."

"What? You are kidding me, right? That'll not scar. Now let me put on my pajamas."

"Some cuts can leave small scars; your skin should be perfect except for aesthetic piercings, of course. But as a gift to you, I'll let you have the choice."

"How gracious of you. No, I don't think I would ever want any piercings. And I am sure my skin will be fine," she tried to put on her pajamas again, and he stopped her.

"We don't wear nightclothes. They are unhealthy and go against the gods. If you want to wear those, you must go to the shrine onboard and make an offering to the gods, right now."

"Well, I'm not going to do that right now," she sighed, left the clothes on the floor, and then just got into bed to get warm. She had gotten very cold without any clothes on and felt like she was sobering up a little; she just wanted to be warm and sleep now.

Tir paid Sera by touching his fingerprint to his IC that he left on his desk, and then got into bed with Kara. Neither one said anything about the day that seemed to have lasted twice as long as any day should.

An alarm went off in the middle of the night. Tir jumped up to put on a uniform and was gone in less than a minute. He hardly had time to say, "We're under attack. Stay here. My guards are still outside," before running out the door.

Kara got up and got dressed too. She was not going to stay in bed while they were being attacked in case this might be her opportunity to escape. She looked for her uniform everywhere but could not find it, so in the end, she had to put on the same dress she had worn the day before. Once dressed and her hair combed, she approached the door and opened it. She had learned half of the hieroglyphics to read decently in Alliance and had memorized the door code by watching Tir. The door slid open, and the two guards were there.

The guards looked at Kara with a bit of surprise that she had opened the door. She hoped they might believe Tir had given her the code. "I was going to go help," she lied, and before she could say where she was going to go help, they were shaking their heads. One guard even pulled his gun out to threaten her.

"No, you're not. Go back in. I'll lock this door from the outside. You'll only go out or get food when Admiral Tir returns."

Kara did not move, so the guard with the gun moved in front of her and pushed her back into the room, hard enough that she fell to the ground. When she rose, the door was locked from the outside. She sat on the bed and lifted the shades to see if she could see any of the battle, but she could only see the ships on the perimeter.

After watching for over an hour, all the ships had changed positions, including the *Refa*, and now she could see much more of the battle raging outside. Tir was finally sending out his fighters, which she thought was a bit delayed. She wondered which formation he would use as she knew from last time their two usual formations were terrible against the Jahay, whose fighters were faster and could maneuver around the larger, more powerful Alliance fighters. When Kara saw that Tir was making the same mistake, she wanted to tell him not to, but then she hoped this was just a ploy. They were doing something new, but no, after five minutes, she saw he was sending pilots needlessly to their deaths because he had not come up with a new plan yet as this was a surprise attack. He had been busy having sex with her instead of doing his job. She thought about it, he, of course, would still win with this tactic only because the Alliance outnumbered the Jahay, but it was wasteful. She knew she should not feel guilty, but she could not help it. He had been pleasuring her instead of working. She went to his computer and sent him a new flight plan, and she knew it was so easy that all he needed to do was send it to his pilots.

Tir was watching his pilots die on the bridge, wishing he would have been more prepared for this battle when he received Kara's message. He looked at it and sent it out to his pilots. Of course, it was so simple but brilliant, and she made it all up hungover, watching from his bedroom window. *Gods*, he thought, *Don't ever let us be equally matched and her not be on my side.*

Kara watched now to see a change, and after 30 minutes, her plan was being implemented. The Jahay, unsure of what was happening, did not know how to respond. Half of the fighters thought the Alliance was falling back, and the other half were falling back themselves, just as Kara had predicted. It was not long before the Alliance fighters had the upper hand and were destroying all the Jahay fighters before they could return to their ship. The battle was over 20 minutes after that.

But it was not until ten hours later that Tir returned to their quarters. He found Kara asleep at the dining room table, which he thought strange. "Kara," he said gently as he came up behind her and lifted her into his arms.

"Wait, no, the food. I'm waiting for some food," she said, half-asleep.

He stroked her hair. "Did you try to leave?"

She nodded against his chest.

"I'll order you some food only because you helped me win that battle today, for which I was very grateful."

"I figured it was partly my fault you were so unprepared, and I didn't want our sex life to slow down because of it," she admitted.

"I'll go against the gods and get you some food. I'm sorry about the orders, but Kara, you are still my prisoner, so you can't leave." He did not need to ask her how she opened the locked door; he summarized that with her new studies of their written language, she had probably easily memorized his code.

He ordered her food and then sat on the sofa with her in his arms. She was not sleeping, but she was very tired and lay against him with her eyes closed. "What did you do after the battle?"

"Study. Wait for you. Think about food." Then she mentally turned off her translator to see if she could understand what he said next.

"What chapter are you on now?"

She was happy she could understand him, but she did not want to risk speaking back, and it was wrong now, so she said in English as he would not even guess she had turned off her translator. "Chapter 34. Almost halfway."

"That's good. Soon you will be able to read almost everything, so I'll have to be even more vigilant." *Gods,* he thought, *She's too clever. She must get pregnant, then gods' willing, her loyalty to me and the Empire will be certain and our destinies set in stone.*

Kara turned her translator back on. She had understood most of what he said, so she was pleased with herself, given that she had only begun to study Alliance a couple of days ago and recognized less than 300 words. Thankfully, Alliance grammar was not very difficult. She lay her head against his chest again as he stroked her hair. She thought, *Enjoy this while you can, Rainer, because you're going to leave soon.* But then that same voice inside her head said, *You're playing with fire.* She told her mind to shush then, and she just peacefully tried to think of nothing but the pleasure of being held by him and his strong grey hand stroking her hair.

After thirty minutes the door chimed, and Mux came in with food that he laid out in the dining room. Kara sprang into the dining room to eat without saying anything to Mux or Tir. She was so hungry. She had not eaten for over 24 hours. She did not even care that it was the same boring vegetables; she ate them as if they were delicious, which they were not. Her body had become used to regular food again, so she often felt hungry.

After she finished, Tir led her into the bedroom, where he took off her dress, put her to bed, and did the same for himself. He pulled her close to him in bed. His naked body against hers. His head resting on top of hers. "There will be one more battle, I reckon," he said softly.

"I think three major battles are left," she countered him. "The Jahay will draw this out for as long as possible. Wouldn't it be better to hunt them down than wait for them to come to you? You have this massive fleet use it."

"I'm waiting to meet up with two more fleets." He was confident she had no access to communications and could not relay this to anyone. "Then they'll come to us. We're more powerful and don't need to chase them down. We have the resources to wait. And," he grabbed her breast and began pulling gently on her nipple, "the sooner the war is over, the sooner it is more likely I'll be pushed into sending you away."

Kara put his hand over her breast to urge him on. Her thinking was that the sooner she became pregnant, the sooner she could gain his loyalty, stay on the ship, and escape. She knew she would never escape if she were left on the Capital Planet. His other hand was caressing her vulva and the top of her thighs now. She enjoyed how he got her to orgasm quickly, sometimes just as much as when he did it slowly. Kara knew he was tired now but appreciated that he would not orgasm if she didn't, or at least he gave it a really good try. She reflected that he was beginning to know her body better than she did herself and made it perform for him. Not long before he made her come with his fingers lightly tapping her clitoris she was grinding her hips back into his groin and loved the feeling of his erect penis on her backside just waiting its turn.

Tir was so aroused that he had to hold her hips firmly in place to make her orgasm, and once she had, he quickly and aggressively pushed his ridged penis into her, holding her close from behind, his hands on her breasts. He couldn't help it, he was rough and guessed she might even have bruises tomorrow. But there had been so much death today. Death he was responsible for, he needed this.

The feel of him going in and out of her from this angle was almost too much pleasure and she felt shaky from the sensations. The feel of his hands roughly handling her breasts and his strong fingers pulling on her nipples was exquisite. She reached back with one of her hands, put it in his long, thick hair, and pulled. She didn't know why but she wanted to pull on something of his.

As if he needed that signal, he moved his hands to her hips and began moving even more quickly. He knew she wanted him to enter her, 'like a dog' as she had said once before, but he wanted to see her now. So, he flipped her on her back and put her ankles together, resting on one of his shoulders as he began pounding into her. He loved the way her breasts moved with each thrust. And the way her cheeks were flushed pink. It was only minutes before he found his climax, some of the excess semen flooding into her brown hair covering her sex was fitting for the way they had just had sex. He lay beside her and pulled her close and the blanket over them.

Kara slept comfortably with the enemy. Her thoughts as she drifted to sleep were, *I've done it now. I've married, slept with a prostitute and now helped win a battle against my allies. I'm a traitor*. But even though she knew the truth and the person she was one week ago would be upset with her now, she could not be that disappointed with herself, having made the decisions she had had to make about her crew, their lives, and her current position. *Nothing in life was ever clean*, she thought, then drifted off to sleep with her hand resting gently on Tir's waist.

In the morning, they were awakened by Mux bringing in breakfast. They got up and ate silently. Afterward, Tir said, "I've got to go. Stay here. Learn the hieroglyphics; there are some children's books there you can try to read too. I might be gone for a long time. Do not try to escape, or else the guards will not feed you as you discovered yesterday."

Kara was not looking forward to a day alone again. "Can you send Doctor John here for the midday meal? I usually eat with him. I will be lonely here all alone again."

"No, Kara, he is working with Siu. If you get lonely, call for Sera or another slave artist to entertain you."

"I'm not going to do that," she said, but as soon as she said it, she thought she might do just that. The thought of her and Sera alone without the interference of Tir was enticing, but then she thought she was so hypocritical saying he could not sleep with her when that is exactly what she wanted to do suddenly.

"Your thoughts are clear across your face, Wife. Fortunately for you, I'm not nearly as jealous as you, and you can have fun with Sera. I don't mind, just don't make it a habit; she is very expensive."

"We'll see. I enjoy the idea of spending your UCs as your prisoner."

"My wife," Tir corrected her as he got up to leave. "Now, wife, you say to me, 'Let the gods guide you.'"

Kara just looked at him blankly.

"Say it."

"Why?"

"Because it is what you do in the Empire. Say it."

Kara reminded herself that she was trying to gain his favor. "Let the gods guide you."

"Let the gods continue to show you the way," he responded to her and then turned and left — the doors locking behind him.

Kara went to the console and began studying. After the evening meal, she had become so bored and lonely that she opened Tir's computer and called Sera. She was no longer in the mood for sex as she had been that morning but rather just someone to talk to.

When Sera arrived, Kara explained, "It's just me. I've been locked in this room all day yesterday and today. I'm lonely."

"I can imagine," Sera said sympathetically. "Would you like to hear a story or do something else?" She smiled sweetly at Kara and innocently touched her arm.

"I'd like to talk to you. I know almost nothing about the Empire, and Tir is not forthcoming with information."

"What would you like to know about specifically? Do you mind if I sit?" Sera asked.

"Let's begin with the classes of society, you and Tir have both mentioned them, but I do not understand."

"In the Alliance, we have three classes, the maximum class, which is what Tir is, the middling class, there are none onboard, and the slave class which I'm a part of, and about a hundred others onboard. Every Alliance citizen then belongs to a symbolic House no matter their class. In that House, they are born into a role or job with very few chances to make choices for their futures themselves."

"What about Tir?"

"He was born into an imperial family, of which there are a few. It had always been expected that he would join the military and become, at the very least, a general. It was not unexpected, though, that he became an admiral as he is a very good leader. Because of this and the exchange of imperial families is near, he has been chosen to be the Emperor's successor. You know this, right?"

"Yes, he mentioned it. But I do not understand how that works."

"Every hundred years, the empress and emperor retire and choose who will lead next from the best of the imperial families. Usually, a new emperor is chosen, and he will marry a suitable woman, and they will rule together until it is their time to retire and choose someone else to take their place."

"But Tir has not chosen someone suitable, has he?"

"Not at all," said Sera honestly. "But he has chosen you for religious reasons as he believes humans are the Lost People, and he's making an example out of himself for what he believes will save the Empire. But because of this, it is doubtful he will ever become emperor."

"Are people that racist in the Empire?"

"Captain Kara, you know it's not just the Empire. Whoever rules the Alliance Empire rules the galaxy. The *galaxy* wouldn't stand for a human empress, much less the Empire."

Kara was completely offended. "Why not?"

Sera looked at this sweet little human and said as she would to a child, "Because the empress is the most powerful person in the galaxy."

"But what about the emperor?"

"A man? He's a consort, a means to an end."

"I don't understand," Kara admitted. "He's the one who has been chosen."

"Yes, chosen to choose his mate. Admiral Tir earned the successor position because of his leadership skills, morality, and dedication to the gods. These qualities will lead him to choose a suitable leader for the Empire."

Kara was awestruck then. "The empress is the supreme ruler, not the emperor?"

"Of course."

"I don't believe you," Kara said. "Why would Alliance men allow themselves to be so secondary to women? They are the ones who keep their women at home."

Sera laughed. "You're seeing this all backward. Alliance women don't want to risk their precious lives out in the galaxy, and so, they make the men sacrifice their lives for the Empire."

Everything was becoming clearer to Kara now. It was as if she had been looking at a book upside down, and now it had been righted for her. "So you're saying as an Alliance woman, I've more rights than Admiral Tir?"

"On the planet, yes. If you were in the Capital City right now he could not hold you prisoner like this. It's all very complicated. There are a set of long rules called The Contracts that set out the compromises made between men and women over the centuries to make things more equal. But what it amounts to is that men are dominant off-planet and women on the planet."

"Then why do you choose to live off-planet?"

"Look at me? I was meant to be a slave artist. I'm richer than I ever dreamed I could be. I'll return soon enough to live a different chapter of my life. As the gods' will it."

"And do you believe we are the Lost People?"

"Many people believe, and many more don't say for fear of being ridiculed, but if Admiral Tir were to bring you back with a child and try to take the throne, I think there would be some unrest because the Empire is split over humanity."

"And I would be killed with whatever offspring if I were to live in the Empire. It's a tricky situation for me."

"We never kill children."

"Well, that is reassuring," said Kara sarcastically.

Sera gave her a disapproving look. "But I'm sure Tir will do his best and make excuses to keep you with him for as long as possible before the exchange and both of your futures will be called into question. Moreover his fleet is loyal to him, and no matter what they may personally feel about him marrying a human, they would never let any harm come to you or sell you to the highest bidder."

"People want to abduct me to get to him?" Kara had never played a political game in her life. This suddenly was all so new to her.

"Yes, to prove that religion might not be real."

"I thought humans were supposed to be Alliance citizens now? I've just sent my female crew on Tir's word they were. That they would be treated decently. Now, what are you saying?"

"They'll be treated well there, but Admiral Tir is supposed to be Emperor. No matter how beautiful you are, no one wants him to marry a lowly human. I mean no offense." Kara showed she didn't care with her hand and nodded for Sera to continue, "Humans are meant to be for lower-ranking members of the maximum who could not find an Alliance wife. Not to be empress. Neither the Alliance nor the galaxy would stand for it."

It was all becoming clearer now why he was adamant that she also memorize some religious prayers to say in public. He told her she need not believe, but she gave the appearance of believing. "This seems like it won't end well at all."

"It's a gamble, but I think Admiral Tir is right in marrying you."

"Is there anyone else to take his place so that he can just remain in the military?"

"There are some others, but they are much lower than he is, and the current Empress does not like them as she likes Tir. That's a problem. It's the Empress who wants you to disappear now."

"What do you think Tir wants to do? Do you think he really wants to be Emperor? Or did he marry me to escape that path?"

"I don't know. He's never shared any of his private thoughts about anything with me. I'm *only* a slave artist."

"Thank you for being so candid," Kara lied.

"This is common knowledge, Kara. You don't mind if I call you that as we have been intimate?"

"Fine. 'Since we have been intimate,' I want to know about secret things in the Alliance," Kara smiled at Sera. "Tell me now about periods. Doctor Siu mentioned a thing called 'the tab'?"

Sera had not been expecting her to ask about that. "Yes, it's a tiny machine that used to be shaped like a tab on clothing, but now it is the size of a very small line of three balls, and they go into your vagina and take care of all the blood and alleviate the pain until the end of your bleeding, and then they come out."

"Does it fall to the floor? You don't wear underwear."

"Underwear is unhealthy. No, it just waits for you to take it from the entrance to your vagina. You'll see." Then she looked over at Tir's small shrine and said, "Or maybe not. Tir has the fertility goddess front and center. I'd say he wants you to get pregnant as soon as possible."

"Yes, he does. But I don't think anything will happen as soon as he would like."

"What do human women do for their periods?"

"We have a little cup, and it catches the blood."

"Oh, that sounds...."

"It's not nearly as bad as it sounds."

"I'm sure it is. No offense, but I don't think anyone in the galaxy understands humanity's desire to 'remain close to nature,' as you call it."

"We've no religion but a strong culture that focuses on the connection between us and our planet. It's difficult to explain to off-worlders.

Tell me about yourself, Sera. How is it that you came to be on the *Refa*?"

"I simply made arrangements to come onboard when Admiral Tir took command."

"Have you known the admiral for a long time?"

"No, only for about a year," Sera was enjoying the look on Kara's face; she could not decide which would win over, jealousy or curiosity.

"And how well do you know him?" Kara wanted to know how many times she had slept with Tir.

"I know him by reputation, of course, and I have met him privately twice, including yesterday."

"What kind of reputation does he have?"

"Religious, honorable, and efficient," Sera could see that these things did not seem to mean much to Kara, so she continued, "He believes in the Empire and will do anything, even marry a human, to see it survive."

"Do you think bringing in human women will help boost your female birth rates?"

"I'm no doctor, but we must try something. The rate of females being born continues to fall, and we are beginning to reach critical levels." Then she paused and continued conspiratorially, "I know that it was always planned from the onset of this war that human women from the Earth fleet would be taken back to the capital as a trial."

"A trial to see if it biologically works?"

"No, we already know that it will biologically work. We've been conducting medical tests on humans for centuries to see if you really are the same as us. This is a trial to see if Alliance citizens would accept human females in society. There were other options, like polygamy."

"But men like Tir would rather have a human wife than have to share with another man?"

"Admiral Tir never has had an issue sharing women for pleasure, but he was so anti polygamous marriages, of men sharing one wife, he spoke in the High Council for human women to become Alliance citizens. This was all his idea, to take you during the war. He said that military women would be emotionally stronger and more open-minded than a human that has never left Earth."

"Yes, that is probably true in some ways." She did not want to mention that a lot of the women she knew would probably like to be married to an Alliance man were all still on Earth; she did not want to give any of them any ideas about just taking more human women. "But what do you think his long-term plan is with us?"

"I think just to show that human women, if willing, can adapt and serve as a stopgap to fortify the Alliance civilization against further decay until we figure out why fewer and fewer females are being born."

"I wish I could get word to my people about this so that we could have some negotiation points, if that is even possible before you begin taking us, maybe to appeal to the Alliance's moral side of this. It's not right to force us into it."

Sera shrugged. "It's tough being bullied, but if I can say anything for the Alliance, most of us believe that humans are the Lost People, so you'll be treated with as much respect as we can offer. This is why you are here, married to Admiral Tir, and not chained up to a medical bed for fertility experiments."

"I don't even want to ask if the Alliance has done that to other species."

"Because you know we have. We did not become rulers of the galaxy by being nice."

"I know; it's just the image you just put in my head was terrible."

"Because it's a terrible thing, but the galaxy can be that way, you of all people must know that. Life cannot be easy for humans, always being the last." Sera paused, taking in Kara's sad expression. "Have you told your family the good news?"

"What good news?" Kara was bewildered.

"That you are married to Admiral Tir."

"I wouldn't call any of this good news. Humans don't marry anymore; we see it as an archaic practice that has no place in the modern world. My family and friends would be horrified. I'm assuming my first officer will let my parents know what has happened to me. Tir, of course, only allows me access to internal communications onboard ship and to access the children's learning programs from the Empire so I can learn to read."

"And I'm sure learning our spoken language too. I've heard that humans like languages, and you can turn your translators on and off." When Sera saw that she had guessed correctly, she said, "Don't trouble yourself; it's nothing to me and I won't mention it to Tir. I also use every opportunity I can to make my situation more favorable. Can you say something in Alliance? I want to hear what it would sound like."

Kara looked at her and said seriously, reciting her learning program, "Chapter one, first hieroglyphic," in what she hoped was acceptable Alliance pronunciation to be understood.

Sera smiled and said sarcastically, "Totally useful in everyday conversation."

"Did it sound clear; nothing came out as nonsense?" If the translators could not translate something, it was registered as gibberish. Kara turned her translator back on then.

"Clear but with a slight human accent, of course. So strange to hear an accent." Sera looked at her and said, "Say this, 'I am human. My name is Kara.'"

"I am ... My name is Kara," she struggled with the unfamiliar sounds.

"Human," Sera said, and Kara repeated the word about six times and then was able to say both sentences correctly. "Gods, you are so adorable," she then said to herself more than to Kara. "Don't let Admiral Tir know. He'll become more obsessed with you than he already is if he hears you speaking our language with that sensual accent."

"'Obsessed' is a strong word."

"That's what everyone is saying. He almost messed up yesterday, which is something he has never done, and it's all because of you."

"But he didn't make a mistake in the end."

"No, but ..." Sera trailed off. "I think he's struggling with wanting to be with you all the time and introduce you to our ways, to show to everyone that he is correct and that it works with a human, but then at the same time, remembering as well that we are in the middle of a war. And he knows that one of these things, either you or the war, will have to wait, as he cannot focus all his attention on both simultaneously, which is what he wants to do. Or rather focus all his attention on you. And I don't blame him."

Kara blushed, remembering what they had done the last time she met Sera.

Sera rose, took Kara's hand, and guided her back to the bedroom as she said, "You're a prisoner here; you might as well enjoy some of the benefits of always being so close to a bedroom and nothing else to do." Kara resisted a bit, and then Sera kissed her quite expertly and said quietly in her ear, "I will teach you to speak Alliance like a native if you teach me how to seduce a human. We both want these things. What do you say?" Sera asked as her hand was already up Kara's dress caressing her between her legs.

Kara turned to kiss Sera as her answer.

Escape

Kara looked at Tir across the dining table. "Is that all you're going to say?" She had been alone all day and was desperate for some conversation.

"I'm not going to share classified information with you. When the Jahay loses this war, which they undoubtedly will, Earth will pay reparations with the rest of the Jahay's allies. I'm not going into any details about it."

Kara frowned. She was exasperated with her monotonous existence as a prisoner on her husband's ship. Every day was almost the same. She was confined to his quarters without any off-ship communication. In the mornings, she studied the Alliance spoken and written language and frequently practiced speaking Alliance with the smart mirror in the bathroom. In the afternoons, she would try and break into her husband's computer to access outside communication or anything that might aid in her escape.

Escape was constantly on her mind. Sometimes she was allowed to meet her doctor, John, the only other human onboard, for the midday meal in the mess hall, but that rarely happened after she tried to run away from Tir's guards and succeeded for about ten minutes in eluding them. Ten minutes is a long time to be gone on an Alliance starship.

Occasionally when she was very lonely, she would ask Sera, the slave artist, aka prostitute, to visit. But Kara tried to limit those intimate visits to once a week because the shame of paying for someone to see you was also exhausting. "I am going crazy here. Am I your wife or prisoner? You must choose."

"If I could trust you, you would not be confined to my quarters, but every time I have given you a bit of freedom, you have proved that you have no loyalty to me. I saved you, Kara. I saved your ship and crew. I have not treated you unjustly. If you were me, would you let me roam around your ship in the middle of a war?"

"I'd never be in your position. I would never keep a prisoner-wife-husband-whatever, you know what I mean, in the first place."

"And you honestly can't imagine a scenario where you would have rescued me, and we would have become romantically involved?"

"I'm not in love with you," she said defiantly, purposely using the word 'love' to annoy him. "This is lust." She looked into his green eyes. "And if I would have rescued you and we fell in love, then you would not want to escape. You would follow me to Earth, and we'd live there forever."

"I like your confidence that I'd just give up everything to live on a little insignificant planet on the edge of the galaxy. I like this fantasy; tell me more about our human home," he said softly. He knew he'd managed to calm her now and he was actually curious about this new fantasy she had concocted.

"It wouldn't be cold and muted like here, human homes are warm and colorful, and we can eat when we want. We can do what we want anytime."

"It is unfair to compare life on a ship in the middle of a war to your home during peacetime."

She ignored him because she suspected that life on any Alliance planets would not be too different from life on his ship, organized, unbending, and predictable. "I have the sweetest little apartment we would live in, with a yellow kitchen with a small balcony. It overlooks a busy street below where the trams go by. I love the sound of the tram bell trams make before leaving the stop. In the early mornings in summer, I open those balcony doors, drink my coffee, and watch the people go by, and I am so happy then." She looked up at him, and he seemed genuinely interested, so she continued, "In my sitting room, there is a sofa which I made myself from a patchwork of old fabrics with different patterns and needlework. I am not an artist, but both of my parents are, so I sometimes like to create things. In the bedroom, I have a four-poster bed that has been in my family for a long time. It hardly fits in my room, and it has curtains on it because the light can be so bright in the summer mornings, and I'd rather have three heavy curtains on the bed than on my beautiful windows where I have curtains only for show."

"It sounds very old-fashioned and inefficient for a starship captain. I couldn't live there."

"Yet you expect me to adapt to your culture here. Humans value beauty over all else, and some of the most beautiful things were created centuries ago. What is your home like on the Capital Planet? I am assuming that is where you are from given you're the successor to the imperial throne."

"My home is modern and functional. As you probably know, in the Empire, most art, except religious pieces or jewelry, is considered frivolous. We use the colors of our planet in all homes. They are grey, yellow, and black. Some more modern people have begun painting a room red here and there, but that is considered almost scandalous. Red is not native to our planets."

"Do you have a red room in your home?"

"No, but I have a feeling if I sent you there, you would paint the whole thing red."

"But you are not going to send me there, are you?"

"I don't want to, but you need to accept your new life. I know that you can feel that this is your destiny. Why do you continue to resist?"

"Tir, destiny does not exist. We all control our fates. We are at war, as stupid as that is for humans to be, and I have an obligation to my people, just as you do to yours. Why don't you just let me go, and then after the war, let's see if we have a true romance? Despite what you have done to me, I would still give you an opportunity."

"Do you ever wonder in a different timeline how that would have been? Maybe we met and married under different circumstances. If

Earth had been our ally instead of the Jahay's, how different the timeline would look then."

"I would be lying if I told you that I never thought about it," she admitted. "But this is the situation now, and I want to go."

"I understand that, but I can't let you go, and even if I did, your people would accuse you of being a spy you've been here too long." He didn't think she realized that because she was still young and idealistic.

"No, they would know you coerced me into marrying you, and I was kept a prisoner."

"No, they wouldn't believe you. It's too convenient, politically speaking, to name you as a spy. No one rises to be a starship captain as quickly as you did without stepping on some toes. And I don't need to know human politics well to know those people you stepped on are waiting for you to make a mistake. I actually think it might be just as dangerous for you to return to Earth as it would be for you to go to the Empire. Kara, this is your future now."

"I can't accept that," she said very determinedly.

"There is a story, I will not tell it to you in its entirety now, because it is too long, but the gist of it is that all people used to have four arms and four legs, but we angered the gods so much they split us in two as punishment. Now we are always looking for our other half to feel complete," he paused making sure she was listening. "When you have what we have, you are blessed to be one of the rare couples in the world to find your true other half. Whether it is fate or the gods have blessed us by putting us together, I don't know, but you are my true other half, Kara. And I know you feel it too."

Tir moved his hand to touch her, and she could not deny, she did feel more at peace when he was near. She did not mention that humans had a similar story written by Plato, because she did not want to encourage him further in his Lost People fervor, so she said nothing.

"Every day, I want this war to end, but at the same time, continue forever so that I can keep you here with me and hope that you start to accept your destiny. But every avenue is a risk. Every day, you learn more and are that much closer to escape. And if you manage to escape, you may die, by your enemies' hands or your own people's, and then whatever our true destiny is will be passed on to others." He looked at her seriously, "Kara, I want to live out our destiny."

She didn't like it when he was so serious like this about his ideology and fantasies. It scared her because she was worried that she might start believing him. She was quiet for a couple of minutes and then said, "I don't like the way you keep me locked away in your quarters. I need to exercise. I need to get out and do something else. If you want me to start believing that this is destiny, you need to start treating me better."

"Now, you are being somewhat unreasonable. I have tried to give you some freedoms and you have tried to escape. As for exercise, the only exercise we do onboard is swordplay, but there is no woman to teach you, and women are not allowed, no, that is not what I mean. It is just that there has never been a maximum class woman here. Women have their own places for swordplay and men are not permitted entry, ever." It was difficult for him to explain his culture to her, and he always felt completely inarticulate, which only made it more confusing.

"I don't care. Let a man teach me then." Kara realized she had said something wrong because Tir looked scandalized.

"You don't understand. In the Empire, men and women are not equal in the way that one role can be substituted for another. Everything is prescribed. A man could not teach you. It would go ..." Kara interrupted him then.

"Go against the gods, I know," she looked at him then and tried to look desperate. "You are my husband. We are as close as two people can be. Surely, you can teach me how to use a sword. How can that go against the gods? Even the gods must understand that this is an extreme and unique circumstance."

Tir thought about what Kara had requested for a couple of minutes, weighing out the pros and cons. "I'll teach you. You must learn at some point anyway, and I can hardly bring a female teacher onboard, especially when we are still at war."

"One more battle, and it'll be over, especially now that Admiral Uikoly of the Jahay is gone."

"Thanks to you," he wanted to give her credit where it was due. She had privately helped him strategize before the last battle, and this war would soon be over because of her. He was constantly impressed with her intelligence, which made him wary of giving her too many freedoms onboard. He worried about her escaping before she truly realized they were meant to be together.

She nodded. She had mixed emotions about what she had done, and she had hoped he would have given her more freedom after she handed the Jahay to him in the last battle. "I have always had to be creative in my strategies, or else I would be dead. I thought you would have given me more freedom after the last battle. That I could at least meet John regularly for the midday meal."

Tir ignored her suggestion as they had had that discussion many times. He changed the subject completely then, "How are your studies of Alliance hieroglyphs going?" He got out his IC as he asked her the question, wrote a couple of sentences, and then showed it to her. This was a game they played frequently.

Kara looked at the sentences and knew all the words but two but read out the sentences in English anyway,

> Every day I am even more amazed by your intelligence. Now let's go to the gymnasium and practice swordplay, which is something that I am good at.

She looked up at him. "I don't know those two words," she pointed them to the small screen.

"Gym and swordplay," he replied. He was amazed at the speed she had conquered the Alliance's written language, and he thought, *Because they are the Lost People, it resonates with her to learn the language the gods gave to us.* And then another thought occurred to him, *Have humans been learning other languages in the galaxy because they are still looking for their true language, Alliance?* Humans were the only species in the galaxy that could turn their universal translators on and off. The rest of the galaxy laughed at them for this. 'Why in all the stars' name would you want that?' people always asked, but he looked at Kara now and wondered if this was why.

Kara was beaming now at the thought of getting out and doing something new and physical. She had not left his quarters in days. She got up from the table and said, "Let me change my clothes," and went into the other room to put on her yoga clothes, tight black pants, and a pink tank top. She did not even care that she would be cold in such little clothing on the Alliance ship, which was kept at a cool 15C. He had consented to keep his quarters at 19C for her.

When she walked into the sitting room, he took in her appearance. "Good." Then he opened the door and escorted her to the officers' gym, which was busy with half-naked grey officers. As they walked along the side, everyone stopped and saluted Tir. He acknowledged them and walked with Kara to a smaller room in the back. They went in. He began looking around the room for something.

Kara just stood near the entrance and watched him. She suspected this must be a room for him alone. "Who do you usually practice with here?"

"Doctor Siu, he is the best swordsman in the Empire," Tir said casually.

"How do you know he is the best?"

He looked at her and smiled. "Because we have frequent competitions throughout the Empire when we are not at war."

"How do you rank?"

"Not well enough that I would enter a competition, but I am standing here, so I have yet to lose a duel."

"And women?"

"They also have competitions, but they are not for male spectators nor are they made public for maximum class male eyes." Then he came over and handed her a heavy blunt sword. "Only women can compete, and only women and male slave artists can watch."

"Male slave artists? That is strange."

"It is rumored that a male slave artist for a year is the prize in the women's competition, but only women know if that is true. It is forbidden to talk about these things with any man, even your husband."

"What is the men's prize?" *Alliance culture is so messed up.* She thought as she asked the question.

"Only the honor of winning."

She looked down at the sword and asked, "A practice sword?" As she tested it, she commented, "It's a little heavy."

"It is a man's practice sword; for obvious reasons, there is not a woman's one onboard. But, I am sure you can manage. You are strong. Hopefully, this will come naturally to you." He watched her investigating the sword. He found her appearance now completely tantalizing.

She was looking at the sword, wondering what it was composed of to look so brown and matte, when Tir suddenly came over and had his tongue in her mouth so sensually that she almost dropped the sword. She thought, *Surprisingly, a worn yoga outfit and practice sword is obviously a big turn-on for an Alliance man.* His hands began to roam then, and she pushed him back a little. "Tir, we can do that later; right now, I want to do something new. Teach me."

He looked at her swollen lips and ran his thumb over them. "You are right, but later. There is so much about you right now that is forbidden, and I cannot begin to explain it, but you will understand in time. You look irresistible to me, but I will do my best to teach you without becoming too distracted. Let's begin now." Tir took off his shirt and put it to the side, so now he looked the same as all his officers who had passed on the way in. He quickly braided his long black hair in a perfect braid down his back, and she wondered then how many times in his life he had done that. He walked into the middle of the room with a practice sword for himself, and she followed. Then they stood across from each other, looking at each other eye to eye with no emotion for about half a minute.

Kara thought to herself, *And now you look enticing to me, but I will not be taken in by your charms.* Just then, Kara had the feeling again that she had done this with him before and tried to shake it. She did not want to say anything because he would tell her it was the work of the gods, and honestly, she just wanted to do something that was not having sex, talking about religion, learning Alliance, or thinking about escape. So, she ignored the feeling and tried to focus.

"Have you ever fought with a weapon like this before?"

"No, I'm from the 25th century."

"Be serious, Kara. In the Empire, we often resolve personal conflict by the sword. You are an Alliance citizen now and will be expected to do the same. It would be a pity if you died in your first duel."

"Fine. I'm sorry I made fun of your culture again. I have never used a sword, no, but I'm no stranger to fighting with a weapon. I hope cheating is allowed?"

"This is the Empire, not only is it allowed but expected. You'll be dead if you attempt to follow some sense of honor. It's funny you should ask that, though. It never occurred to me that humans even knew what rules or honor were."

She gave him a fake smile. "Oh, we know what the word 'rule' means; we just don't care. It's difficult to think about rules and honor when you are the most disadvantaged civilization in the galaxy and every day you survive is a victory."

"I wouldn't know," he admitted. For centuries the Empire had controlled the galaxy, and Tir never considered how less powerful civilizations felt about compromising their morals to maintain independence. But leaving galactic politics behind, he began instructing her then, starting with how to stand, and gave her some tips on simple movements. "Now, I want you to move forward like this," he showed her, and she did it well for someone who had never held a sword before.

While practicing the simplest movements and stances, she asked, "How many duels have you been in Tir?"

"Five serious duels."

She waited for him to continue and was annoyed that he didn't. "And all of these were to the death?"

"Yes."

"Before me, had you ever talked to an off-worlder before?"

"Of course, I have, many times. Why would you ask me that?"

"Whenever I ask you a question, you answer me as if I should already know."

Tir thought about this for a minute, and she hit him hard with her sword in his stomach while thinking. He looked at her with a feigned disapproving look. "All I can say in my defense is that you are the first person I have ever met who does not know all of this about me already or know about Alliance culture in the first place. I am not used to having to explain either." Then he looked at her seriously and said, "I have been in five duels to the death. Four were to protect my place as successor to the Emperor."

"And the other one?"

"It was a private matter."

"I'm your wife," she couldn't believe she was using that again to get him to do something for her. She smiled to herself at how absurd and brutal it was. Then she thought, *That's me, I am a wife barbarian with a sword now.*

"My sister was courting a man who treated her inappropriately. Other options were open to punish him, but he chose a duel. And this, you must never speak of to anyone."

"But surely people wondered why he died?"

"The Empire isn't Earth. In the Empire people die, and we don't always know why, but we never ask."

Kara was shocked by his admission. She had always imagined the Empire to be a place of transparency and rules that were followed. "And my female crew, what if they just die?"

"You have my word that nothing will happen to them. I am not explaining this well. Don't be anxious. Your crew is in no danger. We have very little crime in the Empire, and the little crime we do have is all very personal. Women are treasured above all else in the Alliance. Your female crew is quite safe. I can't think of any circumstance where any of your crew would be facing a duel to the death."

"You're not assuring me with that answer."

He struck her lightly with his practice sword. "I apologize, but I can't explain it any more than that. You must trust me. Now, let's focus on this."

Kara brought her sword up again and resumed the same movements as before, thinking about how vicious the Alliance Empire must be that they legitimately solve issues through dueling to the death.

After an hour of practicing movements and techniques, she began to falter. "I must stop now, Tir, or else I will not be able to pick anything up tomorrow with this hand."

He stepped forward, took the practice sword out of her hand, and then put them both on the floor. Then he took her right wrist up to his mouth and lightly kissed it while he looked into her beautiful brown eyes.

Kara found him so attractive now with his shirt off, and his hair pulled back as if she had never seen it. She leaned into him as he kissed her wrist. She could see the desire in his green eyes and wondered if they could have sex here in his little private gym. His guards were not outside this door, and the door was not locked as far as she knew. She could still hear a lot of his men practicing outside. But she had to admit. She liked the idea that any of them could walk in on them at any moment.

Tir pulled slightly away and looked into her eyes, deciding what to do. A part of him wanted to take her now, but the door wasn't locked, and if he took the time to do that, it might ruin this moment, and he wanted to live out this fantasy. It was forbidden in the Empire for men and women to spar together. Even more, to be in the same gymnasium. Her being here was one of the most popular fantasies played out with slave artists in the Empire. But what made this even sexier for him was that this was real. She was here, dressed in athletic clothing, and he saw her holding a sword for an hour. It was just too sexy, he finally decided, and he could not help himself.

Kara reasoned that it was doubtful any of his men would walk in, and if they did, it would not be too shocking that they were having sex. As far as she understood from Sera, his crew was talking about their sex life anyway. Sera had told her it was mainly because she was human, and everyone was wondering if she would become pregnant with a hybrid child.

Tir was running his hands over her pink top now. He was making her nipples hard, and he was aroused by how they looked through the fabric of her shirt. He was groping her breasts over her shirt while standing behind her. She leaned back into him, and he thought, *Yes, we will most definitely do this.* After many minutes of touching her breasts over the fabric, he put his hands into her shirt to touch her breasts skin to skin. She was grinding her hips against him, and he began attempting to remove her shirt, but after some futile attempts, he could not figure it out; there did not seem to be any buttons or clasps. So, he just scooped her breasts up, so they were held out into the open air with her shirt pulled down, just begging to be sucked. At this angle, he almost thought they looked bigger and fuller, which he found so irresistible. He moved in front of her and began licking, sucking, lightly followed by a little bit of biting and pinching. She was making the most wonderful little sounds as a reaction. As he was still sucking on one of her breasts, he moved his hand down to caress her sex over her tight pants. "You are so wet already," then he slowly took down her pants and began kissing and sucking all around her stomach, thighs, and vulva. Then he made her turn around with her pants still around her knees. "Bend over Kara," and began licking her rear and all around her anus.

Kara jumped from the sensation. The next thing she felt was Tir holding her steady by her thighs and then smacking on her bottom with one of his hands. She smiled with the pain and could not help but say, "Please punish me, Tir. I have been such a bad human."

Tir smiled. *My wife, has more fantasies than I do, apparently.* "Tell me what you have done."

Kara thought quickly about what would annoy him and tried to list them all, "I was disrespectful about the eating times," he smacked her once, and she paused to see if there would be more, and there wasn't, so then she tried to think of something worse. "I was disrespectful about your culture," he smacked her a couple of times then, but she wanted more. "I tried to get past the safeguards on your computer," he struck her a good ten times for that, and she was starting to feel really good then.

"I get a notification every time you do."

"I assumed you did," she said and struck her again.

Then his finger lingered and was lightly circling her anus, waiting for her to say something more. He knew she was enjoying this. "Is there anything else?"

Kara was trying to think. She felt his tone change. Did he know something real and was waiting for her to confess? She couldn't think. She had been alone too much; she could not read people anymore. She must have been quiet for an entire minute because he hit her again; this time, it was harder, and then he asked the question again. "I have had sex with Sera without you and didn't tell you."

Tir rubbed her bottom then and said, "I know you have done that. There are guards at our door. They tell me everything." He knew she wanted more but would not give her what she wanted until she confessed more. "I can use the practice sword to make you tell me how you have been naughty."

Yes, do that, she thought excitedly but said overdramatically, "Oh no, not that."

Tir had to try not to laugh then and thought to himself. She *could never be a slave artist. She really is a terrible liar.* He reached over, picked up one of the practice swords, and stood next to her. She was still bent over with her yoga pants around her knees. He took the sword and rubbed the width of it against her rear.

Kara felt the cold sword slide against her bottom and became so aroused with anticipation. Then, without warning, he spanked her with it, and she felt the tingling everywhere and especially through her sex.

"What else have you done to deserve this, my wild human wife?"

Kara had completely forgotten she was supposed to think of some other things. Her mind was blank with both pleasure and pain. "I had a fantasy about the doctor and masturbated to it." He was silent then. She did not know if she had crossed a line or not. She still did not fully understand how sex and monogamy were perceived in the Empire.

Tir was surprised by what she had just said, and it took him a minute to decide if she was telling the truth or lying. In the end, he decided that she was probably telling the truth. So, he smacked her hard with the sword a couple of times. "Do you wish he would have joined us on our wedding night?"

"Yes."

He smacked her again several times, then put the sword down and rubbed her red bottom. He kissed it and licked her anus. "Would you like the doctor to put his penis in here? The place you told me I could never go."

Tir's tongue was in her anus now. It was such an unusual but good sensation; she thought for a minute that maybe she did want to try that with someone. *If the doctor hurt me, he could probably fix me afterward,* she thought and replied, "Yes, I want you both inside of me simultaneously. Two alien men."

"You are so naughty telling me before you never wanted to do that," he said, but he did not spank her again. He just continued licking her, and now he was moving her down to lay on her stomach while he began licking her vulva and vagina from the back and had a finger in her anus. "We will have to stretch this out, you know?"

Kara did not say anything. There were too many new and pleasurable sensations going on. She loved the feel of her breasts against the cold floor and his hands, fingers, and mouth on her most vulnerable areas while she lay with her pants around her knees. Soon he was making her climax, and then seconds later, he had his trousers down and was pounding into her. He held her by her hair and pulled on it roughly. "Yes, Tir. I am such a bad Alliance wife to you."

Tir loved the feel of thrusting into her like this, he needed her to say something she may not understand, but it didn't matter, "Say 'We shouldn't be here.'"

"We shouldn't be here. It is forbidden. It goes against the gods," she smiled, thinking, *See, I have learned a lot of things from you.* She was rewarded by him turning her over then and pushing her legs down to one side as he began pumping into her roughly and one of his hands pinching her nipples. "This is so forbidden," she said quietly for good measure. Even though she had no idea what was so forbidden, she thought having sex on the conference room table was much naughtier than this. Then a thought occurred to her if they were super playful; she wanted to bring it to the next level for him while he was in the mood to go against the gods. She pushed him back and quickly began sucking on his penis before he could pull her off. She tasted herself on him but loved the idea of going against the gods in every way.

Tir only ever had a slave artist lick and suck his penis before. Kara was so different as it was so wrong in this place and as she was not pregnant yet, but it felt so good; her mouth was so much warmer than an Alliance woman, he could not resist her. He had his hands in her short brown hair, intending to push her back, but it felt too good; he just ended up with his hands firmly in her hair while she pleasured him with her hot mouth. He was going to come soon. He said as much to her, hoping she would stop, but she didn't. She just continued, increasing her speed and pressure until he started to orgasm, and then she was perfect, not letting go, but her mouth became so gentle, guiding the semen out into her mouth. *Gods, I am going to die now. My wife can make me do anything.*

Kara swallowed all of his semen which tasted exactly the same as a human's, and she wondered if they really were the Lost People. She smiled to herself. *After all the other thoughts I have had about the subject, the taste of his semen is what sways me? I am one classy woman.* Kara got up to her feet, pulling his trousers up as she went and then her own. She looked into Tir's green eyes with a devious grin. "Later, you can punish me for that too."

"Don't worry. I will," he said as he tried to adjust her breasts back inside her shirt for her. Then he walked over and put on his shirt. "Let's go. We can come back tomorrow."

Kara followed him out the door. Fewer men were practicing there now. They all stopped and gave Tir the respect he commanded, he acknowledged them, and then walked on. Kara wondered how many of them had heard them inside Tir's private room. It made her aroused again just thinking about it.

When they reached his quarters and went in, she said, "I am going to have a shower alone." She wanted to have a warm shower now and think about everything. "Just tell me one thing, why was it so bad to have sex in the gym?"

"Women have their own areas, and as I said before, men and women never practice with each other. Moreover, we are on a starship; Alliance women rarely leave the planet, let alone would go into that particular room on a starship. It was so forbidden, but every second of that will live in my heart forever."

"Even my mouth sucking all the semen from your penis," she asked as innocently as she could.

"Don't remind me, Kara or I might orgasm again by merely the thought. It was all so immorally wrong. We cannot do that again until you are pregnant. It goes against the gods."

She shook her head in disbelief and thought, *I am so tired of hearing that.* Then she took off her clothes and went into the bathroom. She sat on the toilet, and it adjusted specifically for her. Then she got into the warm shower. Tir had had the engineers take off the safety setting so she could have a much warmer shower than any Alliance citizen could go into without being burned, and she was grateful. She stood under the water for some time, constantly telling the shower that she was not done yet when it reminded her that she had been under the water for too long and it would dry out her skin. Finally, when she got out, her good friend, the mirror, greeted her.

"Good evening, Kara. You're healthy today. Now all you need is a good night's rest."

"Thank you, mirror."

Kara went out into the bedroom, accompanied by a cloud of steam the size of the bathroom door, and found Tir already in bed, probably asleep. She put on her stockings and nothing else, as she liked to sleep with socks on. And she especially liked the stockings Alliance women wore under their dresses as they were even better, warmer, and softer than any human socks or stockings she had ever worn. Even more, they went up to her thighs and never fell. So, she put them on and then got in bed and drifted off to sleep comfortably, thinking all the while, *When I escape, I am taking all the stockings with me.*

In the morning, Tir woke up at his usual time and looked over at Kara asleep. He touched her hair gently before he got out of bed. While he was getting dressed, he looked at her and realized that she was wearing her stockings in bed, as one of her feet was sticking out from under the covers. He smiled as he went over and ran his hands up until he reached the top of her thigh, then pinched her.

"Oww," she said and opened her brown eyes. "What are you doing?"

He playfully grabbed the top of one of her stockings and slowly pulled it down. "Why are you wearing these in bed?"

"I like having something on my feet at night, and I must admit these stockings are divine."

He took her other leg and removed the second stocking. "It is unhealthy, Kara, and I find it a little unhygienic as well."

"Says the man who has no problem having sex all around his ship or licking my anus."

"That is different," he defended himself.

She shrugged her shoulders, grabbed the blanket, and returned to sleep.

"Kara," he said while he touched one of her shoulders. "It's breakfast soon. If you miss it, you'll be hungry."

She didn't move. "I'm not hungry. I'm just tired. Eat without me."

"That is bad luck. Come on. Get up, then you can go back to sleep."

"No, I don't care about food this morning. I'm tired. I think I'm ill. Please let me sleep."

Tir left Kara in the bedroom but was very concerned about her. He wondered if she had caught an Alliance flu; it was going around. He ate breakfast and checked on her again before he left, and she was sound asleep. He went by sickbay on his way to the bridge. Doctor Siu was involved in a private procedure with a patient, so he could not talk with him. But the human, Doctor John, was there, and since this was about Kara, he told him, "Captain Kara was so tired this morning she did not want to eat breakfast. I think she may be ill."

John tried to look the admiral in the eye and not smile at his overprotective attitude. He had noticed that Alliance men talked about women as if they were so fragile and mysterious, he wondered how they ever managed any kind of equality in their civilization. He might have found these tendencies endearing if they were speaking about children or pets, but not adult women. "Does she have any other symptoms besides being tired?"

"She said she was not hungry and just wanted to sleep."

"Maybe she just wanted to sleep?" John was just trying to be the voice of reason. "My captain would say if she were unwell."

"I don't know how long you served with your captain, but she never misses a meal, and she is never that tired. Although yesterday she had a lot of exercise." Tir noticed the doctor's surprised reaction and clarified, "I was teaching her how to use a sword."

"I am sure it is nothing serious. I can go and talk to her later if you allow me?"

"Yes, as long as you take an assistant with you and then report back to me what is wrong with her."

John agreed and then watched the admiral go thinking, *I wonder what life is like for Captain Rainer with him taking such extreme care of her all the time? She might prefer to be alone in the brig rather than have all of that man's attention.* John had not seen Kara in weeks because the admiral did not want her roaming around the ship and escaping. So, he only knew of Kara's current condition through the rumors circulating around the ship about her and the admiral's sex life and threesomes with the slave Sera. He did not know whether to believe the rumors or not. He assumed that Captain Rainer was doing whatever she thought she needed to do to try and escape, even if that meant having threesomes with these grey aliens. He was not one to judge.

John was a prisoner of sorts too, but his invisible chains were to the sickbay and learning about Alliance medicine, which he welcomed as it was much more advanced than human medicine and he hoped that when he returned to Earth he would be able to implement some of it. In return, he shared information about human medicine, which was much more organic-based. It also seemed to him that the Alliance doctors were mainly interested in human fertility. He was surprised when he learned that the doctors onboard had never studied any aspect of fertility and that they were denied access to most medicine and procedures that involved only women. When he questioned this, Siu replied, 'On our planets, doctors are all women. Men are only allowed to be doctors aboard starships and in colonies. When we are at home, women doctors treat us all.' John was surprised by such a professional separation between the sexes, but he accepted it as another major cultural difference between humans and Alliance citizens.

―――

Hours later, Kara woke up and still felt tired. She figured it was all the sword practice yesterday. She rallied herself to get up and dressed so she would not miss the midday meal. And she even cut down on her studies and told herself she only had to do one chapter of hieroglyphics, and then she could go back to bed afterward. She had just left the bedroom when Mux came in with her food and said, "Doctor John will be visiting you after the meal."

Kara was delighted by this news. After she finished eating, which she did faster than she usually did with the expectation of meeting John, she just waited for him in the sitting room. Ten minutes later, John, and an Alliance medical assistant came to the door.

"John," she said excitedly. "It's good to see you." She just nodded to the assistant. "I assume you're here officially?"

"*I* am. Admiral Tir was worried about your health since you missed breakfast."

"I was just tired."

"I'm sure that is all it is, but I have to check because he's so concerned like you're some kind of beloved doll." John was taking her figure in now that he had not seen her in weeks, but it was impossible to discern anything under the Alliance women's fashion for loose dresses.

He took out a small medical device and held it over her as he talked, "How have you been? I have tried to come and see you, but I guess they thought I would be colluding with another prisoner."

"Yes, Tir is suspicious about everything" She sighed. "I've been as well as can be expected. I've been learning Alliance hieroglyphics to pass the time." She wanted to say much more, but the assistant was spying on them.

"I'm sure you are way ahead of me as I only know the ones on the medical equipment so far..."

Kara interrupted him, "Green Doctor, Green."

He looked at her and knew immediately by her expression she was very upset about something. 'Code green' was something used to signal an emergency evacuation. But he needed to keep talking so as not to raise suspicion from the assistant, "Interestingly, I have been sharing a lot of information about human women's fertility. I honestly think they will never solve their problem with fewer Alliance women being born. I hope that whatever is infecting Alliance women does not spread to the human women who have been taken to the Capital Planet. I believe, from the little I've seen, it is something in the environment. On Earth, in humanity's prehistory we had a similar issue with human men. There's evidence human men almost went extinct."

Kara didn't care about Earth's prehistory now. "What about Alliance women living off-planet?"

"You're joking, right?"

"No."

"Captain, Alliance women, except for slave artists, don't leave the planet if they are of child-bearing ages except under extreme circumstances. And slave artists are forbidden to have children if they have chosen that as their profession."

"Making a comparison impossible."

"Exactly," said John. At the mention of slave artists, he wanted to ask her about Sera and the threesome but held his tongue in case it wasn't true. No matter what their situation now, she was still his captain.

"I can't seem to really figure out who has which rights between Alliance men and women."

"I can't either. It's all really confusing," said John. "Like women not leaving their home planets is really terrible, but at the same time, some things for men seem skewed the other way and are just as unequal." He stopped scanning her then and asked, "Kara, you are six weeks pregnant. Did you know?" He wondered if that was what the 'green' was about, aborting the child.

"No. I think you must be mistaken. I can't be," she was genuinely shocked.

John showed her his scan and said flatly, "Congratulations." He looked into Kara's eyes, and they both knew this was trouble. He had thought, like Kara, that even though Alliance citizens and humans were genetically compatible in theory, the thought of mixing two species without heavy medical intervention was impossible.

Kara immediately touched her abdomen. "Is it a little monster? Mixing species like this?" Images from horror movies popped into her mind of deranged doctors mixing species — aliens creating hybrid monsters.

"It's not a monster, Kara. It's only a fetus that will grow into a baby. Maybe with grey skin, but no fangs, horns, or tail."

Kara was listening to all of this. Of course, she knew this was exactly what Tir wanted to achieve. To show that humans were the Lost People and that it was the gods' will that humans be integrated back into their society. But she felt that she had betrayed humans by providing this for him, even welcoming his touch, as it may mean the extinction of humanity. Her escape meant nothing in the scheme of all of this which she really hadn't considered until this moment. *How could I be so stupid?* There are so few of us and so many Alliance citizens, and too few Alliance women.

"I feel sick," she said and got up and went to the toilet to throw up. She was sick from the idea of being pregnant with a hybrid child and what that would mean to all the religious fanatics in the Empire and further repercussions on humanity. All she had been thinking about before was her escape and doing this for herself. She needed to escape now more than ever. After throwing up all the food in her stomach, she splashed some cold water on her face.

"You are dehydrated, Kara. You should drink some water."

"Why didn't you tell me I was pregnant, mirror? I thought we were friends," she said sarcastically to her reflection.

"Pregnancy is not within my parameters. Only men serve on starships."

Kara sighed and returned to sit on the sofa across from John. "Tell me now, what happens? How much longer until it is born?"

"You don't know?"

"Why would I ask you if I knew? What do I know about babies and being pregnant? I know nine months but nature isn't always accurate." She ended her last relationship with a man named Micah because she didn't want to sacrifice her career for a family. She never thought she would be able to become pregnant with Tir. Her menstrual cycle had been crazy this past year, and he was a different species, *Wasn't he?*

Kara noticed his assistant looking at her in shock and reminded herself to curb her comments.

"Gestation in humans is 40 weeks and 45 for Alliance citizens. I reckon we should aim for about 42. Otherwise, you don't need to do anything differently as you are hardly doing anything now. Just try not to become too stressed about the situation."

She gave him a scathing look. "Sure, I am going to have an alien's baby on an alien ship. That might just be the catalyst for the Empire to overtake humanity based on Alliance people's religious zealousness, but you tell me that I should not get stressed out about it? I don't want to be the equivalent of the Virgin Mary for the Empire."

"Kara," he put his hand on her knee. "I don't think this is going to be the green light to destroy humanity. Remember, these people are still quite racist. None of our female crew has even married on the Capital Planet yet. And they have all told me that they are fine, but most men seem to avoid them. I don't think Admiral Tir's plan to push human women into his society is going to work. Alliance culture is just too different."

"You've spoken to them? When? Why didn't you tell me that first?"

"About two weeks ago. They wanted to speak with you, but the admiral wouldn't let them."

"Typical."

"He allowed them to speak to me for medical reasons."

"Good."

"And they were all fine. They live in a little guarded apartment-type building in the capital with teachers who come in daily."

"Teachers for what?"

"I don't remember exactly, nothing out of the ordinary, culture, reading, you can imagine. They were told they would be back in space again with the Alliance Fleet. The High Council has allowed human women the right to maintain their jobs on starships if they want, even though all human women are now considered Alliance women."

"How can they do that? You would think the GC would do something. We didn't ask for this, nor do we want it."

"I guess they can because no one can tell the Empire 'no.' The best we can hope for is that the Empire abandons this plan of integration and sorts their demographics issue another way. First, so as not to destroy human civilization, and second, because humans won't solve the issue, I firmly believe it's something in their environment. It must be so close to them, their daily lives, they're not even considering it." John was lost in thought then.

"Well, me being pregnant is not helping in the hopes they'll give human women up, quite the opposite." She grimaced. "I'm worried about my female crew. It's not right what the Empire is doing."

"I agree, but there's little we can do here and now."

Kara felt guilty then because she could do more, she could kill herself and the hybrid child growing inside her to show that human women would not be subjected like this. "It would be better if they just took us by force than trying to marry us and integrate us in this strange manner. At least then we'd know what we were fighting against."

"Maybe the Empire isn't as terrible as we imagine them to be?" John suggested.

"No. I feel this is all a test to see how docile we are and look at me, I am playing right into it."

They were all quiet for a minute, and then John gave her a hypospray of some vitamins. "Eat well and take care, Captain."

When John returned to sickbay, he decided to tell Admiral Tir about the pregnancy in person. He contacted the admiral through the ship's internal communications and asked him for a couple of minutes privately.

Tir was waiting for him in the conference room. "Captain Rainer," John began, but Tir interrupted him.

"Captain Kara, she is married to me now, and we rarely use our surnames."

"Captain Kara is pregnant. Both are healthy. She should be monitored, though, as this is the first hybrid that I know of in recorded history."

"Good," the admiral said and then dismissed John. He would speak to Siu later about the details. He now needed to decide what to do with Kara. He wanted her to stay with him, but it was unheard of for a pregnant woman to be on a starship in the middle of a war. However, sending her back to the Capital Planet was not necessarily the best idea, given his enemies would use her against him if they could.

Just as John was leaving, the admiral called him back.

"Do human doctors know about female bodies?"

"Yes."

"Do you know how babies are born? What I mean is, would you be able to help Captain Kara deliver this baby here?"

"Of course, Admiral."

"Fine," he dismissed the human doctor and thought, *This changes everything now. I can keep her here, safe, close to me, and prove to everyone the gods want us to bring humans back into the fold.*

———

After a couple of hours, Kara went to the internal communications and called Sera to come and see her. Within 10 minutes, Sera entered, and Kara told her about the pregnancy.

"The gods have blessed you."

Kara did not feel blessed. She felt terrified of what ramifications this may have for humans, but she didn't want to think about it. She wanted to just be with Sera now, like a drug.

Sera picked up on her feelings. "But you've not called me here as a friend today or for the deal we made? You have called me here in a very professional capacity."

"I have called you here to make me forget what I have just learned. To take my thoughts away from myself or else I might end my life."

Sera stood up, took Kara's warm hands without saying anything, and led her into the bedroom. Once there, she quietly began undressing Kara. Her cool soft hands tenderly took off her dress and lingered all over her shoulders, arms, and torso indiscriminately. "Turn off your translator Kara. I want you to hear me in my language as I touch you."

Kara nodded and mentally turned off her translator.

Sera slowly pulled Kara's dress down to her hips and then stopped, edging her fingers around her soft, warm waist. "I also can't believe that you have a child here. There is hardly any sign. You still look so firm, but there is still a long way to go." Then her hands rose to her breasts, holding them gently. "But I should have noticed these, they are bigger and heavier. I just thought you were putting on weight now that you have access to food." She kissed one nipple and looked up at Kara, making eye contact. "How could you have not noticed? They are more sensitive too," Sera said as she blew on her wet nipple, and it became very hard.

Kara felt she was in a different world when Sera touched her body and spoke to her in Alliance. It was so different being with Sera without Tir, trying to comprehend a new language and a new kind of sexual partner all at once. She couldn't think of anything else but the present when they were together. "I don't wear undergarments with this dress. I thought my breasts hurt because..."

Sera smiled at her bad grammar. "I understand, my wild beauty." Sera began massaging her breasts gently then, lightly licking and kissing them. "Alliance women would kill to have a body like yours. You are truly blessed by the gods."

Kara put her hands down to Sera's face and brought her up for a kiss, but Sera stopped her.

"You must ask me."

"Kiss me," she asked, and she obliged.

Sera adored Kara's accent on Alliance and this secret that only they shared, that Kara could speak and read quite well now. But it wasn't just her curiosity of being with a human who had learned Alliance, she also adored just being with Kara. It had been a year since she had been with a woman regularly, and she enjoyed a woman's touch as much as a man's because it was so different.

Sera began running her fingers through Kara's brown hair while they kissed, cupping the back of her head. She felt Kara's warm hands taking off her green slave clothing, and even she was anticipating their lovemaking.

Kara's mouth moved away from Sera's mouth and found one of her earlobes. She tenderly touched the long, ornate earring with her hand and kissed her ear, then whispered, "I love all your embellishments. They are so exotic." She began kissing her way down her neck, past many necklaces to one of her breasts that was also pierced, and a long piece of jewelry hung exquisitely from the nipple. She kissed the nipple as she had done her ear lobe and put her hand on the jewelry, tugging just a little to bring a ripple of pleasure and pain. Then she put her mouth on her breast and sucked her nipple hard.

Sera wondered if she was addicted to Kara's warm mouth. It was amazing the difference a couple of degrees made. Kara's hot mouth and then the cold air brought a new level of oral sensations to her skin.

Kara began kissing her on her mouth again, and then Sera pulled off the rest of her dress, falling to her knees. She brought her hands up both of Kara's stocking legs, stopping where the stockings ended on her upper thighs. She ran her fingers around the top of the stockings, looking up at Kara, who was looking down, watching her. Then she moved one of her hands over Kara's vulva and pulled a bit on the brown hair there. "Never remove this hair here, it's one of your true beauties." Sera was running her fingers through her hair, enjoying the look of increased desire in Kara's eyes. Then she moved her hands back to the tops of her stockings and said, "I remember you don't want me to pull these down as you get cold," she said, kissing all around her inner thighs, around the top of the stockings. Sera then moved to begin licking all around Kara's vulva.

Kara could feel herself becoming so wet in anticipation of what Sera would do. This was exactly what she needed, this pleasure and to be with someone who had no say in her future. Someone to give her pleasure.

Sera finally moved to lick Kara's clitoris and then moved to put her tongue in her vagina as she continued to stroke her sex. It was not long until she brought Kara to climax and then cooled her down with slow, light strokes across her vulva, admiring the hair that had become wet from her arousal. Sera looked up at Kara, "Your cheeks are so pink."

Kara looked into Sera's grey eyes. "I know you like that."

"There is so much I like about humans," Sera said as Kara guided her onto her back and began kissing her down her body as she talked. "I like your patches of hair in the corners of your bodies, your warmth, your different colors," then Kara reached Sera's clitoris directly, and Sera gasped and put her hands on Kara's head. "And your hot tongues. Yes, right there. You are so naughty going in and then leaving," Kara had begun licking her elsewhere, "teasing my clitoris like that."

"I know you like it," Kara then urged her to turn over on her stomach and began licking her vagina, first just skimming the outside but then thrusting her tongue in and out with her hands on her bottom spreading her. Again, Kara thought she tasted like some kind of alien flower, not like a human woman at all, not that Kara had any experience with human women beyond herself. Still, she knew what she tasted like, and then she wondered if this were some slave artist thing. Something they purposely did to make themselves smell and taste like flowers. *A drug.*

"Will you put your fingers inside of me?" Sera asked.

Kara put one finger inside of her vagina and moved it slowly in and out, looking for the sensitive area that would bring Sera a blended orgasm. When she found it, she had Sera move her hips up and had one hand on her clitoris and the other going in and out of her to give her as much pleasure as possible. "Do you like my fingers on your Alliance skin?"

"In my Alliance vagina," Sera corrected Kara's Alliance and then orgasmed. Kara kept her hands gently moving for a minute, then retracted them to move up and to lie next to Sera. Kara caressed her beautiful grey body lightly and casually as they lay next to one another on Tir's bed.

Sera kissed Kara and held her while stroking her soft human hair. "Tir will be back soon."

"Yes," Kara said.

Sera disentangled herself from Kara, got out of bed, and put her clothes back on. "He won't want to see me here when he arrives, not today." She looked at Kara and felt pity for her; she did not believe in the gods and thought she was betraying her people by doing this. "Kara, the gods give each one of us free will. Make your own decision. If you choose to end your life, I will pray for your soul and the soul of that child to reside in the Afterlife."

Kara just nodded. She knew what Sera meant.

Sera kissed her on the forehead as she lay naked on the bed and then left.

Tir entered sickbay, and Siu led him into his office to speak privately. Siu began, "You should send her to the Capital Planet."

"I have thought about it and want to keep her onboard. It is too dangerous at home. People will use her against me. I have also spoken to the human doctor, who says he can oversee the birth."

"This is unprecedented, men watching a birth. People will say we have lost our minds and what if she or the baby dies? It is too risky."

"They won't die. This is meant to be. She is healthy, and their doctor is knowledgeable, right? You have been working next to him for months now."

"Yes, I believe him when he says he can do something."

"It is settled then. She will remain here. We will keep this all a secret until the baby is born. I worry about my enemies wanting to prove that humans are not the Lost People by separating Kara from me and killing her, the child, or both."

"I understand. She could not be anywhere that is safer than on our ship right now. My only concern is her health. An Alliance baby has never been born off-planet before, and I worry we are tempting the fates by pinning all of our hopes to a hybrid baby born with only the aid of a male human doctor on a man's warship."

"Or maybe the gods are trying to show us the way forward. We must keep our eyes open. And for my wife, I don't think she would want it any other way."

Tir went directly to his quarters from sickbay. He found Kara in the sitting room studying hieroglyphics. He did not interrupt her but sat down while she finished. He liked watching her concentrate and found her serious demeanor intoxicating, the way her big eyes focused on understanding the problem in front of her. She looked the same when she was strategizing battles.

Kara closed the program. "I assume John told you I am pregnant."

"Are you not the least bit excited by this news?"

"If it was just about us," she pointed between them, "then maybe I would be. But this is about you and a religious myth that you have somehow turned into law to subjugate human women for your purposes."

"This is about us too. You cannot pretend to be so emotionally cut off from me or us. We are destined for each other," he took her in his arms. "And this is about the future of both our civilizations; we are one species," he said quietly. "This is the gods' will whether humans believe it or not. I believe and will make this happen to save us all."

Kara wanted to say, 'But humans were doing just fine without you,' but she couldn't because the truth was that they weren't. They were barely hanging on to their independence year after year. They weren't strong enough to protect themselves in a galaxy with civilizations bent on conquering as much territory as possible. And humans were thousands of years behind technologically in the galaxy. Human technology was the running joke of most other species. The only thing that had kept them safe was their obscure location in the galaxy, but those days were coming to an end. Humanity needed a new defense. She knew that Tir recognized this, which is why he believed he was saving humans too. However, Kara, like most humans, given a choice, would rather die than enter into an outrageous partnership focused on hybrid children with the Empire.

"We must go to the public shrine onboard and thank the gods for this blessing. Do you remember the prayer?" Tir asked her.

"I am not doing that."

"Kara, stop acting like a child."

She decided she didn't actually care. She said nothing but went to the bedroom, got the necklace, put it on, and then walked out of his quarters.

She walked behind him through the corridors to the main shrine. It was a small room with very little decoration, but statues of what Kara assumed were the Alliance gods lined up perfectly in the front of the room and along the walls. There was a large candle burning at one end of the room, and the smell of incense burning from somewhere else in the room Kara couldn't see. A few other people there looked up when Tir and Kara entered, but no one saluted him as they had done in other areas of the ship.

Tir gently pushed Kara forward and nodded at her. She dutifully said the short prayer he had made her memorize to the goddess of home, who she assumed she was standing in front of, and then he did the same and lit a candle. After a couple of minutes of silence, they left. They did not speak to each other on the way back.

Once in his quarters, he went directly to his own shrine and kneeled before it lighting a candle. She sat on the sofa and watched him. She wanted to be respectful, but she could not believe that he would have faith in religion, something humans had given up centuries before.

Tir finished praying and sat across from her. "I want you to be seen in the shrine daily, giving thanks to the gods."

"Only if I get to go by myself," she did not expect him to grant this request, but she had to try.

"No, the guards will, of course, follow you."

Kara reckoned that it was still better than nothing. "Is there any particular time of day I should be doing this?" All she could think about was medieval women having nothing better to do than go to church and pray as an activity during their days.

"An hour before the midday meal."

"Anything else?" she asked with a sharp tone. He didn't answer her and looked deep in thought. After a few minutes, she asked, "What are you thinking about? You look so severe. I thought this is all that you wanted?"

"It is, but now I am concerned about keeping you safe and this a secret until the baby is born healthy."

"Are there any onboard who would like to harm me?"

"A few, I imagine, but my guards are good and loyal. This is a dangerous time. Everything I have worked for will fall if anything happens to you now."

"We have nothing to worry about except me going crazy from boredom."

"Kara, I know you like to make light of serious situations, but please, not now. I don't want you doing much or seeing anyone, not even Sera, until the baby is born."

"That is a bit overprotective, don't you think? Sera is one of the only people you let me talk to. You can't deny me her visits."

"We cannot risk anything right now. Sera can be bought as many people can be. I will be more than pleased to grant all the freedoms of an Alliance wife once you are holding a healthy baby in your arms and have proven yourself loyal."

"I want a translator," Kara recognized she had some bargaining power now.

"After the baby is born, I promise you an Alliance translator."

"I want to communicate with the female crew you sent to the Capital Planet."

"Limited, but I will allow it in good time."

"I want a ship."

"I am not even sure I can trust you to walk down to the shrine and back. I am certainly not giving you a ship."

"What can I do to change your mind? I would have an Alliance crew loyal to you. It's not as if I could get far. I could be a big help in the final battle. I want to do something."

"I am trying to keep you safe. You are not going into battle only to find an easier way to escape. I may not be as intelligent as you are, Wife, but I'm certainly not a fool either."

"I want to talk with my crew that you sent to the Capital Planet as soon as possible."

"I know you already have had an update from your doctor, so there is no rush."

She looked at him and again wondered what he was hiding. "What difference does it make?"

"I will decide when you can talk to them. Not tomorrow or the next day." He didn't want her telling them too much about her life onboard or that she was pregnant. The Alliance needed to believe she was here by choice and that they were destined to be together.

Kara decided by his tone that there was no way she would find out why she could not speak to them tomorrow. She needed to put him in a better mood to explain his reasoning, so she dropped it for now.

She switched back on her hieroglyphics learning program and began the next chapter. He went out again and did not say where he was going. He did this sometimes, and she did not ask because he was always back within an hour, usually less. She assumed he might have more work to do or was talking to someone, possibly a friend.

After the evening meal, she went to him and put her arms around his neck. Seductively she said, "You still haven't punished me for last night, as you said you would."

"No, but now that will have to wait. I don't want to do anything that might hurt the baby."

"Just a little; I don't think it will hurt the baby. I know you have that whip in your wardrobe."

"Kara, no." He was so aroused thinking about what happened at the gym and how he could whip her now for it, but then he thought about the baby and used all his self-control to separate himself from her physically.

"So, we are not going even to have sex? People don't stop having sex when they become pregnant, Tir."

"This is too important."

"Tir, I need you. I am so lost right now, and I need your physical body to center me in all of this. You are making me betray my people, and I don't believe in the gods' or destiny. It is just us. Just you. I need you to make me believe this is right, or I honestly don't know what I will do."

He turned around and kissed her. In between kisses, he said, "You have me. I swear you do." He put his hands on the sides of her head and looked into her brown eyes. "You are saving everyone. This is your destiny, and you have me. Gods Kara, you have me. But I must be vigilant and protect you and the child or we will both lose everything."

Kara kissed him passionately as she undressed him so slowly and gently; she could feel him begin to relax into the situation completely. When he was naked, she started kissing him everywhere and then said before taking the tip of his ridged penis into her mouth, "See, we weren't going against the gods by me doing this yesterday." *Although it was great that you thought so when I was doing it,* she thought as she began lightly flicking her tongue across the underside of his penis, up and down, to get him more aroused.

Before she took him into her mouth, she moved down to his testicles and began gently licking them and caressing them lightly with her fingers. She was on her knees and looked up at him. They held eye contact for half a minute before she spoke, "Just tell me if you don't like it."

He wanted to tell her, 'To be serious,' but the words would not come out as she was already giving him so much pleasure, and the idea that she would do this again made him more aroused than he had been since yesterday.

Kara looked back down and began kissing the inside of his thighs, licking his penis up and down slowly, purposely avoiding the tip. Finally, after countless minutes of teasing him, she began taking him into her mouth and sucking. Then she would lightly blow on it, and she heard him gasp, 'Gods,' and she smiled.

Tir was way too big even to consider deep-throating him. She hated that anyway, so she concentrated on what she was good at, keeping it nice, slow, and pleasurable. She had never had any complaints before, even though she had to admit that she would not include fellatio as one of her top sexual skills. She looked up at him again and made eye contact just before he was going to come and asked, "Do you want me to swallow your semen, or do you want it somewhere else?"

What a strange question. "Swallow it."

Kara smiled and then continued, she had to bring him back to a high state of arousal, but she was smiling to herself, thinking about the expression on his face when she asked. *Obviously pearl necklaces were not something that Alliance men did,* she thought. He came, and she swallowed it all and then wondered again at the taste of it, being just like human men, *Are we the Lost People?*

Tir looked down at Kara, pulled her up to him, and embraced her. Then he removed her clothing and said, "Let's sleep for a while now." He pulled her into bed with him as he held her close. Tir's curiosity got the better of him, though, and he had to ask, "Kara?"

"Hmm," she was almost asleep.

"Where do human men put their semen if not in a woman's mouth or vagina?"

She opened her eyes and smiled, thinking, *You're going to think this is another dirty human thing; I can feel it already.* "You could have come on my body somewhere, or I could have to spit it out."

"On the floor?" he asked disbelievingly. She could sense the next word.

"Barbaric."

"Why?"

"It has to do with both the gods and hygiene. There is a myth about..." before he could continue, she stopped him.

"I am too tired to hear about your religion now. I want to sleep."

Kara fell asleep in minutes. When she woke the next morning, she vaguely remembered them having very slow sensual sex, which he instigated during the night. She was relieved that she had convinced him that sex during pregnancy was fine. She wondered what other Alliance couples did. *Did they not have sex and just fellatio for nine months?* But then she thought about the number of times he had made her come and reasoned that maybe this was just the Alliance tradeoff between husband and wife, as strange as it seemed. She was happy that she had been able to dispel that quickly. The only thing that kept her sane, she thought, was his touch.

―――

A few days later, Kara was talking to the bathroom mirror, practicing her Alliance pronunciation, when there was a chime at the door. Mux came in with a lot of clothing and other things in his arms. He laid them on the bed and then began hanging the clothes in the wardrobe. She looked at the dress and noticed that it was made from a much finer material than the one she was wearing and asked, "Are those for special occasions?"

"Some are, but most are for every day. Admiral Tir wanted you to have clothing that suited your imperial rank now, especially since you are reluctant to wear the one necklace he gave you."

"How will I know which is which?" she asked, looking at the dresses that all just seemed very nice to her, boxy in that terrible Alliance cut but made of beautiful material.

"I can tell you. Also, in those boxes on the table is jewelry for you. You must become accustomed to wearing it."

"Is this jewelry that the admiral bought for me specifically, or are these pieces he might have already had for a potential future wife?" Kara had found that Mux was a good source of cultural information.

"Both. A maximum class man begins collecting jewelry for a future wife when he becomes of marrying age."

"What is the marrying age?"

"Thirty years old."

Kara looked down at the jewelry, there was a lot of it, and reflected he *had been buying this for a future wife for the last 15 years, for someone he didn't even know.* "I find this so strange." She opened the ornate wooden boxes and saw the most gorgeous necklaces and bracelets. "I couldn't imagine wearing any of this."

"Aren't you happy with the jewelry?"

"It's not that. It is your culture. It is too different. I am sure an Alliance woman would have been very happy to receive this, or?"

"Yes," he answered her patiently. As he saw Kara at all times of the day, he had sympathy for her situation. He knew she was trying to understand their culture, but he reckoned it was just too much at once, they were at war, and it was a very unusual circumstance, her being both Admiral Tir's prisoner and wife. And during a war surrounded by men. It was all so unnatural. "Men are publicly avid jewelry collectors, so potential wives know what they will receive when they marry. Admiral Tir is said to have good taste and values quality over quantity."

Kara looked at Mux, stunned as she often did when he said these surprising things about their culture and tried to keep her mouth closed. It all seemed like something from medieval Earth. She closed the box to the necklace she was looking at and decided to change the subject. "Mux, Admiral Tir said he also ordered some human food. Could you bring some coffee to me and a list of what he bought?"

"Everything is the same as what you took from your ship before, coffee, tea, honey, salt. The human shop owner, was very curious about a human onboard an Alliance starship, and also included two other items and a personal message for you." He pulled an IC out of his pocket, brought up the message, and showed it to her.

> Hello Fellow Human, I hope you will be happy with your shipment. I am also including some chocolate and a bottle of wine in our appreciation and hope you will be a regular customer. Bon Appétit.
>
> Frank, Owner of the Earth Store, Alliance Empire

"Where is the chocolate and wine?" Kara asked.

"I took it to the kitchen to keep with your other things," Mux replied casually.

"Bring all the chocolate and wine here, now." She had not had human chocolate or wine in a year maybe longer. Genuine chocolate was out of her price range on Earth. So she was going to have it now. And she knew from John that she could still have a glass of wine while being pregnant, but she needed to do it before Tir found out and had a heart attack and took it away from her. He had already removed the Alliance wine from his quarters. Even though John had told Tir it was fine, he had said, 'We are taking no chances, Kara.' She was so tired of hearing that phrase from him.

Mux set out an exquisite black dress for Kara on the bed, took some of the jewelry from the boxes, and put it next to the dress. "Put on this dress and jewelry with no fuss, and I'll bring you some of the chocolate and wine as a special favor, even though it's not mealtime. I can imagine how you miss things from Earth." Like many of the men onboard, Mux was understanding of Kara's situation. They admired her and wanted to make her as comfortable as possible, given the unusual circumstance. They were also all waiting in anticipation to see if human women could serve as replacements for the missing Alliance women from their own population, so they looked at Kara as if she represented the entire Empire's future.

Kara took off her dress and put on this other one without asking him to leave. Alliance citizens she had noticed cared little for being naked in front of one another, so she decided not to waste time between her and the chocolate by asking him to leave the room just for her modesty.

She then picked up the necklaces, and Mux came to help her. "You know, we put these on and take them off in an order, shortest to longest and then longest to shortest," then he began putting them on her. After he finished putting on her jewelry, he decided she looked like a proper Alliance woman. "This suits you," he said, taking away the other dress.

Kara thought as he put on the heavy necklaces; *I doubt this is what you signed up for when you joined the interstellar Alliance, poor boy.* "Now go and get the chocolate," she commanded him.

Mux nodded and left. He was back in five minutes with the chocolate and wine. He set them down on the table in the dining room, and she said with delight, "Swiss chocolate and French wine. Open the wine, Mux."

He looked at the bottle and shook his head. "With what, Captain Kara? I have never seen such an old-fashioned device. I don't know how to open this," he pointed at the cork.

"The Earth Store didn't send a corkscrew?"

"There were no devices in the shipment."

"Your sword. You can open it with your sword."

"Excuse me?"

"It might work."

"No. Show me what this corkscrew looks like, and I will replicate one, and never ask me to use my sword to open wine again."

"It goes against the gods?" she asked as everything fun in the Empire seemed to be against them.

"No, a man who would use his sword for foolish tasks is not an honorable man."

"Oh," she said to the young man and tried not to smile. She wondered then if she should wait and see if Tir would use his sword. Then she went to the computer and tried to bring up a picture of a corkscrew, but as usual, she was locked out of everything but the children's learning and the ship's internal communications.

Without thinking, Mux accessed the guest user. "Show me now," he instructed Kara. Mux did not know that Kara would be able to read Alliance well enough to bring up the guest user herself.

Kara typed in 'human corkscrew for wine,' and it came up.

Mux closed the guest's access and then went to make one.

Kara could not help but smile; she quickly opened the guest user again and found external messages. She sent an encrypted message to the nearest human ship, which she knew was the *Silverado*, because she had been helping Tir with their strategy for the next battle. Then she closed the user and went into the dining room.

It was not long before Mux returned, and she was enjoying a bottle of Bandol with dark chocolate thinking about escape. *The gods are telling me to get off the ship and back to Earth if anyone asks about these omens*, she thought as she ate the chocolate and drank the wine. After she had one glass of wine and had eaten half of the generous chocolate box, she left it all on the table and said sternly to Mux, "Do not take that chocolate away. It stays there until I've eaten it all."

"But Captain," Mux protested.

"I'll take the blame with the gods," she said as respectfully as possible. "And I don't think the ship will go down for this one misdemeanor of bad luck, do you?"

He didn't answer her. They just returned to their work of putting away these new things Tir had ordered.

"Can you explain these to me?" She held up some almost transparent stockings with designs that seemed to move on them with the light. Mux just looked at her, shocked, and then realized that he was definitely not the person to be asking because judging by his facial expression, these stockings were no doubt supposed to be sexy. "Never mind. What is this?" she asked, holding up a box with two bracelets.

"Marriage bracelets."

"So, this is what they look like," she said more to herself than Mux. They were two black and silver bracelets with markings on them. Some she understood, and others she didn't. She asked Mux, "What does this mean?" pointing to an unknown hieroglyphic.

"It is the admiral's family name, now your family name."

"Great, I always wanted to be tagged like a dog," Kara said, and Mux gave her a disapproving look.

Kara opened another big box with a large pen in it. "What is this?"

Mux closed the box lid and moved it away from her, "The admiral will explain it to you later."

"Tell me, or I will tell him you let me have wine."

Mux looked at her as if she had betrayed him. "This is for binding tattoos. Some married couples get them."

"Binding, meaning you can never be with anyone else ever?"

"Yes, you will desire no other."

"How barbaric can the Alliance be?" she asked rhetorically.

Mux ignored that commend and simply reminded her, "Captain

Kara, it is time you go to the shrine and thank the gods. You can also pray to the goddess of home that the admiral does not want you to take the binding tattoos. And just so you know, those tattoos are considered a romantic gesture in the Empire."

Kara just looked at Mux in disbelief. She did not understand this culture at all. *How could physically binding yourself to someone be romantic?* But then she reminded herself, *Isn't that what this whole marriage thing is about?*

Kara wanted to go through more of the things that Tir had ordered for her with Mux and ask him more questions about his culture, but she knew she had to go to the shrine. To be publicly seen there. She reluctantly left him to put everything away. She walked out, and immediately, his guards were her shadows as they always were as she made her way to the shrine. It was always busy at this time of day, and she had no doubt that was why Tir asked her to come at this time continually. She always walked directly to the fertility goddess's statue, said the short prayer, waited a minute or two, depending on her mood, and then left.

As she was slowly making her way back to Tir's quarters, she feigned to be tired and asked to go to sickbay. Her guards, of course, took her directly there. She wanted to see John, but unfortunately, Doctor Siu was coming forward to see her as she entered.

She tried to keep her mind as focused as possible on feeling ill, which wasn't very difficult as all she had to do was think about the hybrid growing inside her.

"Captain Kara, please sit down. You must calm yourself."

Damn, she thought, *he is reading my mind.*

"This is not going to be a monster," he tried to comfort her. "It will be a beautiful child to start a new and peaceful chapter in human and Alliance's lives."

"I don't think I can do it. I want to speak with John, I don't know anything about pregnancy, and I don't have access to a computer. I am scared."

Siu nodded and brought John over. Siu did not leave them alone, though.

"Are you feeling dizzy again?" John asked for something legitimate to say.

"Yes, it was my daily walk to the shrine. I always go an hour before the midday meal, but today I felt like I was going to pass out on the way back." What she was really saying was, 'I am going to try to escape when I go to the shrine. I have found a way.'

"Maybe you should change the time, and you won't feel so light-headed?"

Kara was pleased that they were easily talking with a hidden message about when to try and escape, "Tir asked me to go at that time, so I will continue to do so. I just wondered if this was normal?"

John put his hand on Kara's arm. "Yes, your body will change a lot. Don't stress."

Kara smiled and said she felt a bit better, got up, and walked back to Tir's quarters before she missed lunch. As she walked in, Mux had just laid out her lunch. She sat down and ate. He sat watching her as no one was allowed to eat alone. Apparently, it did not matter if only one person was eating, and Kara wondered if this meant that Mux missed lunch every day, and she expected he did. "Why don't you ever eat with me?"

"I'm here to take care of you. I am not your equal."

Kara sighed. She knew that was the answer before she asked and realized she subconsciously needed to be reminded that these people were not her own and never would be. That she needed to focus on escape and not try to make excuses for them or justify staying.

Kara finished eating, and then Mux left. When she was sure he was gone, she logged into the guest account again on Tir's computer and saw a message for her. It was from Captain Jackson of the *Silverado*. He wrote,

> Captain, the next time we are in Tombstone, we should meet, OK? HJ

Kara looked at his message and screamed, "For the love of pandas, why did it have to be Captain Jackson, stupid Wild West freak? What do you mean?" She tried desperately to remember what happened at the

OK Corral, which she knew was in Tombstone. She could not remember, and if she searched for it and someone noticed, she would not be able to escape.

She closed the guest's services and sat on the sofa, trying to remember everything she could about North American history from the 19th century. "Come on, Rainer, your father loved that stuff. Remember," she whispered to herself. "Nothing is ever lost in mind. It only takes longer to retrieve it," she said, trying to inspire herself to remember.

She lay on the sofa. Her eyes closed, then she remembered a name and said loudly, "Wyatt Earp was in Tombstone." Then she thought to herself, *but what did he do? Was there a rescue at the OK Corral? How can I respond?*

She lay on the sofa for another hour concentrating, and then she jumped up, opened the guest computer, and replied,

> I hear that fight is something to see and takes place every two days at the same time, at about noon, but one should dress appropriately if entering from the actors' entrance. It's also rumored that Wyatt always fired a warning shot.

She sent it and hoped it made sense. The last battle would take place in two days. Kara knew the *Silverado* had cloaking technology, and the one thing humans did better than any other species in the galaxy was stealth. The *Silverado* could get in and out during the battle. Humans had the technology to get through force fields quickly, disruptions that would go unnoticed in a battle. Once the *Silverado* was in the vicinity and alerted her, 'with the warning shot,' she would somehow get out of Tir's quarters and get to the *Silverado*.

Kara quickly checked her messages one more time before Tir returned, and she was not disappointed.

> It's funny. You should say that. I have two friends that are actors in that reenactment. They say they never use the actors' entrance, but the spectators are always there by noon sharp. Still, it's always confusing, with the spectators not quite realizing what is happening until the man who plays Doc Holiday says, 'I'm your huckleberry,' often as late as 3 PM. I never heard about a warning shot, it might be too shocking for the crowd.

Kara thought to herself, *Really, Captain? I don't love the Old West, and I hope that you mean you are coming through the main docking bay at noon during the battle, which will hopefully have begun by then.* Just then, Tir walked through the door, and she quickly closed the program. She could see on his face that he was trying to decide if he had just seen anything suspicious, so she took him off guard by saying to him in Alliance, "Welcome home, husband."

Tir was dumbstruck when Kara spoke to him in Alliance. He knew that was what she had used as she had an accent suddenly, and this was a set phrase that only existed in his language as one word. He recovered himself after a minute and then said the appropriate response, "I am home," which was a set response that was also only one word.

Kara's heart was beating so quickly. *Had he seen the message? Did I distract him enough for him to forget? Was he going to take everything from me and keep me in the brig now?* She was watching him, waiting for a reply.

Tir knew he shouldn't be surprised that she learned to speak Alliance so quickly. Humans were known to waste their time doing things like this. He knew that she would never gain the kind of fluency she needed to steal a ship, even though, without a doubt, that was her intention. "You know you have an accent?"

She turned her translator off so she would not be distracted by the English in her ear when she was trying to speak Alliance. "I know, but you can still understand me?"

He smiled at her. Her accent was charming. He had never heard an alien speak Alliance, and now he wanted her to say so many things. "I can understand you. Your accent is pleasing to listen to. What else can you say?"

"What do you want to hear? Maybe you can teach me how you would unlock an Alliance ship?"

"You know you will never be good enough to fool the computer. If I gave you your own ship, we would have to reset everything for you. Our security technology outstrips most of the galaxy."

"Tell me about it."

"Not a chance. But tell me, how have you learned to speak so well? I am impressed."

"The hieroglyphics program and the mirror in the bathroom," she did not want to involve Sera in this. "Humans can turn their translators on and off at will."

"Yes, the galaxy looks at you all and laughs about it. But I am not laughing now. I find this remarkable even though I know you had ulterior motives."

She did not want him thinking about how far her ulterior motives would go today, so she distracted him again. "As you can see," she stood up so he could see the dress and her jewelry properly, "I am suitably dressed now, according to Mux."

"And to me." He took in her full appearance. She was dressed as his equal. "I hope you like the jewelry?" He had never imagined that he would see a human wearing that jewelry when he bought it years before, but now it seems so natural.

"I've never seen anything like these. They're all exquisitely made. I imagine an Alliance woman would have been able to appreciate these much more than I can."

Tir went into the bedroom and looked through all the boxes. He returned to the sitting area with a couple of them. He sat down across from her and handed her a small black box, he knew what she wanted to know, what every woman wanted to know, *What did you buy specifically for me?* "This I bought for you. It is not small because I think less of you, quite the contrary."

Kara took the box from his hand and opened it up. Inside was a small but beautiful barrette.

"I know you don't want to wear a lot of jewelry, especially when you are alone, so I thought, maybe you could wear this in your short hair," he finished and thought, *Gods, I am so inarticulate when it comes to romancing Kara.*

Kara had never been given a piece of jewelry in her life before Tir. His thoughtfulness touched her in an unexpected way. She looked up at him. "Thank you, Tir. Its lovely." She took it out of the box, and he reached over, took it out of her hands, and put it smoothly in her hair. She was always amazed by his actions like this. She couldn't help being reminded of the first time they were alone in his quarters, and he combed her hair.

Tir opened the second box he had brought out; she knew these were the marriage bracelets. He took them out and held them in his hands so she could see them. "Can you read these inscriptions?"

"Yes."

"So, you know what these are?"

"Yes."

"Good. We should put them on now. We will have to repeat the promises to each other again."

Kara didn't know why she was so nervous all of a sudden. She was already married. And pregnant.

He took her left wrist, put the bracelet on her, then put his own on, and said, "Kara of Earth," he left off her surname as they were technically already married, "I pledge my life to you."

She responded, "Tir Zu," she knew he was surprised she knew his surname, "I pledge my life to you." Kara jumped when the bracelets tightened automatically, and she felt a pinprick in her left wrist. "What was that?"

"Just an initial activation to make them ours." He turned her wrist and showed her where it said 'children' on the bracelet. "There will be a number there after that we have a child, and it will continue to grow, I hope."

Kara looked at him in disbelief. "And you all wear these things openly with your names and how many children and how long you have been married?"

"Yes, it is an honor to be married in the Empire."

She looked down at the bracelet now and wished her dress covered her wrists but now understood why it did not. She felt sick again and went into the bathroom but didn't throw up; she just hovered over the toilet wishing she could throw up. Then she got up and splashed some ice-cold water on her face. When she emerged, she said, "Frank from the Earth store sent a bottle of wine and chocolate. I need to eat and drink this now. We have so much to celebrate," She said the last sentence sarcastically.

Tir followed her into the dining room and took the wine. "Not this."

"How do you not know this is just as dangerous?" she asked, holding up the chocolate.

"Very little happens on this ship without my knowledge, especially about you." He set the wine on a side table, poured them some water, and sat down. "This is a strange situation for us both but Kara, this is destiny. We are meant to be together. The gods have blessed us. You will see."

"I am so tired of you saying that. I am here against my will and now seriously married."

"You were 'seriously' married months ago too," he said mocking her.

"I guess being tagged like a dog with all my personal information on my wrist makes it real."

"You mean you can't lie to yourself about it?"

"Yes," she confessed.

He brought back the wine and poured her half a cup. "Relax. You are no one's pet." Tir looked at Kara and remembered Siu's advice not to put extra stress on her, so he decided not to bring up the binding tattoos now.

"With all you Alliance men running around after me, I feel like it. I am used to taking care of myself. You won't even allow me to walk to the shrine and back alone."

"It is for your protection."

"At least let me eat with John tomorrow. I hate Mux watching me eat, knowing he misses his lunch because of me."

"You can have the midday meal with John tomorrow," Tir said against his better judgment. But he rationalized that she was pregnant now. She knew the risks she would face in the Empire or on Earth. She wouldn't want to leave. He didn't realize that humans saw fetuses as non-beings until they could survive by themselves, and that escape was still very much on her mind.

The next day after visiting the shrine, Kara met John in the mess hall for the midday meal. Although the guards shadowed them, the mess was louder with so many voices, the guards could not fully concentrate on her conversation with John.

"I was invited to the OK Corral," she said out of the blue, "by the captain of the *Silverado*."

"Unfortunately, you can't go," John said after a couple of seconds, trying to figure out if she were talking about escape or if she had completely lost her mind. "Remind me again, what time does that start? At night?"

"Before lunch tomorrow. At the same time, I usually go to the shrine to thank the gods for the child."

"Ah," John said as if this was the most boring thing in the world. "I expect I will be very busy in sickbay then; we're going into battle, probably in the morning. Siu has said to expect the worst as the Jahay will see this as a last-ditch effort."

"Yes, the Jahay are known to even ram their ships into enemy ones," she agreed, and then they held each other's eyes. She knew he would not be able to join her. Guards did not follow him, but he would be killed on sight if caught trying to escape. As the admiral's wife, she would always have to be taken alive, or so she assumed.

"I'm sure you're learning a lot that will help humanity when you return."

"Yes," he agreed. "You should think twice about going to the shrine so much now that you are married and with child, Captain. It's dangerous. You don't know who's against you."

She dismissed his warning with a stern look, and then they said their goodbyes, which would hopefully be goodbye for quite some time.

———

That night Tir did not come back to his quarters until very late. "Is everything alright?"

"Yes, just last-minute changes for the battle tomorrow."

Tir got into bed, pulled her close to him, reached his hands down, and pulled off her stockings without saying anything.

She became immediately aroused by his hands on her legs and cuddled closer to him.

He then put his hand on her hip to keep her at an acceptable distance. "I just need to sleep now." And true to his words, Tir was asleep in minutes.

But Kara's mind was racing from his words, *What if the plans have changed so much that the* Silverado *can't rescue me?* She told herself that no matter what happened, she needed to get to the docking bay by noon, and she willed herself to sleep, and she had a small thought she tried to stamp out, but couldn't that said, *And revel in these last moments next to him in the silence, because you'll miss this.*

The next day the battle was more vicious than anyone had expected. The *Refa* was hit several times, and the ship rocked with the impacts. Everyone had to be at their stations, and Kara was left only with one guard. She still went to the shrine as she always did. She only wore her barrette and marriage bracelet, though, as she did not want to be burdened by all the other jewelry. She also wore three pairs of stockings under her dress. She was not leaving without those. When Kara walked out of the shrine, the *Refa* was hit again, and this time the lights went out momentarily; Kara did not wait. She saw this as her sign from the gods. She ran as fast as she could away from her guard even though the lights going out affected her more than any Alliance man as they could see perfectly well in the dark.

There was so much confusion that she had lost her guard in no time, then she began running towards the docking bay. It was so obvious that this was where she would go, she knew the guard would sound the alarm, and this would be the first place they looked, but it was also where she was supposed to be rescued. She was running through corridors, trying to remember the way, but just as she saw the main doors, she was hit over the head by someone from behind her and crumpled to the floor with feet all around her.

Kara awoke in complete darkness. Her head hurt. She touched her head and winced. She could feel dried blood there. She tried to feel where she was, but she just felt cold metal. *Great,* she thought, *I'm in a transport storage unit.* She wondered if she should scream for help or if it was better to remain quiet and see if she could somehow figure out a way out of the box in complete darkness without a weapon or tool. She decided to try the latter first. Her fingers traced every inch of the box, and she could not find anything that felt like a latch. She sat back and thought, *You were right Tir. The ship is not safe, and now I have been abducted by your enemies instead of my people.* Suddenly Kara felt very tired again and decided just to sleep. Soon she would either die or be let out of the container, she reasoned.

When she woke up next, she was in a bed, and when she sat up and looked around the room, she was surrounded by all the sights, sounds, and smells of everything human. It was all so overwhelming. She began to cry tears of joy.

Kara immediately got out of bed and felt dizzy, but it was only a minute until she steadied herself and walked out the door to her room. Wiping her eyes, she smiled that the door had just opened. It was unlocked; she was no longer a prisoner. She walked out into the ship's hallway looking for someone, but it must have been in the middle of the night as no one was there, and the hallways were only dimly lit. She decided to go back into her room then and ask the computer. One thing for certain she knew, she had been rescued by her own people, and she was no longer a prisoner. Relief continued to wash over her as she brought up the ship's general computer on the desk in her room and found out that she was indeed aboard the *Silverado,* and the mission was classified. She apparently was not even cleared to see it, so she had no idea if she was the only one who had been rescued or if they were heading back to Earth.

Satisfied that is all the information she was going to get now, she got back into bed and thought about everything that had happened in the last months and made her plans now that she was free. The next thing she would do was try to get her female crew home before they became pregnant.

She quietly apologized to the unborn baby inside of her, "I am so sorry," her voice was barely a whisper, "I hope that if there is an afterlife like your father believes in, you will find it in your heart to forgive me for what I must do. I must protect humanity at all costs, even you, little one."

The next morning Captain Jackson was at her door with his doctor. She sat up. She thought *The fates were cruel*. The *Silverado's* doctor was her former lover, Micah. They had been madly in love until she abruptly ended it because she didn't want to have children. It was ironic she was here pregnant with an alien man's child now. Kara ran her fingers through her hair and then looked down and realized she was still wearing Alliance clothing, and nothing was more repellant to human men than Alliance dresses.

"Captain Jackson, thank you for retrieving me," Kara said, then to the doctor, "Micah, you don't know how good it is to see a familiar face."

"We could not let those zombies take one of our best, Captain." 'Zombies' was a derogatory term humans used to refer to Alliance citizens because of their grey skin. "I'm just happy to see that you're mostly unharmed. We ran some tests on you when you came onboard. The doctor is willing to abort that hybrid now. Micah insisted we wait for your consent, but I tried to tell him you would want it out of you as soon as possible." Captain Jackson was happy that he was not female as he could not imagine anything worse than having an alien growing inside of him.

"We can do it right now," said Micah. He sympathetically put a hand on her shoulder. "I'm sorry for what they put you through, Kara. It must have been terrible." Micah imagined her being tied down and raped or restrained in a medical bed and artificially inseminated at best.

"I'm sorry we had to knock you unconscious. We had to make it look like pirates so that it did not look like a human operation," Captain Jackson explained. "It's so strange that they took you all prisoner, to begin with. Your crew told us some crazy story about wanting human women, but we couldn't believe it until now," he trailed off with a disgusted look. "Those damn zombies."

Kara nodded understanding. "The Alliance has a demographics problem. There is at least a 7% decrease in the female population, and they want to use human women to fill in the gaps."

"What the ..." Captain Jackson said, his blue eyes reflecting his anger. "So, they want to create half-Alliance half-humans because their fertility is failing? Over my dead body. Doctor, abort this abomination. There will be no hybrid zombie kids in the galaxy just because the Empire has a problem."

"They believe humans are the Lost People from their ancient mythology. They think humans and Alliance are the same species."

"Religious fanatics. I am sure they are suffering from too much inbreeding or something," Captain Jackson said disdainfully. "The war is over as of this morning. Yesterday was the final battle. Admiral Tir and his crew were too busy to notice your abduction until it was too late. It is good that no one in the galaxy has figured out yet that we have cloaking technology. Just one more human trick; it is so convenient for the rest of the galaxy to think we know nothing and have nothing."

"I wish we had cloaking technology on all of our ships," said Kara, "including mine. Where is the *Dakota*?"

"Waiting for you in orbit around Earth."

"Are we on our way there now?"

"Yes. Once you are on Earth, I doubt they will pursue you further, but now we need to be concerned about them abducting women. If it is not one thing, it is another."

Kara had no idea how long Tir would pursue her or what he would do now. "I had so much information that would have helped the Jahay in the war, what a waste."

"It was doomed from the beginning, Captain. Thankfully, the Jahay are not a threat on our doorstep anymore, and I guess we can thank the Empire for that at least. It is a pity we won't slip back into obscurity now if they pursue this Lost People nonsense. It will be good to say the baby died as soon as we reach Earth, maybe then they will think it is too difficult to hold on to human women and too difficult to combine the species."

"I will message the admiral that the baby died to stop the search for me. Maybe the Empire will pursue another avenue for their demographics issue, and we can work on getting my female crew off their capital planet."

"We will have to leave your female crew to the diplomats. There is no way we could get them off the Alliance Capital Planet. No doubt some deal can be struck when they come for the war reparations."

"Is it his? I mean, Admiral Tir's child?" Micah asked, horrified. "Kara, I promise you, if I ever get the chance, I will murder him for raping you," he promised fervently.

Kara wanted to tell them it was far from rape, but she couldn't. She knew if she admitted that, she would be subjecting herself to suspicion of being a spy, so she said nothing, and she felt guilty about that because she knew Tir was one of the last men in the galaxy who would ever rape a woman. *I am sorry, Tir, but I must do this or risk being accused of being a spy by my own people. They would never understand. Humans are just as racist as Alliance.* She thought, hoping in a futile way that her thoughts would somehow reach him.

Micah looked at Kara. "You are physically fine. I'll prep sickbay and come and get you when I'm ready. In the meantime, you should try and relax. I'll have some other clothing brought to you so that you can burn that," he said, looking at her Alliance dress with revulsion.

She thanked them both, and then the captain left her with an invitation to dinner for tomorrow evening. She, of course, accepted. She needed to find out everything that had happened in the months she had been away.

The doctor lingered. "Kara, is there anything else you need?"

Kara looked at Micah. They had been passionate lovers the year before. She could not deny that she still found him very attractive, he was tall and muscular with brown skin and light brown eyes.

Micah looked at Kara, and his heart was beating fast. He was still very much in love with her. He wanted to take her in his arms and tell her it would all be okay. She was looking at him now in a way familiar to him. So, he took a chance, sat next to her on the bed, and put his hand on her cheek lightly. "What a mess," he said softly, "but we have you now." And then he slowly kissed her. Chastely at first, but then soon his tongue was testing her lips, her mouth, and it felt so right for him to have his Kara back.

Am I really kissing Micah now? She mentally questioned her morals and her sanity. His mouth felt so warm compared to Tir's, and the stubble on his face rubbing against her skin a little roughly made her question what she used to find attractive, which she now found somewhat repulsive. *Have I forgotten what it is like to be with a human man?* She found his touch soothing but not right sexually. She gently pulled back but was still touching his chest. "Micah, it's so good to see you, I can't even express it properly, but I've been through a lot. I don't think I can do this now."

"Let me comfort you, Kara. Let me bring you back to humanity," he began kissing her again, and she consented for a time, until she felt guilty and she pulled back again.

Kara could see the desire in his light brown eyes, and for a couple of seconds, she thought that maybe she should do this, to separate herself from Tir with this completely physical action with a human man. That by sleeping with Micah, it would end her confusion. But then, she brought herself back to reality. "I can't do this. I'm pregnant with another man's baby. I feel terrible." *And I married him*, she thought, but she was not going to mention that barbaric act, but she could not help but look down at the bracelet when she thought of her marriage to Tir.

"Not another man, a zombie, an Alliance, and he raped you. You owe him nothing." Micah felt sorry for her and just held her close to him. He noticed that she smelled differently and concluded it must be the different soap she had to use or food that she had had to eat on the Alliance ship.

"I still feel..." she trailed off; she did not know what she felt, except that sleeping with him would be wrong, even though her body thought it was a good idea. She realized that she really did have feelings for Tir and that as much as she wanted to escape and be free, she would still miss him and his touch. She didn't want to be married, of course, but she wished that things could have been different, and they could just be together, but that would never be. She would return to her old life, and if anyone ever tried to take her again, she would die fighting.

"I understand. We can take care of the pregnancy. None of this is easy. This child represents too much to the Empire to let it live. Think of what would happen if those floodgates opened, we would not be able to protect ourselves."

"Micah, but I feel like I'm going to kill an innocent, and I know I'll regret this for the rest of my life, but I know I can't keep it either. I just wish all of this had never happened. I'm thinking of just ending my life to make it all easier…"

"Don't do that Kara. How could you regret killing a child conceived by rape from a monster…."

"He's not a monster."

"Don't tell me you have feelings for that zombie? Was it rape or not, Kara?" Captain Jackson had questioned him about what kind of woman Kara was before they decided to help her. He was concerned that she was a spy for the Empire and Micah had put his reputation on the line by vouching for Kara.

"I don't know," she admitted quietly, looking into his eyes, hoping she would find some understanding there.

"Stockholm Syndrome," he said, confidently diagnosing her and hoping she was not a spy. "Stop thinking about him. He's convinced you to think that you liked him, maybe loved him, by the way you're talking. Kara, listen to me; we've rescued you. It'll take some time, but you'll recover and see your captors for what they truly are, vicious criminals. They abducted you and raped you for their greedy purposes. Give yourself time to readjust. I'm going now and will return shortly. Relax, you've survived this. You're strong, and you're safe."

When Kara was alone, she opened the computer and accessed her messages, she had so many, but there was one that stood out that was sent only five hours ago. She could read the sender's name in Alliance, 'Admiral Tir Zu,' she opened it, not knowing what to expect.

Kara,

I know you were taken and are unable to return. I will come to Earth for you.

Tir

Kara looked at the message written in Alliance. She knew he had done that on purpose. Her tears began to fall silently and hit her hands as she hesitated to send a reply. If she replied, he would know where she was, but she decided he was not coming after her now anyway, so she wrote,

> Tir,
>
> The baby died. Don't come for me.
>
> Kara

Bought

Tir read Kara's message and wondered two things, first, if she had been forced to have an abortion, and second if she never wanted him to find her. He got up from his desk and went to pray in front of his small shrine in his quarters. He moved the fertility goddess back and moved the god of war forward. He lit a small candle and prayed for forgiveness. He unsheathed his short sword and cut the center of his left palm, letting the blood snuff out the candle flame.

Tir was angry. Furious with himself for not taking better care of Kara. He prayed loudly, "Please forgive my negligence and allow me my wife back. I'll not be so careless ever again. I will not lose her or our fate so easily."

Tir had gone over their last day together in his mind repeatedly. He realized now that he should have addressed her concerns about their child being the catalyst to destroy humanity more seriously. He had thought it was so absurd. He had just dismissed her worries. And because he had not taken her fears seriously, he had not bothered explaining that that was not what the Empire had in mind. Tir tried to console himself that his mind had been preoccupied, that they had been at war, and he had not had the time or patience for her small human concerns. But he could not forgive himself for the death of their child, and he only had himself to blame. It did not matter if she chose to have the abortion, if she was forced to do it, or if she lost the child from the stress of the escape itself; he put the fault on himself for not being able to adequately convince her of their destiny. That should have been his priority. His fleet could have done their part and won the war without him.

Tir had thought a lot about their relationship as well. Physically they were well-matched and clearly attracted to each other. But again, he blamed himself for not being as emotionally attentive as he should have been. He knew she was struggling with everything that had happened, but he thought there would be time to help her settle into her new position as his wife in the Empire after the war. For this misstep, he blamed himself for her running away. He knew humans' reputation well enough to know they would make it look like an abduction so that no one could be blamed, but Tir knew in his heart that she had chosen to leave. She had escaped.

He had interrogated her doctor, who pretended to know nothing about it, but as Siu confirmed later, Kara had told him she was leaving. Tir did not think it was worth threatening the man over it. Doctor John did not go himself and seemed genuinely interested in trading human medical knowledge for Alliance medicine, which made Tir even more incensed, that Kara chose to go when her crewman decided to stay.

Tir looked directly across at the small white statue of the god of war and said quietly, "I'll go to Earth and bring her back. I'll right this wrong. Do not give up on us. We will fulfill our destiny."

The gods heard Tir's prayers in their palace in the Alliance heavens. The goddess of home rose and took the god of war's hand while saying, "I must admit, you were right. This will be the making of Tir."

The god of war's idea was to separate Kara and Tir. He did not think that Tir valued Kara as much as he would need to accomplish what they needed both of them to do. "Trust a man to know a man's heart," the god of war replied. "Now, it's time you make sure that Kara doesn't die or kill the first baby that will reunite the Lost People with their Alliance brethren."

"She won't. I made the enchantment so strong, and there's no chance she will doubt her connection to Tir."

"You've been wrong before," the god of war pointed out.

"A millennia ago," the goddess of home replied as she disappeared into the smoke.

After Tir finished praying, he returned to his computer. He buttoned the collar on his uniform, and opened a video message, RVM, to his mother, a senior member of the High Council. His fleet was not far from the Empire's border, so they could talk in real-time.

"Tir," she said, pleased to see him on the screen. "You're not coming home, are you?"

"No, I've requested that I be the one to go to Earth and oversee the war reparations and at the same time retrieve my wife." This would normally be left to someone below him and a diplomat.

"Are you going to publicly kill her for leaving you? It is your right and the law." Tir's mother had been shocked when he had told her that he had married Kara. So much so that she had not replied to his message for days.

"No." He looked at his mother, scandalized. "I'm going to bring her back. She was abducted. She didn't leave me." This was a lie. They both knew she escaped but running away from your spouse carried heavy consequences in the Empire.

"Are you sure you want her back alive?"

"Mother, have some sympathy."

"Tir, I do. But I think you are so blinded by your infatuation for this human sorceress you can't see the real situation. The rumors of you two have even reached us here on the Capital Planet. All of your fights and your sex in every area of your ship and during a war. Everyone thinks this wild human has driven you mad, seduced you with witchcraft. No doubt that was your plan all along. I know you, my boy, you want to make human women look so sexually irresistible that every Alliance man would want to marry one, despite their low social standing. And if I'm going to give you anything, it was well-played until she ran away, I'm sorry, I mean, was abducted."

"Abducted. She was abducted. She didn't run away from me. Please remember that. Now, I need the High Council's permission to offer the human government UCs, weapons, and technology. I'll be there in three days."

Tir's mother sighed. "How much do you think they will ask for? Remember they did lose this war; you shouldn't have to offer them much."

"You know this is about our future relationship with Earth too? We want humans to like us so that more women will volunteer to join the Alliance. I don't want to make it a habit of targeting human ships to take the women and send them to our homeworlds. I'll offer the human government minimal compensation, but for them, of course, this will seem extravagant as they are so poor. I'll also need access to our House accounts to secure the release of Kara. They are undoubtedly doing it to make it expensive to get her back."

"Humans certainly are living up to their reputation in the galaxy as being untrustworthy and impulsive, aren't they? And you are sure you want her back? Maybe you should let her stay in prison to teach her a lesson. Or do what you should do as her husband and execute her."

Tir sighed; his mother could be intolerable sometimes. "Mother, do I have access to the accounts or not?"

"Of course, you do. I hate to see you having to buy your wife back, though. It's embarrassing for us all. After you get her back, I think you should kill her as is your right. We need to communicate that our culture and laws are not to be trifled with."

"I don't think that is the right message to send. We want human women to come to us. That was decided in the High Council, as you know. If we start executing wives, no one will come."

"Maybe that's how it should be then. Maybe it's better men share wives as I suggested."

"No," said Tir firmly. "It's my fault Kara let herself be taken. I wasn't the best husband to her when she was onboard."

"You were at war. You had other things on your mind Tir. She should have honored her marital pledge to you."

"That's true, but I also mistakenly assumed she would be happy to marry me, which was not the case. She did not feel honored to be an Alliance citizen or my wife. And she's not religious either, so she had nothing to guide her, and I didn't take the time to explain things to her properly. I thought our physical connection would be enough for her to accept her destiny, but it wasn't. This is my fault. I'll bring her back and comfort her, I'll not kill her. Furthermore, I'll not bring her home directly. I plan to keep her with me on the *Refa* and make amends for my past behavior."

"Why would she not be happy to be married to you? There's nothing wrong with you. She is a lowly human, and you are the best of the Alliance. Why didn't she feel honored that you chose her?"

"I don't think she ever saw herself getting married or doing anything but dying in that war on her little ship. It was quite a surprise to be thrown into marriage, no matter how attractive she might have found me. And humans have been isolated for so long, they still see themselves as quite important in the galaxy, despite every fact and every other species telling them the opposite." He could not help but smile then. "In some ways, it's good they have some pride, no matter how misplaced. It'll make it easier for them to act like Alliance citizens once they accept that they are the Lost People."

"It's good that they are so attractive, or else they would already be punished for this pride. And did you tell her that you were the successor to the imperial throne? Maybe that is why she ran away. She feared being killed for it."

"I told her I was the successor, and she was unimpressed and uninterested. I think she was more upset that she might have to do something rather than command a starship. I know it does not make any sense, but humans seem to be focused on the wrong things, as we have often noticed."

"Gods Tir, I still can't believe you married a human. Anyway, we digress. It helps that her own people have imprisoned her. It doesn't make your behavior look so bad, but you shouldn't keep her on your ship; you should send her home to us to learn what is expected of an

Alliance woman. Your sister Hez is so curious to meet her. If you intend to keep her, she should be here with us so that we may take the necessary steps to train her."

Tir closed his eyes to calm himself, but he didn't like Kara being referred to as a person who needed to be tamed. In the weeks he had shared with her, he had realized that there was some joy in human behavior and that he didn't want all her human spirit to be thrashed out of her just to become a second-class boring Alliance woman. "No, that will not be necessary. I'll keep her here with me." *And I am worried about how my sisters would treat her, an alien, a human.*

"If she becomes pregnant, she'll have to come home to us. Your doctors cannot help a woman on a starship. It goes against the gods, Tir. Whatever you are thinking about, abandon that plan."

Tir did not want to go into that with his mother. He knew she would be very upset by the whole thing and would not help him now with the High Council. "Of course," he said. "Now, about the High Council's approval?"

"I'll push this through and arrange a new rendezvous with the new Ambassador to Earth. We can't have old Tui there anymore now that we need to do something other than monitoring the comings and goings of humans. We will all be praying for you. May the gods grant you success."

"Even if I'm unworthy," he answered his mother in response to the set phrase, and they both signed out.

―――

A small ding at Kara's door in her quarters onboard the *Silverado* announced an ensign's arrival. "Here are some clothes for you, Captain. Do you want me to take that Alliance dress and throw it out an airlock?"

Kara forced a smile at the young ensign. "Thank you, no. I'll take pleasure in doing the honors myself." Kara took the human fleet uniform from the ensign and dismissed him.

She began taking off the Alliance dress and realized it was impossible to do without thinking of Tir and how he touched her so tenderly all over her body. She tried to dispel those memories from her mind but couldn't. In the end, she just let them play out as she undressed, and tears were streaming down her cheeks silently. She smiled sadly as she took off two of the three pairs of Alliance stockings she had on and folded them with the dress. She left one pair on. Kara could not help but remember the touch of his cool grey hands on the stockings less than a day before. She tried to think about something else as she put on some underwear and a bra that was supposed to be her size but was too small now, then zipped up her human fleet uniform. Once she was dressed, she looked down at the folded black Alliance dress and decided she would keep it. She did not want to admit to herself why, so she just put it in the small closet and closed the door.

Kara looked at herself in the mirror and thought, *This is the first step, next step, stop crying.* She wiped her eyes. Then she noticed the barrette in her hair and gingerly touched it. She looked at her reflection; her eyes were red. "Take it out, Rainer," she commanded herself quietly, and then, with shaky hands she removed the barrette and put it in her pocket. Kara considered putting it with the dress, but she wanted to keep it close. Tir had given that to her, and for all the awful things he had done, there was a small part of her that did like him and an even bigger part of her that could forgive him now that she was out of the situation and back with her own people. Finally, she tried to remove the marriage bracelet, but it would not budge even after several attempts of serious trying. She decided that it didn't matter for the moment because there would be very few humans who knew what it was, and as long as she wore long sleeves, no one could see it anyway.

Another ding at her door, and Micah was there. "Are you ready, Kara?" He could see that she had been crying, and he felt sympathy for her.

"Yes, let's go," she tried to speak without emotion. She had mixed feelings about this abortion. She had never thought about abortion before. It had never occurred to her that she would have to consider it for herself, but here she was now, and it was the moment of truth. *Unprepared*, but then she thought, *Is anyone ever prepared to think about abortion until they need to decide for themselves?* She tried to console herself that this was the right thing to do. It was a hybrid child, so easily conceived that it would only increase the chances of humanity being all-consumed by the much larger Alliance Empire. But without any way to stop it, she heard Tir's voice in her head saying, 'It goes against the gods, Kara.'

She did not doubt that this absolutely would go against the gods if there were any real gods. But she was not religious, and she quieted that voice in her head down by thinking, *This has nothing to do with my or Tir's religious beliefs, but everything to do with taking life and whether or not I believe that this is a life and if it is indeed a life, what this life would represent to both of our civilizations. The birth of a returned people, if humans are the Lost People as the Empire believes, or the beginning of a wave of hybrid people that could wipe out the uniqueness of humanity, wiping out both Alliance and humanity. Come on, what do I think? Is this the start of a beautiful and harmonious relationship? Or would Tir's and mine hybrid child represent the beginning of the end for humanity? Undoubtedly, whatever is responsible for low female births in the Empire will also begin to affect human women. What do I think? Yes or no to killing this fetus?*

Micah spoke to her as they walked into sick bay, but she was not listening. All she kept thinking was, *Am I a murderer of an innocent, or are these just cells? Am I saving humanity or just proving I am a savage as all the other species in the galaxy claim humans to be?* As they walked into a deserted sickbay and Micah led her to the back, she was overcome with angst and confusion. She followed Micah's instructions, though, and laid down on the medical bed after removing her clothes, but after a few minutes said, "No, stop. I can't do this, Micah."

"Kara?" Micah asked as he put down his scanner.

"I know it sounds like I've lost my mind, but I can't do this now. It's still early enough that I can do this back on Earth, right? I'm too confused to make this decision now."

Micah sighed. "Kara, I can't force you to do this, but as your friend and your doctor, I highly recommend it and a good therapist to speak to when you return to Earth. You've been through a lot." Micah was also disappointed not to be the first one to look at a human-Alliance hybrid and be able to write a paper on it.

Tears were in her eyes, and she said softly, "Don't be ridiculous, Micah. We were never friends," He gave her a sympathetic smile. "I need time. I'll do it. I just can't right now, but I need you to record it as an abortion so I don't look suspicious. I know I won't keep it."

He gave her a disapproving look. "I understand your concern, but I can't do that," this hybrid would not just be a normal abortion; it would be saved and studied. Every doctor would want to see it, so there is no way he could get away with a lie. "I don't think you have anything to worry about. No one will think you're a spy. It doesn't make any sense. The Empire has already proven that they can take what they want from us without asking. They don't need to seduce any humans to be spies. But I know that some people, like Captain Jackson, think too highly of Earth and like to believe we are worth spying on. And there are those onboard who find it odd that you were so effortlessly rescued and that your doctor remained onboard the *Refa* as a prisoner. I'm not going to lie, it looks awfully suspicious and then if you don't go through with this abortion…"

"Please, Micah, listen." Tears were falling freely down her cheeks. "I've killed so many in this war, I just can't right now, but Captain Jackson will think I'm a spy if I don't, but I'm not." She took his hands in hers and looked him in the eyes. "You know I'm not a spy. I've done everything I've ever been asked to do in the human fleet and as a citizen."

"I know you aren't a spy, but that's because I know you. This hybrid is an abomination, Kara. You're so confused." He put a hand on her shoulder and said, "Trust me as a friend and as your doctor and do this now. Get this zombie hybrid abomination from your body."

"Please, Micah, give me more time but mark it as done, just between you and me for old time's sake. Will you do that for me?"

"The best I can do is to note that you came here for this procedure but nothing more. I'd also ask that when you're ready, and I'm sure once you come to your senses you'll be ready, you do the abortion with me. As for everyone else, Captain Jackson won't ask but assume it's done if I say nothing. If anyone asks, this falls under doctor-patient confidentiality, so I'll not say one way or another, but that only goes so far. If I'm asked in a court of law or ordered by the captain, I'll tell the truth. And if you wait too long, the truth will show itself soon anyway."

"I understand, Micah, thank you. I owe you."

"You owe me nothing, Kara. I always knew you had a conscience in there somewhere. I'm surprised it's showing itself now for this hybrid child." Micah could not forget their last argument when they were still lovers. He had wanted to become more serious and have a child together, and Kara had said to him coldly, 'I never want to be a mother to a child we would produce.' And now he looked at her and wondered, *Are you a spy, Kara? Do you want to live as a wife to this zombie? Do you think you love him?* And jealousy and despair rose inside him as he watched her walk out of sickbay. He hadn't thought it possible to hate Alliance people any more than he had yesterday, but today he found out he was wrong. He hated what they had done to his Kara.

―――――

Kara spent the rest of the day in bed. The *Silverado's* psychologist came to see her, but Kara sent her away. She said she would like to be alone today. The psychologist said that she would return tomorrow.

Kara lay in her bed and looked at the metal ceiling. She was happy to be back with her own people, but she questioned herself why she was not thinking of the future, why she couldn't get the abortion. She put her hand on her abdomen imagining a little Tir and Kara mix there. *I have taken so many lives in the galaxy. I don't know if I can take yours. But if I keep you I must disappear because you represent bad things, through no fault of your own.*

She fell asleep thinking about everything that had happened over the last few months, and of course, there was just one person she kept thinking about, Tir. She wondered if he was in pursuit of the *Silverado* now or if he would have given up and decided that maybe he was wrong, and they were not destined for each other after all. She had no idea how Alliance marriages worked. She wondered if they could be just as easily dissolved as they were created.

Kara awoke in the early morning and felt sick. She got up, went to the toilet, and was happy; nothing in human bathrooms talked. She threw up. Between the acid taste of vomit, she saw and tasted a bit of the chocolate and thought about Tir again. Then she whispered to the vomit-filled toilet, "Stockholm syndrome," and flushed it.

Once the nausea had passed, she went to the *Silverado's* mess hall and got herself a coffee and a piece of bread. She did not like all the curious looks the *Silverado's* crew were giving her, though, and ended up taking her coffee and bread back to her temporary quarters. There, she sat in front of the computer and began reading about everything of interest that had happened since she had been taken prisoner aboard the *Refa*. Nothing she read surprised her.

The human fleet had tried to stay back and out of the war between the Jahay and the Empire as much as possible to keep human causalities low. Kara read it and thought, *We are not even ashamed about this.*

No humans were elected to the Galaxy Court this year, not that a human had ever been elected to the Galaxy Court. Every year, a new Galaxy Court of 10,111 members was elected from all the galaxy's civilizations. The only requirement was that a civilization must have a universal technology rating of at least three. Humans had a technology rating of barely four, and because of that, other species did not think humans could be trusted to sit on a committee that tried to keep some unbiased record and order in the galaxy. Humans were always complaining that the galaxy was prejudiced against them, but Kara had a different reflection after being aboard the *Refa*. She had to admit, the Alliance was much more advanced and maybe it was right, the galaxy's distrust of humans. It was not just human technology that was unevolved but, if she were being brutally honest, some of human culture as well, there was very little societal structure which meant there wasn't much cohesion, unlike many of other cultures in the galaxy. And without unity they were unstable politically. Kara, of course, preferred human culture to Alliance. Still, she had to admit, she could see where other civilizations might find faults with how humans governed themselves and interacted with other species.

A new restaurant on Earth had opened, encouraging diners to masturbate during the dessert course with a vibrator specifically designed to accompany the dish. She thought, *And we wonder why no one takes us seriously?*

Then she was surprised to see breaking news across the bottom of the news screen that Earth's government had already set a date to begin negotiating war reparations with the Empire. *That was fast,* she thought, *But of course they are. The Empire wants to keep all those human women from the* Dakota *without drawing too much attention to themselves. And probably retrieve me,* she also thought solemnly. She closed the computer. She didn't want to think about it.

It wasn't long before the entire day passed. The psychologist, as promised, had come back to see her, and they talked for hours about her capture, captivity, and abortion. Kara did not say whether she had had an abortion or not. She just let the psychologist believe that she had. She also didn't mention getting married because the psychologist didn't think to ask, as she was mainly focused on Kara's readjustment into human society after being kept as a sex slave. That is the term the psychologist had used to describe Kara's situation, 'sex slave,' and Kara to her shame did not correct her. The psychologist had assured her that the rapes were not her fault, even if she had not fought back. Kara did, at this point, try to say that it had not been rape any of the times, but the psychologist had already made up her mind about what had happened. Kara felt incredibly guilty now that Tir was a documented rapist. The psychologist asked her to sign off on their discussion, and the information received. Kara hesitated signing her name.

"Do you mind if you change that? He didn't rape me," Kara said.

"I understand that you are confused. This is called Stockholm Syndrome. I have written that here too. It's because of this. You are trying to protect your captors. Please sign Captain Rainer," the psychologist was forceful now, and Kara knew that she was not going to back down. But neither could she.

"I can't sign this. It was not rape. If I sign this then it becomes a lie."

"Captain, I understand that you believe it wasn't rape right now, but I guarantee you, once you're back home and can process all of this, you will see it clearly. *You* were raped on the *Refa*. I'm signing you up for regular sessions with someone on Earth to help you work through this.

Just relax. None of this is your fault. Given some time; this will all become clearer to you."

Then the counselor left, and Kara felt even more confused. *Did Tir rape her?* she questioned herself. *No, it was not rape. Forced marriage absolutely, but she wanted him every time, as wrong as that was.*

That evening Kara had dinner with Captain Jackson in his quarters. She was happy to have human food again. It was so delicious. She ate a lot and kept telling Captain Jackson how good it all was. Unfortunately, the price of the pleasant food was that she had to listen to a lot of nonsense propaganda about how if humanity were just given a chance, the rest of the galaxy would provide us with the respect Captain Jackson thought we deserved. Kara did not believe any of that. She saw the facts as they were, and humans were undeniably almost last in everything because they were the last to this galactic technology party. She wished that people would accept that and start from there, but then she reasoned sweet-smelling lies were always better than the truth. She listened to the captain politely, thanked him again for rescuing her, and hoped she would never have to have dinner with him again.

On her way back to her temporary quarters, she ran into Micah, who she suspected had been waiting to pass her in the hallway. "Kara, I want to talk to you."

"Is this about my health?" She did not want to be alone with him right now. She had had some wine and was emotionally vulnerable. He would only add to her confusion.

"Not officially. I'm just worried about you as a friend."

"I'm fine, just ask the psychologist."

"Yes, I read her notes. I don't think you should be alone right now." He began walking with her towards her quarters.

When they arrived at her door, they both stopped. She purposely did not open the door.

He touched her cheek as if they were still lovers. "Kara, let me comfort you."

"Micah, we are no longer together. Please…"

"But Kara, part of your confusion is that you have been with aliens. Let me remind you...." His hand was on her arm, gently stroking her with his thumb.

Kara felt weak. She wanted to be held, but then she looked at him and thought, *But not by you.* "No, Micah. I want to be alone. Goodnight."

Micah accepted her answer and then wished her a goodnight while thinking, *There is something not right about all of this. We had always comforted one another even when we were not exclusively lovers.*

Kara entered her small quarters and sighed. She looked in the mirror and said loudly, "I don't know you anymore. Turning down Micah?" Sex with Micah had always been something that she sought for relaxation. He was perfect in that way. Even before they had a serious relationship, they had always had a sporadic sexual relationship. Now she was turning him down when she could probably benefit from jumping back in with a human.

She took off her uniform and all her other clothing, everything but her Alliance stockings. She turned off the lights, got into the bed, closed her eyes, and began thinking about Tir and wishing she could both have him and her human life. She ran her fingers over her sensitive breasts and down to her inner thighs. She remembered how he always used to kiss her there. She started to feel her arousal increase at the thought of what was next. She brought her fingers up to stroke her vulva and pull a little on the hair there, just like he liked to. She could hear his voice in her head saying, 'And I like this distinctly human hair,' as he would pull on it. Then she slowly rubbed her labia lightly, long and wide strokes with her entire hand, while she thought about him. The way his hands would touch her. It was not long before she changed to using her fingers and rubbing her clitoris, lightly at first but then faster, with much more pleasure to quickly bring herself some release. She remembered how he had promised her to know her body as well as his and to get her to climax within minutes, just as she could do for herself after a year of marriage. She smiled to herself and thought, *You had almost managed to be able to do that after only a couple of months.* She drifted off to sleep with her hand still on the top of her thigh as Tir used to do.

The next morning, they reached Earth, and Kara was relieved when she walked into the familiar Earth Space Port One. It was loud, noisy, and utterly human. From there, she and Captain Jackson took a transport down to headquarters. Once at HQ, they were ushered through some rooms. After waiting for about an hour, she and Captain Jackson were finally confidentially talking about her experience during the war on the *Refa* with her superiors. She did not mention the marriage, and they didn't ask. Kara was told that she would need to speak to the Earth Ambassador to the Empire about negotiating for her female crew and provide him with as much information as possible about the Alliance. Their human ambassador was on her way back from the Empire and would arrive tomorrow. Kara was dismissed then, and she thought that the worst was over.

Kara went home. She stood outside her apartment building, and the smart technology recognized her and opened the door; the same happened with the door to her apartment. It all seemed so ordinary, as if the last year, the war and Tir had never happened. After she walked in, she sat down on the sofa that she had made and cried for so many things, for being home again, for the loss of a baby that she knew she couldn't keep but couldn't find it in herself to get rid of either and for never being able to be with Tir again. She began to wonder if this was what love felt like, this complete aching for someone, or if this was destiny. She wiped her tears and thought, *Destiny, it's so ridiculous.*

When she had no more tears Kara went into her small yellow kitchen, and opened the door to her balcony; even though it was autumn and a bit chilly, it did not feel cold anymore after all her days on the *Refa*. She watched the people go by below and tried to balance her emotions by the familiar rings of the trams going by and the sound of the people's footsteps. After several minutes she closed the door and poured herself a glass of wine. She drank it while she looked at her empty, colorful apartment and wondered if this would be her future forever, alone here.

She didn't finish the small glass of wine because it didn't taste right to her. So with nothing else to do, she went into her bedroom, put on her pajamas, and called her parents on a video call. They were very happy to see her. She did not tell them she had been abducted, married, or any of that. She just said she had been away with the war. Her family operated strictly on a the-less-information-the-less-awkward for us basis. They liked each other but were not close. Her parents were artists, and she was in the military; there was very little middle ground. Her mother called her a murderess once, and that was when she decided to keep them at arm's length. It was just better for everyone.

Kara then checked her messages, but she didn't have any messages from the one person in the galaxy she wanted a message from, so she closed the blue velvet curtains on her ancient four-poster bed and went to sleep. As she drifted off, her mind wandered to the time she told Tir about her apartment and this bed, and she could not deny that she missed him. She suddenly got up to retrieve the barrette from her uniform pocket and held the cool piece of jewelry in her hand as she fell asleep.

Kara was dreaming about Tir. He was putting the barrette in her hair, and she kissed him. His cool grey lips promised more kisses to follow. She told him that she loved him for the first time, which made him so happy. He picked her up and kissed her even more passionately, refusing to put her down for several minutes. When he finally set her down, he took off all her clothes except for the barrette. He was kissing and licking her whole body as she stood naked in front of him. Suddenly Doctor Siu was there too, watching, as he had done at their wedding ceremony, and Kara was even more aroused at the thought that they would both touch her. Tir whispered, "Do you want Siu to lick you too? He's so curious about humans."

"I want him to," she replied and opened her legs wider.

Then Siu was there, his grey eyes meeting hers as he began to lick her vulva slowly. Then Tir joined him. Their faces next to each other, looking at her from between her legs, giving her so much pleasure, commenting on her exotic human taste.

After they almost made her come, they began touching, kissing, and licking her. She had never had four hands and two mouths on her at once before, and she found the situation intoxicating.

Sui was groping her breasts with his skilled hands, and Tir was kissing around her inner thighs, occasionally making her jump with the sensations.

Kara was suddenly awakened by a noise outside. She opened her eyes and couldn't remember where she was. But it only took a couple of seconds for her to be comforted by the familiar sounds of the city around her. It was early morning. The tram bell rang. She smiled, I *am home*. She pushed back the velvet curtains, got out of bed, made herself a coffee, and then checked her messages again. She almost dropped her coffee when she saw one from Earth's Ambassador to the Alliance.

> Captain Kara,
>
> Please read the following article and meet me in my office as soon as you can this morning.
>
> Ambassador to the Alliance Empire
>
> Lora Lane

Kara opened the attached article, which brought her directly to the GC's information page and an article about her recent marriage. Their military identification pictures had been used. She read the short article and swore out loud. The article made their marriage look romantic and like some kind of Cinderella story. She knew, of course, that he had told her that he was an important person in his society, that he was the successor to the Emperor, or that he had been. But it had all just seemed so alien and outside her comprehension. But now, looking at it in black and white, she understood why Tir had told her that if she escaped, her own people would think she was a spy, as outrageous as that was. But she had to admit, the galaxy must be looking at this article and saying to one another, 'This cannot be real, a human?' She hoped that people would question the Empire's motives, but as she read through some of the comments on the galactic gossip pages already discussing it, she realized that people weren't that clever. She was being accused of a lot of things; espionage, deceit, and witchcraft, which she particularly liked. "Better to be a witch than a spy," she said quietly out loud to herself.

Kara took a long hot shower and then put on her uniform and went to speak to Earth's Ambassador. However, her morning took a very unexpected turn as she was arrested as soon as she walked into the government building. When they put handcuffs on her, she did not try to claim ignorance or innocence to guards who knew nothing but that she should be arrested. It was not a long walk to HQ's jail, and she was put into a cell. She didn't need to ask why she had been arrested. She knew why. They thought she was a spy. There was no window, so she had no idea how much time had passed before she had a visitor.

An older woman with silver hair, deep wrinkles, and bright pink lipstick came in. She was wearing an old suit of the same hot pink as her lipstick. She looked at Kara and said, "I am your legal counsel. You're being tried as a spy, which is no surprise to you unless you are really stupid. If you don't want to go to court, you can tell the man who has been impatiently waiting to see you all day in the hallway, I was late," she explained with a smile, "every little detail and this won't go to court. This can all disappear. I told him, though. I don't think you are the type to give up any information like that to save yourself. That you consider yourself honorable and that he had been sent on a fool's errand. He didn't like that, as you can imagine. So, what is it going to be, Captain? Me or the unnamed man in the hallway?" She hoped Captain Rainer would choose to go with her rather than make a backhanded deal with the military. She had heard the rumors that the captain was still pregnant with the hybrid child, and no doubt the military would squeeze all the information out of her about the Empire and take the child for scientific research. And she had morals too, she didn't want that on her conscious if she could do something to stop it.

Kara stood up and moved to stand in front of the older woman with just a transparent forcefield between them, "Counselor, I am not a spy."

"Sure, you're not. But, you did send all of your female crew to the Alliance Capital Planet, while you stayed aboard Admiral Tir's ship for months, and then just you were able to 'escape' at the end of the war. Now, this morning, we read that you are married to this zombie meant to be the next Emperor of the Alliance Empire. Tell me, Captain, if you are not a spy, then what are you?"

"Why would I be married so openly if I were a spy?"

"Well, that is the thing, isn't it? You *weren't* open about it. You mentioned it to no one until now. Don't you think that is a bit suspicious?"

"I was embarrassed about being married which is why I did not mention it. I just wanted to put my whole Alliance experience behind me. I thought if I had left and didn't mention it, the marriage would have just disappeared. I am not a spy. I was forced to marry an Alliance man. I was forced to send my crew away. The alternative was death not only for me but my entire crew. I might have chosen that for myself but I couldn't do that to them."

"Sure. Sure. Now, do you want to go to court, or do you want to tell all your Alliance secrets to the man from your fleet waiting behind me? If you talk to him, a deal will be struck with your *husband*," she spat the word, "who is on his way here."

"I am not a spy."

The older woman sighed. "Look, between you and me, I think it's better if you tell them all you know, and maybe then they will grant you pardon since you are so naïve and were forced into this. Maybe if this is your lucky day, you can have your old life back."

"This is absurd. Why would the Empire need to spy on us? We have nothing they want." But as soon as she said it, she knew she was wrong.

"If they wanted nothing, then why did you tell Captain Jackson they wanted human women? Now, are you going to go with me and do this the hard way or go with the guy behind me?"

"I want to go to court. I might have been naïve being coerced into marriage and sending my female crew away, but I would never betray Earth. I have dedicated my whole life to protecting humanity. I am not going to settle for some plea bargain that says I am a traitor."

"Fine," said the older woman. "It doesn't matter to me. I have no shame in having my name connected to yours. I will get my name in galactic papers, something unheard of for a human lawyer. So, I'll register the documents, and we will begin to go through the motions.

We will both go down together. So, I imagine this will go very quickly as our government will want this done before the Empire arrives."

"When do they arrive?"

"Your husband is traveling at top speed and should be here in three days. I suspect the next three days will seem very long for you. I've already put in an order for you to be monitored so that you will be treated well, but you know how things are here; someone knows someone who's paid someone off. So, I hope I will see you alive tomorrow."

Kara watched the woman go, and as she opened the door, she heard her say, "I told you, you were wasting your time. She's all mine. She's not taking any offers. Captain Kara Rainer claims she isn't a spy."

Kara sat down on the small cot and thought, *What would be the benefit of trying me as a spy?* And it was not long before she realized it was obviously for more leverage against the Empire. She wondered if her people would really abuse her while she was in this cell. *If the Empire was as strong and ruthless as they were rumored to be, wouldn't that defeat the purpose of keeping me here? They would have less leverage if I were beaten up.* However, it did occur to her that if they threatened her with physical violence, she probably would tell them more about the Empire, and then they would have even more leverage, and her heart sank. *I might still be having that abortion from being tortured,* she thought with a heavy heart. It also occurred to her that if Tir wanted her back, he might negotiate harder if she had been injured. She could not help but be reminded of how he looked after her physically, almost as if she were a precious jewel.

———

Tir's first officer slid a memo across to him on the open computer screen between them in the conference room. Kara had been arrested as a spy. Tir looked at it unemotionally. "This was expected. They are barbarians."

"They think this will give them more bargaining power."

"And this is why no one likes dealing with humans." Tir had the

Empire's new Ambassador to Earth brought in. "The humans have arrested my wife for espionage. I'd like you to remind them that she is my wife and an Alliance citizen and that by the Galaxy Court ruling of 4587, no citizen of dual-citizenship can be tried for a crime without the approval of the other government."

"This is true, Admiral, but we still have an ambassador there, and I think he may have," the new ambassador trailed off.

Tir was angry now. He didn't know if the old ambassador had already been bought by one of his enemies. Earth had never been a desirable outpost and all he knew was that Ambassador Tui was against human women being made Alliance citizens. "Tell the old ambassador that if the humans harm my wife, he will be held personally responsible." Then Tir dismissed them all.

He sat in his empty conference room and looked again at the article that the GC had run about their marriage. He wondered who on his ship had sold them that story. But the damage was done. Before the article had run, he had hoped to go to Earth and convince Kara to return with him by offering her whatever she wanted, a ship, him, anything. Now, he knew he would have to bargain for her. He didn't want to do that, but he knew her people were holding her for this reason alone. Tir would have to buy her and the other women like slaves, and again he thought, *Why are the Lost People such ruffians? Why do they not know their place in the galaxy?*

Kara heard someone enter the hallway that led down to her cell. As far as she knew, she and the one guard were the only ones here. She stood as close to the forcefield as possible to see who was walking toward her. She was very surprised to see an old Alliance man. He had grey hair to match his grey skin and a very unhappy expression. She stood waiting, and when he reached her cell, he stopped and just looked at her for a good minute before speaking.

"As an Alliance citizen, I am here to make sure that you are treated within reasonable comfort while incarcerated on Earth. You look okay. Are you okay?"

"Who are you?"

"I'm Alliance Ambassador Tui."

"Where is Admiral Tir?"

"He's not here."

"Seriously. You know what I meant," Kara said sharply. "Where is he?"

The old man laughed. "Young love. I remember that. Enjoy it, young lady," he sighed and said, "Your husband is on his way, no doubt, to secure your release at any cost."

"How will he do that? I'm going to court. I'm being tried as a spy."

"Captain, no one really thinks you are a spy. It's what you humans call 'smoke and mirrors.' You must realize that. Your government only wants better leverage when they negotiate with us about you, the other human women on the Capital Planet, and human women going to the Empire in the future."

"My government isn't going to auction me or anyone else off like livestock," she said defiantly. "Humans don't work like that."

"Yes, they are. Your government sees this as an opportunity to get military weapons, Alliance technology, and UCs. There is no doubt about it. You, being tried and convicted as a spy, only makes you more expensive. And the human government knows that Admiral Tir will pay a lot to have you returned to him."

"I don't believe you. I'm an asset to my people. I've served them. I've just fought in a war for them."

The ambassador raised his eyebrows at her. "Why would I, of all people, lie to you? I'm here to help you. I know your lawyer. Tell her nothing. Remain silent for the next three days. Your husband is coming, and the less you say, the easier this all will be." He was quiet, then slowly got out of his computer and grabbed a nearby chair. "You seem so innocent in the way of politics for someone who has jumped in the deep end. I've read your reports, and you said very little about your time in captivity which is good. I also have your crew's reports that say the same as yours. Now," he said sternly as if talking to a child, "you need to remain quiet. Do you understand?"

"Why should I believe you?"

"Has the Empire ever done you wrong? Has any Alliance citizen ever broken their word to you?"

"How about a forced marriage and sending half my crew off to marry aliens?"

"Has any of your crew been forced into a marriage?"

"As far as I am aware, no."

"Was your marriage really 'forced'? I've got a record from Doctor Siu as the witness who described you both as very willing on your wedding night. Are you going to dispute that? We have witnesses for these purposes, so no one is ever forced."

Kara said nothing.

"I also have receipts showing that the slave artist Sera often visited you and you alone. Overall, I'd say that you fell into Alliance life well aboard the *Refa*. Alliance clothing was bought for you, jewelry given to you, and human food brought especially onboard. Captain Kara, it does not look like there was too much 'force' involved in your marriage or your time as Admiral Tir's prisoner."

"You don't understand. Sera was like a friend," Kara said, feeling foolish. "And I was forced to wear those clothes as the ship was so cold, and they were warm."

The old ambassador wasn't having it. "No, Captain Kara, slave artists are never your friends. I suspect she is the most probable person who sent those details to the GC to announce your marriage. The unhappier you were, the more money she made and when you left she wanted to squeeze the last UCs out of her relationship with you by selling that information. She probably thought it was a pity it took so long for them to publish it, a whole three days. As for the clothing, I would say that Admiral Tir was thinking a lot about your comfort, and again, it does not come across as a forced marriage at all. He seemed just as willing as you were. Some might even say it was fate, and I'm an old romantic so I will be cliché and say, 'star crossed lovers.'"

Kara hit her hand against the forcefield in frustration. "You are twisting the facts."

"I am telling you how the rest of the galaxy sees this. Now, I am going to tell you how this is going to play out. Tomorrow your quick trial is going to begin. No matter what you say, you will be found guilty and convicted as a spy. Then the human government has the right to keep you here incarcerated until we can seek an injunction from the GC, which could take months. But don't worry, your government doesn't want you to be incarcerated; they want to sell you. The human government recognizes that you are leaving with us, one way or another, and they want to make as much money as possible from the deal. Desperate people do desperate things and the whole galaxy knows humans are desperate."

"I don't want to return with Admiral Tir. I want to live my life here, in the Terran Solar System, where I am supposed to be. I am human."

"The moment you married, living here would never be an option. Even if Admiral Tir dies, you are still a member of his family and are expected to live on the Alliance Capital Planet in his House."

"What?"

"Didn't he tell you about the *Obligations and Rights of Marriage*?" The ambassador answered his own question, "Of course, he didn't. I would leave you with a copy now, but I am not allowed to give you anything, unfortunately. I will ensure you have a copy in English, as well as a copy of our laws, the Contracts, and everything else you might need to know about the Empire, so you do not have to count on your husband or his family for information. You know Admiral Tir is a very respectable leader and a good man, but details do elude him occasionally." The ambassador could see this information had made her very upset, so he tried to cheer her up. "Everyone in the Empire is talking about your great romance, did you know that?"

Kara didn't speak. She didn't care. She was so angry at everything this man was telling her.

"It is said that Admiral Tir knew you were his other half from the moment he saw you, which is why he strongly insisted you marry so quickly. Now he feels completely responsible for your abduction and incarceration. Not only is he coming here to get you personally, which is something people in his position would never do, but he has also signed himself up on the Grand City Temple Wall. The whole Empire is in rapture over his affection for you."

"What does that mean, 'signed himself up on the wall'?" She was sure this was going to be another brutal ritual.

"He will take whatever public punishment the gods assign him in this life for how he has mistreated you. He blames himself and his behavior for your lack of faith in your destiny together. It is a way to try and appease the gods before they give up on you both."

"Who decides this punishment?"

"The High Priestess will pray to the goddess of home for guidance, and then she will tell Tir what the punishment will be."

"And this is public?"

"Yes."

"When will he do this?"

"As soon as he returns to the Empire with you. He will stand with you before the Grand City Temple and receive his punishment." The ambassador took in her slightly horrified expression. "It is his way of asking forgiveness from you and the gods. You know I believe this is more than just propaganda. I think he really does blame himself for your ending up in this situation."

"He is right about that. It is his fault. I don't want to be his wife. I want to stay here."

"You want a lot of things you cannot have. You have been given a gift, a destiny. The gods ignore most of us, but you and Tir are special. Why are you so afraid of taking the extraordinary path that has been laid before you?"

"I'm not afraid. I just don't believe in this destiny."

"What difference does belief make? The path is still there before you. You are still married to Admiral Tir, one of the most powerful men in the galaxy, and he adores you. The Empire still needs human women. I know you do not hate Admiral Tir. The entire Empire heard the rumors about your romantic encounters aboard the *Refa*. And even in your own accounts, you never mentioned rape, and I do not think this is Stockholm syndrome either."

"I didn't mention the forced marriage either. Don't try to convince me I was wrong about being forced to marry or being kept as a prisoner. I was both."

"A very well looked after prisoner. Do you think I spent the last ten years on Earth and don't know what humans find taboo? I know that you could never marry willingly; it is too distasteful for humans. But I also know that you would have never agreed to consummate the marriage if you did not want too either. Would you like me to read Doctor Sui's report out loud to you now?"

"That's not necessary."

"I didn't think so. The gods have chosen a new life for you, Captain Kara. It is a good life. Stop following this childish dream that you will always be on Earth defending your little blue planet in a broken down ship. That future died in the war. Your new future is a more meaningful one and will change the course of the galaxy." Ambassador Tui took in her unreadable face and continued, "You have a choice, you can become a full participant in your new life or be dragged along, making each day torturous for yourself and Admiral Tir."

"I can't be married."

"You will have a better life in the Empire. Admiral Tir's records show that he offered you a ship when you had proved yourself loyal."

"He did say that, but I thought he was lying."

"Alliance citizens rarely lie. Here is my first cultural tip: we will avoid the truth but rarely lie."

"How can I unmarry?"

"It is called 'divorce,' not unmarry, even though that sounds very cute when you say 'unmarry.' And unfortunately, as I said before, you are going whether you like it or not. You will realize that everything I'm telling you know is how all of this will play out tomorrow. All the good you have done for humanity doesn't matter. Your government will find you guilty as a spy and only grant you clemency on the terms you return to the Empire with Admiral Tir, never to return to Earth again. Don't feel sorry for yourself, most people in this galaxy have no choice about their lives, but at least your 'no choice' is to be with a man you like and who honors you."

"So, there are no divorces in the Alliance?"

"When you are released from this cell, I will give you a copy of the *Obligations and Rights of Marriage*, and it will answer all of your questions. I will leave you now and remember, say nothing for the next few days. It will be easier that way. Nice to meet you, Captain Kara Zu of the

Alliance. May the gods grant you wisdom and never let you dwell in darkness."

Tir was only a day away. He had received a report from the Alliance Ambassador on Earth who had seen Kara. She had been told to remain quiet about everything. Tir looked through all he could find about human laws regarding marriage. Because the practice did not exist anymore, they had no laws regarding it now, which was both good and bad for his position as the Empire and the GC still saw marriage as legally binding. However, the difficult part was that he was going to have to prove that she was an Alliance citizen before she became his wife, and that was something that the humans were not going to like.

The High Council had granted human women status as Alliance citizens three months ago, but this was for the sole purpose of solving their population problem and was done quietly. First, so there would not be a mad rush of eligible Alliance men just going to steal a wife and second, so that the GC did not immediately deem the law a violation of the Agreement of Respect for Galactic Species. The Empire hoped that human women would trickle in, and it would be a natural integration process between individuals who cared for one another.

Tir sighed and said to no one, "I am sorry, Kara."

When Tir had read the ambassador's report, he looked for anything that would signal that she was abducted and had not wanted to leave him, but he could find nothing. However, the ambassador noted that she was still wearing her marriage bracelet.

Just then, his computer indicated that he had a message from his mother. It was a video message sent from her office. "Tir, I know you said you were not going to leave your human with us, but I think that is foolish, and I have prepared your house for her." Tir looked at the screen and thought, *Of course, you have mother, let's hear it.* "I have enabled the water to go to very warm temperatures, and in the bedrooms, the temperature will also be able to exceed what we would find comfortable. I have also had the viewer programmed with all the entertainment from

Earth that the Empire has bought over the years. I think that you should bring her home to us and let her settle. May the gods light your journey." Tir closed his computer and went back to bed, thinking about how much Kara would hate living on the Capital Planet, but he had to consider his mother's words; *Maybe she was right? Maybe Kara would be happier there with women around her.* But that did not feel right, so he dismissed it. He can't let his loyalty to his mother guide him now. All he wanted was for Kara to be back with him forever by his side or at least in his fleet commanding her own ship, and nothing scared him more than the notion that she did not feel the same way.

———

Kara's legal counsel came back the next morning. She was wearing the same hot pink suit and lipstick. Kara wondered if it was rented, which was why she was wearing it on consecutive days, to get the most use out of it. Most people only owned about five complete outfits and rented the rest. Kara even owned less because, most days, she was wearing her uniform.

"You look tired," her counselor said disapprovingly.

"I had nightmares," Kara said, getting up and standing in front of her cell, waiting for the guard to release the forcefield.

Once she was out, the women began walking side by side. Kara noticed the lawyer smelled like cigars and pleasantly reminded her of her father. "I heard the Alliance ambassador came to see you yesterday."

"Yes."

"He even left his guards outside so that no one would be able to get to you during the night."

"I didn't know that."

"He's not stupid," she said as they walked quickly up some stairs. "But he could have told you so that you could have at least slept better." She paused before the doors to the courtroom. "Now we are going in, and all you need to say is 'not guilty'...." Kara interrupted her.

"I was told by the Alliance ambassador to say nothing, and I think I will take his advice."

"Don't you want to prove your innocence?"

"I am not a spy, but since everyone already thinks I am. I will have no chance for a fair trial anyway. You know that."

"Absolutely, but then why didn't you speak to the man behind me yesterday?" her lawyer asked frustrated. "Well, you are here now; we are going in. I am still making a plea of not guilty for you. If you refuse to speak, that is your right, but then I will have to give up representing you."

"Then what will happen?"

"Honestly, I don't know. This is the most exciting thing that has happened on Earth in a long time, maybe ever. People are fascinated that you are married to an Alliance Admiral, and the other half the population is convinced you are a spy for aliens." She sighed, "Listen, you have the public's ear. The government did not count on that GC piece on you and your husband sounding like a true romance. Some people even say he is not bad-looking for an alien. This means, despite the outcome of your case, you will still be able to say something about what is happening, and people will be on the edge of their seats listening. Those rumors about the Empire needing women, you will have one chance during your public trial to speak directly to the people. But remember to be fast, the government will cut you off quickly if what you're saying doesn't benefit them."

Kara was taking all of this information in and trying to decide what she should do.

"Of course, the Empire wants you to say as little as possible. They do not want to be incriminated for just taking human women; they want more. They are going to come here and try to negotiate for you and more women. If you say nothing, they can spin whatever story they want, and it will be too late for you to say they are lying if you only say so afterward. This is your only chance, Kara, to spin this the way you want people to see this."

"Thank you. Just promise me you will stay with me and wear that same hot pink suit all the days of the trial. It gives me confidence."

"Really? This color is supposed to relax you and give you peace of mind. I promise. Now let's go in, we are already late, but it is okay because I know the judge and we were out late drinking whiskey last night at his favorite cigar bar, so he doesn't care. And between you and me, he is a softie when it comes to romance even with an alien."

Tir and his fleet were close to the Solar System, but he could not get there fast enough. The Alliance Ambassador to Earth had just sent him a message telling him that Kara had not taken his advice and was pleading with her case. There was nothing more that he could do but make sure Alliance guards were stationed outside her holding cell to ensure she was not harmed, but even that was no guarantee.

Tir left the bridge and went to sickbay to talk to Siu. He went into his office and waited for him to finish seeing a patient. When he joined Tir, he asked, "What's happened now?"

"Kara is defending herself, saying she is not a spy instead of staying quiet."

"Do you think she will say that she had an abortion?"

"I don't know." Tir and Siu shared a serious look. In the Empire, an abortion of a healthy fetus was forbidden, and people responsible for abortions were given severe punishments that often resulted in death. "I can't tell the ambassador to tell her not to say anything, and there is no way to get word to her, not that she would listen or take me seriously. I think she must be the only person I have ever met that does not take the Empire or me as seriously as she should."

Siu smiled. "I think she takes you seriously fifty percent of the time."

Tir wanted to smile but couldn't. There was nothing his friend could say to lighten his mood. "I have to ask you something that has been on my mind lately."

Siu knew already what he was going to ask because he could read Tir's thoughts but allowed him to continue.

"Do you think Kara cares for me or was this all in my head?"

"She cares for you. There is no doubt about that. But for her, marriage was so taboo; I think that was the thing that made her want to reject you. That and you probably talked about religion too much, and again, for humans who abandoned religion centuries ago, it must have felt strange, almost frightening, for her."

"But it wasn't rape?"

"No."

"The ambassador has sent me a list of the crimes they are citing the Empire for, and 'the rape and forced impregnation' of Kara is on it. I can't help but wonder if she said that I raped her, and it makes me question myself even though, logically, I know she would have said it to keep from looking like a spy, possibly..." he trailed off.

"You did not rape her, Tir, and if she said those things, it was only to keep herself safe, which didn't work anyway. The humans want a better deal, and if Kara starts talking about forced marriages and rape, they will get a fantastic deal. Hopefully, there will be no mention of an abortion."

"We all do," replied Tir solemnly. If it came out that Kara had willingly sought out an abortion, not only would she most likely be put to death for it, the Empire's plans of integrating human women would be abandoned. It would be more likely that human women would just be harvested and used for their fertility like animals illegally. He did not see any scenario where the Empire would leave the humans alone now.

The next morning Kara found herself in court next to her lawyer, who was wearing the same hot pink suit and was called to the stand. Kara was asked her name and rank and how she came to find herself on the *Refa* in the first place. Then she was asked, "Did any of your crew witness this forced marriage?"

"No."

"Did any of your crew witness you agreeing to marry him?"

"Yes, through coercion. The admiral threatened to execute my male crew if I did not marry and send my female crew to the Alliance Capital Planet," she was trying to stay as calm as possible. "My first officer and communications officer's lives were threatened in front of me by the admiral on the *Refa*."

"But did Admiral Tir kill anyone or just threaten to kill before you agreed to marry him and send your female crew off to his home planet in enemy territory?"

"Because I sacrificed myself no one was killed," she said. "I was not willing to risk any crew member's life to check the validity of his threat."

"Unfortunately, it appears you put up very little fight making it difficult to prove you were coerced."

"You're saying I should have let one of my crew members die to prove that I was forced to marry Admiral Tir? What nonsense is this?"

The audience in the courtroom began loudly talking amongst themselves.

"Order," the judge said. "I will have order here."

The prosecutor continued, "Captain Rainer, I find it difficult to believe that you, a fearless and outstanding captain in our fleet, would have been so easily fooled unless there was something in this for you too. It just doesn't make sense. You gave not only yourself to the Empire for months, but your female crew forever."

"In exchange for their lives, they are all still alive. Imprisoned but alive."

"That is true, but for how long and what kind of lives are those women leading in the Empire? Are they able to freely return home? No, they are not; you sold them."

Kara looked at the prosecutor defiantly. "I have always been loyal to Earth and would never sell one of our own to aliens."

The prosecutor knew he had already proved his point then, and they moved on, "How would you describe your time on the Alliance ship *Refa*?"

"I was a prisoner."

"Really? Were you kept in the brig? Starved? Beaten? Harmed in any way?"

"No, but I was restricted to quarters with armed guards."

"Your own quarters?"

"No, I had been forced to marry Admiral Tir, so he kept me a prisoner in his quarters; none of this was my choice."

"I might have believed you if you had not been found wearing an Alliance dress and jewelry and pregnant with his baby when you escaped. Do you deny any of that?"

"I was forced to do all of those things. Did you expect me to escape naked?"

"How many times during the war did you try and escape?"

"Many times."

"So, it is just a coincidence that you escaped during the last battle? I find this difficult to believe, and so do your rescuers, and I quote from Captain Jackson's report, 'It was almost too easy of a rescue from one of the Alliance's best ships. We should keep an eye on Captain Rainer as there is something here that is not right.'"

"I was only able to access communications days before I escaped because I had finally learned enough of the Alliance language to access it. And my guards became more relaxed after I became pregnant."

"Yes, about that, are you still pregnant with this hybrid child?"

Kara looked at the prosecutor and said nothing.

"Captain, we are waiting for your answer."

"I sought an abortion aboard the *Silverado*."

"Yes, I have the report that says you went to sickbay, but I have no confirmation of what happened there. A hybrid fetus would have been studied, and there is no record of it. Are you still pregnant?"

Kara did not answer.

"You will answer the question, Captain," the judge said firmly.

"I did not have the abortion because I wanted to wait until I returned to Earth. Before I could organize it, I was arrested."

"Would you like to have the abortion now? I am sure it can be organized easily."

Kara did not answer.

"Why are you reluctant to abort a hybrid fetus? Is it because you plan on returning to your alien lover? I am sorry, I mean your *husband*. I have no disrespect for our galactic friends and their archaic practices."

"No, I am only reluctant to abort the fetus because it is innocent."

"You have killed so many Alliance people during your time in the human fleet. It is difficult for me to believe you would want a hybrid zombie monstrosity growing inside you if you did not love Admiral Tir. There is certainly no place for this hybrid child on Earth. Every human who called themselves 'a patriot' would kill it, especially if it had been a product of rape. Yet you don't, and then you sit there and have the gall to tell all of us that you are not a spy for the Empire."

"You don't understand." Kara felt betrayed on all sides now, but she had already been warned about this, so she decided this was her moment to say what she needed to say and hoped she would not be silenced too soon. She began speaking quickly without preamble, "The Empire believes they can solve their demographics problem by integrating human women into their society."

The judge slammed down his hammer for silence.

Kara ignored him and continued, "They are very religious and believe we are the same species, but what is affecting their women will eventually kill us too."

"That is enough, Captain Rainer," the judge said and motioned to the guards to take her, but Kara kept talking as she struggled with the guards.

"Listen! We are all in danger. The government is going to make a deal to trade wom...."

Kara was led out of the room by guards covering her mouth so she could not speak. She hoped that her outburst had been covered on the world broadcast and that people listened to her. The guards led her back to her cell roughly. However, they were much gentler when they saw the Alliance guards step forward. She was left in her cell then. A robot administered her food and water. All she could do was sit and wait to see what would become of her.

Kara didn't know if days had passed or only hours. There was no window in her cell, and the robot that fed her seemed to come at random times. She was exhausted and tried to sleep, but it was difficult because her thoughts haunted her. She only fell asleep when she thought about Tir.

She dreamed Tir entered the cell, apologizing for everything, and he said that she could live here on Earth and that it had all just been a misunderstanding. When they reached her apartment, she invited him in.

"It looks exactly how you said it would look," he said.

"Is it too much red for you?"

"I don't know. I haven't seen all the rooms yet. Maybe you can show me the bedroom?"

Kara took Tir's cool, grey hand, led him into the bedroom to her old four-poster bed with the velvet curtains, and asked, "Now, what do you think?"

Tir took her in his arms. "Not too much red at all, but I am very curious how it would feel to lie down in such an ancient bed." Then he kissed her, and she realized she had missed him so much.

Kara began undressing him then, and he her.

"You always look so sexy in your uniform," he said as he unzipped it.

She led him to her old-fashioned bed when they had removed each other's clothing. She closed the heavy, velvet curtains, and they were almost in the dark. "I hope you don't mind," she said between kisses, "I don't want to give the neighbors an alien and human sex show."

"I can see in the dark just as well as in the light," Tir said and began caressing one of her breasts gently while he kissed her. Then his hand moved lower and began stroking her in such a familiar way, it was not long before she orgasmed, and he was slowly moving in and out of her. "I have missed you so much, Kara."

"Stay on Earth with me," she was saying in her dream, and suddenly, she woke up. She was sweaty. The robot was there delivering some food for her. Beeping at her to accept it. She wondered if she had a fever to cause such a dream. She then questioned if Tir had been having sex with Sera while she was gone and became jealous, and she tried to reason with herself, *What do I care?* But, of course, she did care a great deal. None of this was clear. It was all very messy. And the thought of his having sex with the woman who probably sold their story to the GC before she could sort out her life on Earth made her irate.

And after what she witnessed in the courtroom she knew that what she had been told by her human lawyer and the Alliance ambassador, that they could not see any scenario where she would walk out and have her old life back, was correct. So she assumed they were both right in that she would also be sold to Tir and be forced to leave Earth as an outcast and traitor. Kara began crying for her lost human future. She felt adrift.

―――

Tir and the delegation from the Empire went down to their embassy in Paris immediately upon reaching Earth. Tir wanted to see Kara directly, but both ambassadors bid him wait until they had reached some agreement with the humans. He did write her a note in Alliance, though, and summoned a guard to take it to her. It read,

Kara, I am here. You will be released today. Please say nothing more. Tir

A few hours later, they were all sitting at a table with the human government, calmly discussing war reparations and what was to be done with human women; those already on the Capital Planet and those yet to be 'volunteers' as potential wives.

"We cannot just let you take some of our women. They can go freely, of course, but to take is against Galactic Law," the President of Earth said.

The old Alliance Ambassador answered him, "First, they were taken as prisoners during wartime, and now, I have reports here that say the female crew from the *Dakota* that was relocated to the Alliance Capital Planet are happy and content to remain there and now serve with the Alliance Fleet. So, you could say the former crew of the *Dakota* has remained in the Empire by choice and legally changed their status from citizens of Earth to citizens of the Empire."

"Captain Rainer reported they were forced," the president said but was interrupted by Tir.

"You will refer to her as Captain Kara; she is my wife," Tir said evenly.

The president was annoyed. "Your *wife*, yes, the spy. She has been tried and found guilty. I assume you think she will return with you?"

"Come now, President, this is all about plus and minuses. The Empire is willing to give Earth 700,000 UCs, 25 transports, 15 laser weapons, and 18 eternal batteries in return for letting the human women from the *Dakota* remain on our capital planet, the release of Captain Kara, and a constant stream of human women coming to the Empire for potential work, if they so choose, with the offer that they take Alliance citizenship and agree to marry an Alliance man. We would ask only for volunteers, of course."

The president, the vice president, and the human ambassador to the Empire all whispered together. The president replied, "For the release of Captain Kara alone, we would ask for that. We need more. And if you want a steady supply of human women to create zombie half-breeds as well, we need a lot more than your initial offer. A million universal credits, 50 transports, 15 laser weapons, 20 eternal batteries, a seat on the GC for the next twenty years, and two alpha starships."

"For that, we would also require that 100 human fertility experts are relocated to the Empire, and we also take 1,000 human women with us now. *Willingly*, of course," the new Alliance ambassador added.

The President of Earth looked at his team and then nodded. "Done. It will take us a couple of weeks to organize…" he was interrupted by Tir.

"You have one week," Tir said sternly. "Now release my wife."

———

Kara heard lots of footsteps down the hallway that led to her cell. She stood up, trying to see who was coming. It was a mixture of Alliance and human guards, two Alliance men who were officers and three humans, two who were her superiors in the fleet, and one government official she had never seen before.

They stopped in front of her cell, the forcefield was lowered, and one of her commanding officers began to speak formally, "Captain Kara Rainer of

Alliance Imperial House Zu, you are formally and dishonorably discharged from the human fleet as of today. You have been found guilty of espionage. However, your prison sentence has been commuted from imprisonment in the Europa mines to banishment from Earth and all human colonies. You have one week to settle your affairs here and leave forever."

Kara just looked at the general who spoke and said nothing for a few seconds because she was so shocked at what he had just said. After a few seconds, she found her voice. "What did you sell me for, General? After all I have done for humanity? I won't forget this. I'll not rest until I have my due for what you have done to me today."

None of her fellow humans answered her or made eye contact. They just stood there, looking everywhere but in her eyes.

An Alliance officer she did not recognize stepped forward. "Captain Kara of Imperial House Zu, you have been given a commission in the Alliance fleet under Admiral Tir that will commence after a suitable amount of training in the Empire. Now if you will come with us. We will escort you to the Alliance Embassy so you may formally accept your position and pledge yourself to the Empire."

She looked at them and thought, *This is it. My own people have sold me.* "Wait, I want to go home and put my things in order."

The Alliance officer assured her that she would be able to do that afterward and be accompanied by Alliance guards for her safety.

Kara allowed herself to be led to the Alliance Embassy. Once there she entered a massive room where five Alliance men were waiting. She recognized two of them. One of the men was Doctor Siu, and the other was Ambassador Tui. She wondered where Tir was, *Why isn't he here? No doubt he orchestrated all of this.* Everything was almost becoming too much for Kara and she struggled to keep her emotions in check.

Doctor Siu greeted her first, "Captain Kara, it's good to see you free and," he was holding out his scanner, "reasonably healthy." He smiled when he passed her abdomen with the scanner but said nothing more.

"Doctor, I'm surprised by the way events have played out. I never thought to see you again, especially under these circumstances."

"Captain Kara," Ambassador Tui addressed her. "Now that Doctor Siu has deemed you healthy, you must take an oath to the Alliance

Empire. After these small formalities, you will have a week to organize your affairs. Are you ready to begin?"

She looked at the old ambassador. "Yes," but could not help but think, *Please do not let it involve a religious blood ritual.* But just as soon as she thought about it, the ambassador brought out an ornate silver dagger, and she knew it was not just for show. *My new people are absolute savages.*

"Captain Kara, take the dagger in your right hand and repeat these words to me, Captain Kara of House Zu of planet Earth, do pledge my life and soul to the Alliance Empire. I solemnly vow to follow the gods' will for the enduring survival of the everlasting Empire."

Kara took the dagger and thought hopefully, *Maybe I just hold it.* "I, Captain Kara Zu of planet Earth, do pledge my life and soul to the Alliance Empire. I solemnly vow to follow the gods' will for the enduring survival of the everlasting Empire." As soon as she finished, the ambassador took a strong grip on both hands and quickly cut the center palm of her left hand with the dagger. Blood dripped to the floor, and someone brought a small candle so that the blood would drip on it until it was out. *And, of course, there was going to be something with blood, the gods, and a weapon. Welcome to the Empire, I am officially a barbarian now.*

When the candle went out, Doctor Siu came over and said, "I'm sorry, I cannot heal that wound as it is ceremonial and must heal according to the gods' will."

Kara took the disinfectant gauze in his outstretched hand and held it against her left palm. "It's fine. It was just a bit of a surprise," she lied, not about the wound but the symbolism of it. She was no longer a citizen of Earth. She felt as if her whole heart had been ripped out.

"I will see you aboard the ship at the end of the week. Come and see me then," Siu said and then left.

"As I promised you, Captain," said Ambassador Tui, handing her a small reader, "Here are the *Obligations and Rights of an Alliance Marriage* in English, all our laws, religion, the Contracts, and our history."

She took the reader from him and thanked him. Then she was assigned two guards who escorted her back to her apartment. They waited outside her door and would presumably be there all week as she had one week to put her affairs in order. One week to say goodbye to her human life.

The first thing she did was open her messages, scanning for the only person in the galaxy she wanted to hear from, and there it was. A message from Tir sent a few hours ago.

> Kara,
>
> I am finishing up everything with your government and will come to you tonight for the evening meal.
>
> Tir

Kara looked at the message again and began to cry. *Am I just going to accept him back?* she wondered, but then reminded herself, *He freed me, but he got me into this mess, to begin with. But my humanity sold me.* She thought about that for a long time. *I was sold by my government.*

She hit reply.

> Tir,
>
> I have one week left on Earth and no food in my apartment, so we are not eating here. Make a reservation at the famous restaurant where our regions called France and Spain meet. The restaurant is very old, and it is legendary. You will have to bribe them for a reservation, something you no doubt are good at now. I will meet you there for the evening meal.
>
> K

She did not need to specify a time since Alliance people always ate at the same time, but she smiled, thinking about how uncomfortable he would be when the meal did not end precisely after an hour. She was almost looking forward to him, saying, 'This goes against the gods.'

Kara looked at the clock. She had two hours to get ready and get there by transport. She assumed that she had the use of the Alliance transport she had used with the guards to come to her apartment.

After a couple of sad minutes, during which time she allowed herself to uncharacteristically feel sorry for herself, she rallied and thought, *It is done. It was out of my control. I must make the best of this. My life with the human fleet and my future on Earth ended the day I was taken prisoner. I could have died. I will see it as my old self died then, and this is the new me. Banished from Earth, married to an alien, and pregnant with a hybrid.*

Then she got into a hot shower and began thinking about what her new life would be like in the Empire. She wondered how long she would be kept as a prisoner now that she was banished from Earth and had no job or home to return to. She pondered if she should escape and become a galactic pirate.

After her shower, she stood in front of her closet. She still had the Alliance dress she escaped in, but as she assumed she would have to wear one of those for the rest of her life, she opted for a human dress. She pulled out her favorite black dress, it had a collar with silver embellishments with matching embellishments on the arm cuffs and across her breasts, but her décolletage was only covered by black transparent silk. The rest of her breasts and midriff down to her thighs were covered by more embellishments and regular black silk, but after the dress reached her mid-thighs, it was purely transparent black silk again down to her ankles. She wore no undergarments with this dress, not even stockings, as they would take away from the flashes of flesh through the transparent sections of the dress.

When she looked at her appearance in the mirror, she realized she needed some makeup too. *This is my last week on Earth to be completely human.* She put on smoky black eyeliner and lipstick. Then she saw the barrette he had given her and put it in her hair. The only other jewelry she wore was her marriage bracelet. She looked herself over and thought, *Yes, this is how I imagine myself looking when something important happens to me.*

Kara walked out of her front door, and the guards followed her silently. She hadn't expected to be followed by galactic gossip drones, wanting to get all the information about her and Tir now that she had been banished and had officially accepted her place in the Empire. "Get away," she said to them as her guards motioned for them to leave. Then they all got in the transport, and she told them where to go.

Once there, she told her guards to find some food somewhere while she ate. They refused, of course, but stood outside the restaurant. She knew Tir was not there yet as there was no other Alliance transport outside the restaurant. The galactic gossip drones were still hovering though.

She walked into the beautiful restaurant and was immediately met by the hosts who were expecting her. At once, she was led to a table with a stunning view of the mountains and ocean and offered her a glass of champagne while she waited. She noticed that the people around her were already whispering about her; she wanted to turn to them and say, 'Yes, it's me, the spy, and I am meeting my Alliance husband who bought me from our government a couple of hours ago.' But she said nothing. She just looked at the gorgeous view and tried not to think about all the other people at the restaurant who would live out their lives on Earth. *I'm saying goodbye to Earth this week. Don't ruin it by caring what strangers think.*

Tir was only a couple of minutes behind Kara. He saw her transport when he arrived. He took a deep breath before walking in. He did not want to meet her so publicly before they had had an opportunity to talk. Still, he had to remind himself that she probably hated him for everything that had happened and wanted to spend as little time as possible with him privately until she was forced to, so she chose to meet at a restaurant. He had had to pay a lot of UCs to get them a table, as the restaurant said they didn't want the bad publicity of having Kara there. He had Ambassador Tui pay them three times what they asked for to get them to accept them.

Tir was led to a table with a panoramic view of the ocean and mountains. The staff were polite, and he thought, *As you should be considering the amount of money I paid.* He did not recognize Kara at first. He had never seen her like this. He approached the table, and she noticed him and stood up. Tir was speechless. She was wearing a very sexy dress. He liked it but did not want her wearing it in public. It was so suggestive with its black transparent panels and silver embellishments. It made one think she was wearing nothing at all underneath. And she had painted her face. He had noticed that other human women did this, but he had never considered that Kara would do this. He found her so exotic at that moment. He did not know what to say as he looked at her.

"It would have been nice if you would have been there when I was released."

"I did not want you to say that I forced you to do anything else. You took what was offered by the Empire freely this time," he said honestly.

"I wouldn't say, 'freely' as I had no other options beyond piracy. But I guess I should be thanking you in a way," she said quietly.

"You would make a good pirate."

She shook her head.

"Kara, you owe me nothing," he said quietly, "But I owe you everything and I am sorry you left." He wanted to touch her but using his willpower not to. In the Empire, men and women, even married couples, did not often touch in public, especially when they had an audience like now.

The hostess held out Kara's chair, and she sat down again, and he sat across from her.

"You are wearing the barrette I gave you," he had not noticed before because he was so shocked by her dress and makeup.

She inadvertently touched it. "Yes, I told you we would have always been lovers under different circumstances. In an alternate universe, I'm sure we are lovers and live on Earth."

"And this must be our favorite restaurant," he added.

"Yes, we celebrate everything here," she said wistfully.

"I'm sorry that I was not there when you were released today and that you were imprisoned." He had wanted to give her time to think about everything that had happened alone, even if it was only a couple of hours.

"You did warn me. I just couldn't imagine that it would turn out this way."

"Are you okay? Nothing terrible hidden under all that face paint?"

She frowned at him. *Does he think I look bad? Is this a black lace lingerie situation?* "This," she motioned to her face, "is considered attractive on Earth. And yes, I am okay, but I am hungry."

"You are always hungry, Kara. As for the face paint, it is very attractive. Almost too attractive with the dress."

"Please don't call it face paint. It's called makeup. Face paint is what clowns wear."

"What is a clown?"

Kara just looked at Tir, astonished for a second. "They're terrifying creatures that live on Earth. Just be happy you've never seen one." He seemed confused, but before he could ask her any more questions, the servers came over then and began explaining the menu. Neither one was listening as the spell was broken, and they could hear people talking about them, both the good and bad, from all around them.

"I'll not be having the wine pairing," said Kara quietly to the waitress, and she nodded. When she saw Tir's look, she explained, "I don't feel like it."

"You're a terrible liar Kara, I'm glad we are still three at this table."

She nodded.

"It was confusing when you told me otherwise in your message, and then in court, you said the opposite. Sui told me of course you were still pregnant and all was well, but…"

She interrupted him, "I know what I told you. But I couldn't do it." She looked at him and then admitted, "I can't believe my government just sold me like that."

"Do you want to eat here? We should go somewhere private to discuss all of this."

"Yes, I want to eat here. I have one week before I am banished from my planet, and I will have to suffer through tasteless Alliance food for the rest of my life. This is the best food in the galaxy even if only humans recognize that."

He smiled at her and remembered the day she sent her crew from the *Refa*. She had said to him he would love Earth too in her patriotic speech. He reached his hand across the table and touched hers, "Kara, of course, it is."

After the first course, she asked, "What was I sold for?"

"It was a negotiation."

She looked annoyed by his correction so he continued without explaining himself, "Humans will have a seat at the GC guaranteed for 20 years, some UCs, a couple of alpha ships, and transports, and weapons. You were not cheap, but I would have paid much more if they would have demanded it."

"How much of it was from your own assets?"

"Are you worried I spent all my money on you?"

"I'm only curious because people will talk. I want to know how much the Empire paid for human women and me in particular."

"I paid half a million UCs and my family will assure a human has a place at the GC. The rest was from the Empire's coffers."

Kara was speechless for a minute. Half a million UCs were more than she would ever earn in her lifetime, more than a dozen lifetimes. "I'm glad I know now. It makes it a bit easier."

"I know this will hurt for some time, and I will try to make your transition into the Empire smoother than before to lessen that pain at least."

Kara looked at him in disbelief, *Was Tir being sympathetic?* "So do you trust me now?"

"Not completely. I will still consider you my prisoner until you hold a healthy baby in your arms."

"Please don't call me your prisoner; wife is enough."

"Kara, you will soon realize that I have always wanted that. I don't want to look over my shoulder to ensure you are not running away all the time. That not only hurts my pride but my heart."

"That should be easier now that I have nowhere to run." Then in the middle of dinner she announced, "I want to go back to my place now."

Tir didn't question her. He nodded, and they left. He assumed that part of the bribery he had given the restaurant included their price for the food. No one stopped them on the way out. They got into his transport, hers trailing behind with her guards, and flew to her apartment.

They didn't speak, but she took his hand and led him into her apartment building. Once inside, she began kissing him. She could not help herself. *This is exactly what I need to ground myself in this new reality.*

Tir's hands were on either side of her face kissing her passionately. He loved the feel of her and the smell of her. This all felt so right. It was not long before his hands began roaming over her breasts, rubbing and pinching her nipples over the fabric. Soon, he had his hands searching for the clasps to remove her dress, but he could not find them, so after a couple of minutes, he took his sword and said, "I hate to do this to such a beautiful dress, but I cannot wait any longer, and you will never wear it again anyway. It's too sexy." He cut the dress off to reveal her completely naked underneath. "Gods, Kara, you were completely naked under that dress? You are so naughty. Come here." He dropped his sword, and she went directly into his strong arms. He held her naked with her legs on his shoulders and his mouth on her vulva. "You smell so divine," he said as he began kissing her there as he held her. He made her come easier than with his hands having her rear as he alternated between licking her clitoris and putting his tongue in and out of her vagina. After she orgasmed, he pulled his head back from gently licking her sex and asked, "Where is your bed?"

"It's in the back, behind you. The old-fashioned one there with the blue curtains."

Tir carried her in this position, her legs around his shoulders, into the bedroom, and then he gently laid her down on the bed, taking in her beautiful naked form, and began kissing her body all over.

Kara closed her eyes and just enjoyed having him touch her again. Soon he was licking all around her upper thighs and vulva again. He was teasing her, and then finally, his tongue was on her clitoris, with his fingers inside her, bringing her wet sex to climax again and again.

"I have missed watching you come so much. I have missed those sounds," Then she came so hard, and he continued, "And your pink cheeks," his hand lightly caressed her cheek. Then he flipped her on her stomach and said, "And I have missed dominating you like you like," he grabbed both of her wrists and held them behind her as he began thrusting into her. "Have you missed this?"

"Yes," she said breathlessly, and he stopped for a second. "Yes, I said. I have missed this. Don't stop now." Kara had missed this so much. He was holding her wrists and thrusting into her, and she would come again.

Then he was coming, and they were on her bed, holding one another.

After several minutes he put his hand on one of the velvet curtains, "Your apartment is just as you described it."

Kara had momentarily déjà vu from her dream when she was imprisoned. But she settled her mind after a minute. "I want to stay here for my last week on Earth. You don't have to if you find it too primitive."

"It is basic, but I would like to stay with you. I know this week will be difficult. You will need to say goodbye to everyone."

Tears began streaming down her face. "I can't believe I'm banished." She said to his naked grey chest as he held her close.

"I know, but they couldn't find you guilty as a spy and then just let you serve in the Alliance fleet without any punishment, could they? You know your people. I tried to prove that you escaped from, but they would not have it. It had all become too public and worth too much money for them to change the story." He ran his fingers through her hair, "I promise you I will make this up to you."

His last words reminded her of something Ambassador Tui had mentioned. "What is this about you putting your name on the Grand City Temple Wall?"

"To make things right with the gods and to make things right with you." He put his hand on her abdomen. "I was afraid you would have been forced to abort the child."

"I may be destroying humanity by doing this, but they just sold me." She tried to hold back more tears while she thought, *They sold me. After everything I've done.*

"You are not a traitor, Kara. You are far from it. You will still be able to help humanity by being my wife, and maybe your banishment will be lifted in a few years. Trust in the gods. Trust in the Empire and trust in me."

She didn't say anything for a long time, but just enjoyed their naked bodies intertwined as she listened to the tram bell outside.

Tir sat up and looked at her. "I didn't know if you were asleep."

"No, I was just trying to think how I will explain all of this to my parents. I mean of course they probably know, but you know…"

"We should do it tomorrow."

"They are going to hate you."

"I would expect no less."

"What did your parents say about you marrying me?"

He didn't answer her.

"Tir?"

"Let's close these little curtains and let me punish you for escaping," he slapped her bottom reasonably hard to get her attention. "I don't want your neighbors watching us again."

"They're just curious, you know, a human having sex with an alien," she smiled as he swatted her again. "I find it sexy they're watching. Let them watch. I'm leaving Earth anyway." She could feel herself become aroused again, thinking about her neighbors watching them. Watching him spank her.

"Looking at this bed and these wooden posts, I'm looking forward to a wild week with my human wife. I will get some ropes…" he trailed off as he began getting her into the position he wanted. "But first, your punishment for escaping wife and wanting the neighbors to watch."

A few days later, Kara was going through her belongings, deciding what she should take and what she should throw away, when there was a chime at her door. She checked the screen, and it was Doctor Siu. She unlocked the doors to allow him entry.

"I'm surprised to see you here, Doctor."

"I wanted to check in on you and run a scan," he said as he walked into her apartment.

"You want to do that right now?"

"Are you busy?"

"Not particularly. Tir has insisted on buying me some human jewelry, so he is currently in Italy. I was going through my belongings."

"It won't take long," Siu said, producing a hand-held scanner.

"Would you rather we went into the bedroom?"

"You don't need to remove your clothing, but we can do it wherever you are most comfortable," Siu answered her.

"I think I would be more comfortable in the bedroom then," Kara said, turning and walking towards her bedroom.

Siu quickly took out his IC and sent a message to Tir,

> Return now, friend. Your wife has invited me into her bedroom.

And then he followed Kara into her very human bedroom.

Kara laid down on the bed, looked at the handsome doctor she had had more than a couple of fantasies about, and asked, in a purposely seductive tone, "Are you sure I don't need to take off my clothing?"

Siu smiled. He could read her thoughts and decided he would enjoy this little foreplay until Tir joined them. "It's not necessary, but if you have some concerns, please remove your clothing."

Kara then added, "I'm so tired. Would you mind helping me take off my clothing?"

Siu put his scanner on the bedside table and sat on the bed next to Kara. He looked into her utterly human brown eyes and touched her face. He could read and feel all of her lustful thoughts. He used his clairvoyance to intensify them, this was against the law on the Capital Planet, but there was no law against it on Earth.

Kara felt a wave of lust flow through her, she looked up at Siu and wanted him badly, "Please, Doctor, I feel so hot in these clothes, but I'm so tired. I don't have the energy to take them off myself."

Siu ran his hand down the side of her face, past her neck, and then onto the curve of one breast, "Do your breasts feel tender? Too tender for me to touch?"

Kara did not want him to go slowly, she wanted him to ravage her. "They don't feel too tender. Maybe there is something wrong. You should touch both of my breasts to make sure."

Siu put his other hand lightly on her other breast, gently kneading them both, "And this doesn't hurt at all?"

Kara looked into his alien grey eyes. "No, it doesn't hurt. But I'm still so hot."

Siu then moved his hands down the curve of her hips and legs. She was wearing human trousers, which he hated. He quickly took those off. "I'm so glad you'll be permanently in the Empire now; these human clothes aren't made of the best materials." Then he ran his fingers up and down her warm legs, finally circling the top of her thighs and around her black underwear. "And wearing these undergarments are bad for your health. I must remove them immediately." He took off her lingerie and threw them over his shoulder onto the floor somewhere. Siu was not disappointed by her glorious human sex, interestingly covered in brown hair. It was just how he remembered it. He bent down to smell her sex as his fingers lightly caressed the entrance to her vagina. "You smell divine, Kara. Do you mind if I taste you? May I lick you?"

"Please," Kara replied, wondering if this went against her marriage contract. She could not remember, but his tongue was on her sex, and she could not think.

Siu loved the taste of this exotic human. He hoped that Tir would arrive soon because he would make her come quickly, and he didn't know if he could resist taking her after he had witnessed that. Her squirming with the muscle contractions and becoming so wet and ready for him.

Kara put her hands in Siu's hair as he began licking her with such perfect strokes. She thought she might die of a heart attack. *Of course he knew exactly where to lick, he was a telepath.*

Siu brought her to climax and then began kissing her stomach and pulling up her shirt. She was wearing more undergarments which he tsked at and took his short sword, cutting both the undergarment and her shirt off without too much effort. He was rewarded with a magnificent view of her taut and perfect breasts. He began sucking on a nipple while his other hand pinched and played with the other nipple. Siu knew it would not be long before he could make her come again.

Tir could hear his wife's moans of pleasure from the living room. He continued into the bedroom to see Kara naked on her human bed and Siu sucking her breasts. "I can smell your sex from the other room, and it is intoxicating," Tir said, getting both of their attention.

Kara opened her eyes, saw Tir, and wondered what he would do now. Despite what he had said, she wondered if he would be jealous.

Siu immediately felt Kara's insecurity about the situation and used his clairvoyance to calm her and assure her this was all okay by Alliance customs.

Tir began removing his clothing, and when he was completely naked, he said, "Siu, take off your clothes. I've wanted to share Kara with you for a while. Is she not the sweetest you've ever tasted?"

Siu still had both his hands on her nipples, caressing them as he answered, "She most certainly is. I'm so glad you made it here in time; I didn't know how long I could last. But I'm reluctant to leave these gorgeous pink nipples."

Tir stood behind him and looked down at Kara, looking at them both with overwhelming desire in her eyes. "Kara, you are so magnificent. Will you share yourself with Siu too? Two alien lovers?"

Kara did not need to think about it. "Yes, I want to be with you both. I've fantasized about this ever since our wedding night."

Siu reacted to her words and let go of her nipples to move back and quickly remove all of his clothing.

Kara watched Siu undress and was turned on by his impressive and handsome body. He was thinner than Tir but still very athletic and beautiful in a streamlined way. His penis was fully erect, with the ridges bulging from the top length of it, but his penis did not have Tir's size or girth.

Tir moved Kara to the center of her bed, and both men joined her, one on each side.

"Should we close the curtains?" Siu asked seeing prying eyes of curious human neighbors.

Tir looked over his shoulder through to the neighbors' window where they had some spectators. "No, let them watch if they want. Let this be Kara's final goodbye to Earth."

"I want them to watch," Kara said rather breathlessly.

"Good," replied Siu, "Now, about these breasts," he said as he began sucking on them again.

Tir moved down and began licking her vulva and all around her vagina, including her anus.

Kara had never had so much attention from two men, and her body was on fire. She wanted them both so much, and it was apparent that they had shared women before as they seemed to work well together.

Tir quickly made Kara orgasm again, he said for good measure. She was so wet now that he stuck his finger into her vagina and then took it out, gently easing it into her anus. She had said before that he would never be allowed to put his penis there, but he wondered if she would go back on her word today or let Siu do it. Tir watched her reaction to his finger inside her anus and was pleased. He leaned down and whispered in her ear, "Do you want us both inside you simultaneously?"

Kara heard his question. She thought about it for a second. Tir's finger in her anus felt so good, maybe it would feel good to have Siu's penis in there.

Tir was watching Kara, he inserted another finger into her vagina simultaneously, and she moaned. "Kara, what do you think?" he whispered again.

Siu left her bed quickly and returned with lubricant. He expertly spread it in her anus and then said to Kara, "Will you let me in?"

"Yes, only the doctor. You're too big, Tir."

Tir was disappointed, but this was not the first time a woman has looked at his penis and said 'no' to anal sex.

Siu gave Tir a satisfied look and moved to the end of the bed.

Tir lay his body on top of Kara and kissed her passionately. His hands were roaming over her sexy and familiar body.

When Tir lay on top of Kara and began kissing her and filling her with his penis, she almost forgot all about Siu until, in the middle of his slow thrusting, Tir flipped them so he was on his back, and she was on top. She tried to rise to straddle him but felt Siu's hands on her shoulders, easing her back down toward Tir. All the while, Siu was kissing her back while his fingers worked her anus. Tir began sucking on her nipples, and she was in ecstasy. She didn't care anymore about anything, not about Earth, her trial and being accused of being a traitor, or her oath to the Alliance Empire. All she could think about was the pleasure she was experiencing now. She just wanted these men to take her like this and never stop.

Siu had never put his penis into an anus so tight and warm. He almost came just having his fingers in her. He kissed Kara's sweet back and then removed his fingers and slowly replaced them with his penis, saying in her ear as he did, "Tell me if this hurts you, precious human." He did not stop kissing her seductively while he did it. Once he was sure he was inside and not hurting her, he gave Tir their usual signal, and then they began to both have sex with her.

Kara had never felt like this before. She had two beautiful men having sex with her all at once. She felt like gentle hands and glorious sensations were coming from everywhere. She wanted this to last forever.

"Gods, Kara, you are so beautiful right now," Tir said as he looked up at her, "And I'm so turned on by watching Siu use your anus like this while I'm in you."

Kara couldn't respond, it was all new, and she was overwhelmed with desire.

Siu continued to move so slowly. He was waiting for Kara to demand more, and it did not take long before she reached behind to touch his hip and urge him a bit more. "Do you want me to go faster, darling human? Do you like this?"

"Yes, faster," she said. "Both of you faster."

Siu rubbed a cheek in front of him. "Of course, faster, and how about a little harder too?"

"Yes."

Siu took her hips in his hands and began moving more in earnest. He could feel Tir's penis on the other side of his. They had all never been so close, but it felt so right.

Minutes later, Kara was demanding, "Faster."

Both Tir and Siu responded without words, trying to all come at the same time. Tir had his hands on her breasts, and Siu had one hand on her clitoris.

Kara had never come so hard in her entire life, and after they finished, they all lay together in an entangled mess of sweat, semen, and lubricant, all with her human neighbors still watching.

Kara looked up at her neighbors and gave them a little wave. "Goodbye, Earth and humanity. I will be back, and I will never forget how you treated me."

Thank you

This is my first book and I want to thank you for reading *Married to the Alien Admiral*, Book One of the Renascence Alliance Series. This series will continue to follow different human women throughout their own adventures and struggles in the Alliance Empire.

The next book, *Married to the Alien Doctor*, follows Junior Doctor Dru, one of Kara's crew from the *Dakota* who was sent to the Capital Planet. Her story is very different from that of Kara's. Not only because her story takes place on the Capital Planet but because she is a very different person. Whereas Kara embraced Alliance sexual practices, Dru shuns them, but despite this, she still must build a life for herself and find a husband in the Empire.

Here is the direct link to *Married to the Alien Doctor* if you want to jump right in. Married to the Alien Doctor

Thank you again for joining me in this Alliance world.

Best wishes,

Alma x

Teaser from Married to the Alien Doctor

Dru looked at her reflection. She had just showered, and she wondered if she should wear her hair up tonight. It was the Year Assembly. Madame Bai had told her that this was the largest Assembly all year and that most eligible men of the maximum class would be there. She also hinted that her Mr. Mystery would also probably be there and reveal himself to her tonight in a romantic gesture. Dru certainly hoped so, she was tired of being ignored. Last night, before she fell asleep, she decided that she didn't even care if her Mr. Mystery was ugly or old, if he was someone to talk to, she would take him for courting at least when she came of age.

She looked at herself again in the mirror and decided to leave her hair down, she thought she looked better this way. Dru also put on some of the makeup that she had bought so many weeks before from the Earth Store. It just made her feel better. She wanted to look her best, not her Alliance best, her human best, if she were finally meeting her Mr. Mystery tonight. And if she wasn't meeting him, even more reason to look her best as it would be a long night not talking to anyone, standing in a corner.

But then she reminded herself, Dera and Ket will be there so she will at least get five minutes of conversation or more. She hoped more when she thought of Ket, but she didn't get her hopes up too much. She knew he was popular among the women and Dera never spoke to her about her brother and she couldn't think of a clearer sign indicating that she shouldn't put her hopes for a courtship or marriage there.

Dru's door opened and without any kind of acknowledgement, a grumpy slave sauntered in with a small package. Dru was naked and took the package without question and then the slave left. *I'm almost enjoying the rudeness of my slaves,* she thought with a smile. Dru set the package down on her desk and then went to her closet to get her one formal dress. She put it on and then the necklace Mr. Mystery had given her and her ID necklace. Once she was ready, she sat down at her desk and opened the present. She assumed it was from Mr. Mystery. She took out the black card with the meticulous silver writing and read it,

Drusilla,

I hope this will help us find each other tonight.

Dru wondered what could be in the small package. She quickly opened it to find a silver ring with a small clear stone in its center. However, when she put the ring on her finger, the stone quickly began to change color in the most fascinating and beautiful way right before her eyes, as if it were filling with a different color smoke that was constantly moving like rain clouds shifting above the ocean. She was fascinated but didn't have a clue as to how this ring would bring her any closer to Mr. Mystery.

She looked at the card again, no name. But when she opened her desk drawer to add it to the other cards, she noticed that the handwriting on this one and the last one that came with the flowers was identical. She took out all the cards and spread them out across her desk. She saw that only these two matched. She knew the flowers came from the Earth Store and that this ring today was from a completely different store, so Mr. Mystery must have written these two himself. She was charmed by that and thought, *His handwriting is impeccable, I hope he isn't overly religious.* In the Empire, one's handwriting reflected their closeness with the gods.

Dru wondered then if her Mr. Mystery had been a doctor at the symposium, as he had to have been on planet both then and now. She didn't have the energy to get the list of potential Mr. Mysteries out again and cross examine it, as she had gone over it too many times already and in a couple hours, she would know who he was anyway. But first things first, she had to figure out how to work the ring, so she opened a RVM to Madame Bai.

"You're not wearing your hair up?" was the first thing Madame Bai said when she saw Dru on the screen. "And human face paint, really? Tonight is the Year Assembly."

"I think I look better this way," Dru defended her appearance. "But that's not why I'm calling. I've a question. I just received this." She held up the ring that now instead of being clear was midnight blue. "But I don't know what it is or how it works. How is it supposed to help me find the man who put the ban on me?"

Madame Bai looked at the ring through the screen and smiled. "It's a location ring. The man who has given it to you is on the planet or in orbit, that is why it is midnight blue. The closer you come to each other, the lighter the colors will be. When you are in the same room, it will be clear again and will become very warm. It is symbolic that there is nothing standing between you anymore but the warmth of your hearts."

Dru looked at the ring. "Nothing except I am not of age to be courted yet and I don't even know this man. He is a stranger. How can there be warmth in our hearts for one another?"

"Not necessarily a stranger. Anyway, all that matters is that he is revealing himself to you tonight and you can choose whether or not you would even enter a courtship with him after your birthday which is not too far away. Remember everything he has given you is without prejudice," she reminded Dru. Madame Bai had realized with a lot of the human women that they felt obligated to men who gave them things and she always needed to remind them that the men did that with the knowledge they may be rejected. And that they need not cater to any men's feelings that they don't naturally return. "You can't have a relationship with a man you don't feel attracted to. Everyone knows this. You'll know when you meet him how you feel. Trust in the gods."

"I will," she said knowing full well she still didn't believe in the gods.

Every day she went to the shrine in their building and said her prayers, but they were still hollow for her.

"Enjoy this evening as much as you can," Madame Bai said warmly to Drusilla and then ended the conversation.

Dru looked at the ring and asked herself, "Who are you Mr. Mystery? And do you already love me?"

―――

Here is the direct link: Married to the Alien Doctor, Book 2

Also by Alma Nilsson

Books written in 3rd person omniscient:

Married to the Alien Admiral, Book 1

Married to the Alien Doctor, Book 2

Married to the Alien with No House, Book 3

Married to the Alien Admiral of the Fleet, Book 4

Abducted by the Alien Pirate, Book 5

Restaurateur in the Alliance Empire, Book 6

The Ward of House Rega, Book 7

The Disciple of the Alien Goddess of Home, Book 8

Jewelry and Couture of the Alliance Empire, Book 9

(Book 9 is not a romance but a small informational book about Known Jewelry)

Seven Days on the Capital Planet, Book 10

———

Books written in 1st person with two POVs:

Married to the Yuletide Alien, Book 1

Married to My Alien Valentine, Book 2

Married to My Midsummer Alien, Book 3

Married to the All Hallows' Eve Alien, Book 4

The Alien I Fell in Love with on Walpurgis Night, Book 5

———

You can find short stories exclusive to the newsletter about characters living on the planet Hogo in my newsletter:

Alma Nilsson Newsletter

About the Author

Alma Nilsson is an author of science fiction romance. In her alien universe, females have always controlled galactic politics, and humanity is the outlier. All doors are always open in her books.

She holds higher degrees in anthropology, art, and linguistics.

Printed in Great Britain
by Amazon